# SCHEHERAZADE'S NIGHT OUT

# SCHEHERAZADE'S NIGHT OUT

Craig Shaw Gardner

## BCA
LONDON · NEW YORK · SYDNEY · TORONTO

This edition published 1992
by BCA
by arrangement with
HEADLINE BOOK PUBLISHING PLC

CN 2552

First published in Great Britain in 1992
by HEADLINE BOOK PUBLISHING PLC

10 9 8 7 6 5 4 3 2 1

Typeset by Keyboard Services, Luton

Printed and bound in Great Britain by
Richard Clay Ltd, Bungay, Suffolk

This one's for Barbara,
with no excuses.

*The Prologue, in which we manage simultaneously to reiterate certain points of difficulty while once again starting anew.*

Then it is my turn?

I will tell you therefore a story of life and death, of dreams unforetold and places no able man has ever seen. My tale shall hold within its bounds the hidden secrets of beasts and the true nature of men, and it shall range from the distant day before there was a Baghdad to a time far after every one of us is gone from this earth, and ifrits and magicians are thought of as nothing more than childish fantasies.

Not, of course, that my humble excuses for story telling are in any way exceptional. But I digress.

You have heard from the others now, concerning the glories of Baghdad, and the wonders of other lands. And both of these men, clever Sinbad who was once a porter, and bold Ali Baba, who once cut wood to survive, have proven themselves to be noble adventurers and grand storytellers. It would be almost impossible for an unassuming tale spinner like myself to best their stories of magic and terror, and I must admit that I have, by and large, led a somewhat less venturesome life than these men, as is suited to my sex and station.

But this is not to say that my story is without drama, for, in a certain way that you shall see, my very life depended upon my every word, for, were my words to fail me, my head would quickly be separated from my shoulders.

Ah, I can see our captor takes an interest now. Yes, even a great *djinni* such as Ozzie might appreciate the effect of the spilled blood of maidens. But I will talk of more than blood, and more than maidens.

For, while you shall see that my life has always hung near the blade of a headsman's axe, I have also discovered certain more subtle dramas as well, but no less strange for their relative calm. For my existence has been a life hidden, by and large,

1

from the world of men, within your world and yet totally separate from it.

So it is that I have discovered that there are stories within stories, thoughts within thoughts, and lives within lives. And it is now my task to unravel all these stories, thoughts, and lives for you, and hopefully reveal those truths that hide within truths.

So I pray you to grant me the proper time and attention, so that I might tell you the most unusual story of Scheherazade.

## Chapter the First,
## *in which certain unfortunate errors*
## *are quickly cut away.*

Know now, that while I tell my own story, it is the story of many others as well. First and foremost is it the tale of two mighty kings, one named Shahryar, who ruled over the great city of Baghdad, and his younger brother, the great King Shahzaman, who ruled the neighboring kingdom of Samarkand. And both these rulers reigned over their kingdoms for a full score of years, bringing peace and prosperity to all their subjects, and thus both were known throughout each of their kingdoms, and indeed throughout the entire civilized world, as being among the fairest and most beneficent of rulers.

But a man is more than a throne and a talent for judgement. So it was that the elder of the brothers, Shahryar, who was known to his people as the tall king, found himself with a violent longing for his brother and childhood companion, whom he had not seen in all of those long years that the two of them had ruled their separate domains. He therefore sent his trusted vizier to visit his brother, King Shahzaman, who was still, for all his years and wisdom, known as the younger king to both his subjects and those of the neighboring kingdom.

And the younger king, hearing of his brother's longing for reunion, readily agreed to such a meeting. He then prepared his court for a prolonged absence, having long discussions with his own major-domo, and his chief of eunuchs and his chief among slaves, telling each of them to tend to their particular duties, and to take special care to watch over his wife and to protect her from all trouble, for he loved the woman dearly.

Oh, but that fate can change any and all without warning, and that no man can control his Destiny! So it was that, mere moments after he had departed from his court, the younger king remembered a certain item in his apartments that he had wished to present to his brother as a gift. No sooner had he returned to his

3

apartments, however, than he discovered not one but two forms residing upon his wife's favorite couch.

Now, one of these individuals was indeed the king's wife, which one might not find surprising. However, the second form – which was pressed so close that you could not tell where the perspiration upon one naked body ended and where the sweat upon the other unclothed form began, not to mention certain other fluids that one might share between a male and female – this second form was the chief among slaves, that very same man whom the king had so recently exhorted. Never had King Shahzaman imagined, when he had issued his instructions, that the tall and agile slave would protect his wife quite that closely.

Well, Shahzaman had little choice in a matter of this nature. There was nothing for it save to have both wife and slave beheaded. But, once he was done with this onerous task, not only was he an additional quarter of an hour late for the beginning of his journey, but this unfaithfulness business had placed him in a temper unbecoming to a reunion with his brother.

And yet, a promise is a promise, and a king is nothing if he does not fulfill his duties. So it was that King Shahzaman traveled to the neighboring kingdom. And his brother, the tall king, King Shahryar, greeted him joyously, and Shahzaman did his best to reciprocate the emotion. But, despite his best efforts, the younger king found he had little appetite for the grand banquet that evening, and did not even deign to glance at the sumptuous entertainments which followed. Indeed, his thoughts plagued him that entire night, so that the following morning found him still awake, with hollowed eyes and sallow complexion.

His brother asked him what was amiss, but the younger king did not wish to trouble the tall king with his domestic difficulties, and blamed the long journey for his malaise. At that, King Shahryar declared that they should both go on a great hunt together, for it is in such manly pursuits that even kings might forget their troubles. But the younger king had no heart even for this sport, and bade that his older brother go without him.

So it was that Shahzaman stayed behind while his host proceeded to the hunt, and the younger king did retire again to his chambers, and attempt there to rest, although his thoughts still would not allow sleep to come.

Now it came to pass that, as the younger king was in this restive state, he did hear a great commotion in that garden that lay just beyond his quarters. Curious even in his misery, Shahzaman arose and, treading quietly, peered from out of his darkened doorway at the unbelievable scene beyond. For there, frolicking among the vast array of cushions that littered the center of the gardens, were twenty male slaves, and twenty female slaves, and at their center was the queen of this kingdom, and wife to his brother, King Shahryar.

And the slaves all paused in their merrymaking, as if waiting for a signal from their queen. And for her part, the queen smiled very sweetly upon one of the male slaves, who was tall and very well muscled, and furthermore was endowed with a prodigious gift of manhood, for I have neglected to mention that all the slaves, male and female, were entirely naked and, indeed, even the queen wore but the flimsiest of robes.

'Come to me,' she said to the fortuitously equipped slave. 'And you know how literally I do mean those words. You should consider them nothing less than an order from your queen.'

Then did the slave smile upon the royal woman, and take her in his arms. And the queen further remarked, 'We will make these cushions know they have been used!' as she drew the slave down next to her with great cries of 'Let us do it!' and, 'Whoopie!' and other sayings especially coarse and shocking coming from the conversation of a lady of such refinement. And then did all the other slaves do the same, naked men and women mixing without discrimination, so that the entire mound of cushions, and the pathway of stones that led to the gardens beyond, became a mass of bouncing and giggling nudity.

Truly, the younger king was astonished by this course of events, and found himself watching the drama for a substantial period of time in order to discern the finer details. But there comes a time when even a king must make a judgement, and so it was that Shahzaman said to himself, 'As bad as is my misfortune, my brother's is twenty times worse.' And furthermore, 'Truly, though I was presented with the leavings of a diarrheic bird upon my brow, my brother has been gifted with the similar gifts of a whole herd of oxen.'

And with that, and another hour or two of observation of what passed in the garden beyond, he found that his grief had passed and he was once again able to eat and drink and sleep with the grace of a king.

When, upon the following day, his brother returned from the hunt, King Shahryar discovered that the younger king seemed much improved in health and demeanor. So it was that the tall king asked his brother again for the cause of his malaise and, this time, Shahzaman answered, repeating how he had returned to his palace to discover his wife in the arms of a slave and how, as his brother most readily agreed, he had both of them immediately beheaded.

'Still, though,' the younger brother continued, 'did I suffer for my misfortune, both pining for my lost love and much angered by her gross treachery, until—' But with this word the younger king took on the countenance of most profound regret, and ceased to speak entirely.

But his elder brother was astonished by what his sibling related, and bade him to continue. So it was that the tall king prompted, 'Until?'

But the younger of the two was extremely reticent to continue since, in his relief at finally finding himself able to relate his misfortune, he had neglected to consider that the latter portions of his story might contribute to the misfortune of another.

'Until?' His elder brother, who no doubt was not fully cognizant of the other's dilemma, replied a bit more forcefully as he pulled distractedly upon his beard.

But instead of a more direct reply, the younger king said, 'Perhaps it is better that I end my story here, for to continue would no doubt cause you great consternation and grief.'

Howsoever, his brother, the great King Shahryar, thought otherwise. 'Until?' he demanded as he pulled even more distractedly upon his brother's beard.

King Shahzaman only shook his head, a difficult feat when your beard is being wrenched.

But still did the tall king bid the younger to continue, or he might have to consider a beheading of his own. And further did Shahryar remind him that Shahzaman was in Shahryar's kingdom, with Shahryar's army, and Shahryar's headsman, and Shahryar's extensive network of prisons and torture chambers.

'Then again,' Shahzaman replied with a wisdom common only in kings, 'perhaps I am compelled by brotherly duty to speak.' So did he tell his brother what indeed happened after 'Until,' especially concerning the night that he had witnessed his brother's wife with the forty slaves.

But when the younger of the two was done, the elder brother declared that he could not believe in such a thing, and had to see it with his own eyes.

Then did Shahzaman, who still realized the possibility of the headsman's axe, suggest that his elder brother loudly announce that the two kings would now embark on a hunt together but, instead of doing this thing, they would instead both secrete themselves in a corner of the palace with a clear view of the garden.

Shahryar agreed to this plan and quickly made it so, announcing that he would hunt again on the morrow. But while he sent a full complement of hunters and attendant servants out into the great forests beyond the palace, he and his brother stayed behind within a secret place and then moved quietly to a balcony overlooking the gardens.

Mere moments passed before the queen reappeared in the garden and around her frolicked the forty slaves, and all were clothed, or rather unclothed, precisely as before. And, after a verbal exchange between the queen and her primary slave concerning bananas, melons, cherries and other fruit, all further proceeded in much the same manner as Shahzaman had previously related.

And there were many calls of 'Whoopie!' that arose from the garden, and even, I am afraid to relate, an occasional 'Hotcha!' Shahryar did witness this spectacle in his garden in every detail, first with disbelief, then with anger, and lastly with an ever-growing sadness. His grief doubled with every whoopie that rose from down below.

At last, he had had too much of this display, and so he said to his brother, 'Why must both of us, though we be kings, have to face this misery? I cannot bear to stay within this palace another instant. Come, we shall take to the road, until we might find someone who might explain why we must be so miserable, or until we might find someone who is even more miserable than we two kings!'

And Shahzaman, seeing his brother's grief, discovered his grief rekindled as well. So it was that both kings left the palace by a secret way, and took to the road, leaving their fate in the hands of Destiny.

The two kings traveled, day and night, until they came to a meadow by the great salt sea. And in this meadow was a tree of substantial age and height, and a modest pond of fresh water. The kings paused there to drink the fresh water and rest beneath the tree. But soon did a great black column of smoke rise from the sea, as if the ocean itself was on fire. The two brothers cried in fear and sought the safety of the upper branches of the tree, as that blackest of black smoke whirled its way towards them, until, upon its arrival on the beach, the smoke cleared to reveal a huge *djinni*, the size of

7

three men standing one upon the shoulders of the others. And this *djinni* carried upon the top of his head a great ivory box. But it was the box who spoke: 'You may put me down there.'

'Yes, most beloved,' the *djinni* said hurriedly, and placed the ivory box, which was worked with intricate designs and set with many precious stones, upon the ground only a small distance from the pond and the hiding place of the kings. And then did the *djinni* call out in his great and booming voice: 'Come out, come out, Oh Sulima, and do your dance for me!'

Then did the lid of the box push open, and a woman of perfect size and form stepped forth. She was dressed all in the finest silk, in a gown whose color seemed to change with every movement she took beneath the sun, so that one moment her dress was the blue of the sky, the next the red of blood, and at a third moment the yellow-orange of wildflowers.

'I do as you command!' the woman said to the great *djinni*, and she began to dance, her arms and legs shifting back and forth to subtle rhythms, and so graceful and regular were her movements that neither the *djinni* nor the two kings could tear their gaze away from her.

'Most wonderful!' the *djinni* called to the maiden after he had yawned most prodigiously. 'My beloved Zzzzzzz.' And the last word was nothing more than a snore, for the *djinni* had fallen fast asleep.

'Now he has been placed out of the way,' the woman called loudly and with great merriment, 'which of you in the tree will be first?'

'Who?' Shahzaman called out in surprise.

'Which tree?' Shahryar added.

'Oh come now, my fine gentlemen,' the woman Sulima rejoined. 'I have known you were there from the moment I popped out of the sea. Now which of you warriors will be the first to try your fine lance upon me?' And with that she smiled and snapped her fingers, producing tiny flames within the palms of each hand.

The two brothers turned to look one upon the other. Shahryar made a gracious wave of his hand towards the younger king. 'You were most recently my guest, and guests shall always go first.'

But to that, Shahzaman replied, 'Oh no, my dear brother. I insist that you are the elder, and thus must go before me in all things.'

Thus did they argue for some moments, with much gesturing and suggestive waving of eyebrows, until Sulima interrupted.

'Enough! Someone must pierce me quickly, or I shall wake the *djinni*, and you shall both experience a death too horrible to describe!'

Well, there was nothing for the kings to do but obey her command. And once they had both done her bidding, and were well weary, Sulima shouted a final 'Whoopie!' and further stated, 'You are indeed experienced riders!' Then did she tell the two kings that once she was a mortal woman, but had been stolen away and ravished by the *djinni* on her wedding night. Since then, she had learned the way of *djinn*, and had made good use of them.

'Pardon me,' she said, as she reached beneath her silken gown and pulled forth a necklace.

'What is that?' Shahzaman croaked, for his voice was much strained from his recent endeavors.

'It is a necklace of seal rings: five hundred and seventy rings long,' she replied, 'for I demand the seal ring of every man whom I enjoy. Come, quickly give me yours, or I shall dance again, and lull you into such a slumber that you shall still be asleep when the *djinni* awakes, and terrible will be his vengeance!'

With an argument like that, what could the kings do but hand over those rings with which they placed their seals of office upon important documents. And she laughed mightily as the two kings crawled away with what energy they could muster until they at last found a place hidden from that meadow, and fell into an exhausted sleep.

But when they had at last awoken, Shahzaman remarked unto his brother: 'If my fate is like a diarrheic bird, and yours the leavings of a herd of oxen, the *djinni*, for all his power, must contend with a fate the likes of all the offal in greater Baghdad.'

'It is time to go home,' Shahzaman agreed.

These were the events that led to my introduction into the tale. These, and three hundred-odd beheadings.

## Chapter the Second,
## in which certain brides have a tendency
## to lose their heads.

So it was that each of the kings went his separate way and
Shahzaman returned to Samarkand, and thus left our story for a
time. And Shahryar returned to Baghdad, that great and fabled
city that is the envy of all the world, but he was still greatly troubled
by what he had seen.

On the moment of his return, he had his wife beheaded, for this
had seemed to work well for his younger brother, and further
treated all those forty servants whom the queen had consorted with
in a similar fashion. But still could the king not take his ease. His
queen was gone, and he found something missing within his life.

Therefore did Shahryar go to his grand vizier, a stately man
known as Aziz. And he said to his trusted servant, 'Go among my
people, and find me the most beautiful of women. For I am lonely
without my queen, and desire to take a new bride.'

Aziz hurried to obey, choosing a beautiful young woman from a
family of substantial prominence within the city. And, upon the
vizier's return to the palace with the new bride, Shahryar declared
that he and the girl would be married that very night, for, since he
was king, he could make short work of all the necessary authoriza-
tions. So it was that Aziz made all the other preparations and, as
the sun removed itself from its watch over the earth, the king and
the young woman were married most solemnly. After the brief but
festive celebration which followed, the king then took his new
bride to his bedchamber so that he might relieve that burden
placed upon his heart.

But, at that moment when he first rested his hand upon the
tender skin of the young woman, a profound change occurred in her
appearance. First did she take on the countenance of his former
queen, whom he had so much loved before that day of deceit. And
she smiled sweetly, as if to say, 'Did not I have the most beautiful
of heads, before you deigned to cut it from my body?'

11

With that, the king called out in fright and turned away as he withdrew his hand from her perfect young form. And his new queen, who only wished her new master the greatest of pleasures, asked, 'What is the matter, Oh king? Is there something about my imperfect form that displeases you?'

Surely, the king thought, I have had a delusion, for I have been much strained by the recent passing of events. So he turned back to his youthful bride again, hoping that his vision of his former queen would have vanished. And, indeed, when he regarded her again, she no longer resembled his former bride. Instead, to King Shahryar's extreme discomfort, she had taken on the countenance of that woman who was woman no more, but through her union with the *djinni* had assumed certain characteristics of that unholy race. Her eyes seemed to be lit by twin flames, and she threw her head back and laughed as she cried, 'You are such a fine rider. Once I have loved you, you shall never forget me! Once I have loved you, you will long to love me forevermore!' And, having said these things, her laughter then redoubled until it filled the king's ears and seemed like the only sound in all the world.

In a great fright, Shahryar pulled forth his own scimitar and separated that laughing head from the beautiful body. But, once life left the body before him, it no longer resembled the almost human consort of *djinn*, nor was it the likeness of his unfaithful queen, but instead the body of the beautiful young girl.

The king summoned his slaves and had the body quickly removed. At first he had thought he was deluded by grief but now believed he had fallen victim to the vile magics of Sulima, the lustful woman who was truly woman no more. This was a most disquieting turn of events, even for one of such majestic demeanor as Shahryar.

But no king would admit defeat after but a single battle. He therefore summoned again his faithful vizier and informed Aziz that there had been an unfortunate accident, and the king was therefore no longer among the married. But all was not amiss, for Shahryar believed that this accident had done a great deal to clear certain difficulties from his mind.

He therefore ordered Aziz to go forth on the morrow so that he might find the king another marriageable girl. Shahryar would then be married again upon the following evening, which would no doubt result in a union both far more satisfying and of longer duration.

So did the grand vizier go forth upon the following morning, and he located a second girl of marriageable age from a family of great respectability. And, that evening, the wedding and feasting proceeded in such a manner that all indications pointed to Shahryar having found a new queen at last. The king led his new bride to the marriage chamber but, as his slaves were removing his many wedding robes, he heard a voice say close by his ear in a tone of great jest, 'We will show these cushions they have been used!' And a second voice added in a tone of even greater ribaldry, 'It is time I once again witnessed your lance!'

Almost before Shahyrar was aware of the movement of his arm, his sword had once again come free of its sheath and his newest bride's head had lost the acquaintance of her body.

It was then that King Shahryar realized he truly had a problem. Not only was he losing bride after bride, but he was also receiving no satisfaction of his manly needs. If he was forced by this curse to behead young girl after young girl, the least he could do was ravish them first.

So it further occurred that the king once again spoke with his grand vizier. And, in giving the good Aziz his new instructions, the king stated, 'Let us be done with this marriage business. I bid you to find another girl of comely appearance and graceful manner somewhere within my city's walls. She shall be my consort, and it will be her honor to help me recover from my grief.'

Any wish of the king's became the vizier's wish as well. Aziz therefore once again left the palace and, after some little search, found a reasonably attractive young woman of marriageable age from a family of somewhat lower social standing, for this business about the beheadings had been getting about in the upper reaches of society.

Still did the night-time come, as it surely must at the end of the day. And, upon this evening, since there had been no wedding to waste his valuable time, Shahryar found himself within his chambers at a much earlier hour. And also present was the maiden, guided there by the faithful Aziz, who then had prudently taken his leave.

The girl stared most humbly at the floor as her king approached.

'Take off your garments,' Shahryar instructed, 'for you are to be ravished by a king.'

'Most certainly, sire,' she replied, as she began to remove her outer garments.

Surely, Shahryar thought, this would be different from his earlier nights. Truly, then, he should finally be able to facilitate his male requirements. And after that all-important easement, who knew? Well, of course, there could still be a beheading, but it no longer seemed quite so required. For the first time in ever so long, the night appeared to be alive with possibilities.

Still, however, was the king wary of a repetition of the events of the last pair of evenings. So it was that he instructed his young consort in the following manner: 'I caution you, if you value your life, you will not discuss overmuch the use of cushions.'

'Cushions?' she asked, her eyes still studying the floor. 'No, I will certainly not mention such a thing, if it is your wish.'

Yet even hearing that word 'cushions' come from the young woman's lips made the king shiver. Would the curse visit him this night as well? But surely, she was only responding to his request. And yet, were that the case, why should he feel such unease?

'And lances!' the king therefore added with all speed. 'I do not want to hear a word about lances!'

'Whyever—' the young girl began, but then paused to giggle as Shahryar reached to undo his belt. 'Oh, those sort of lances! My girl friends have told me much about riding—'

'Oh bother!' the king muttered distractedly. For as soon as those words had come from her mouth, his sword was out and her head was off.

Certainly, he thought thereafter, he might have acted too quickly with this particular maiden. And yet, when one was a king, one could not be too careful. There would be other nights, and other maidens.

So it proceeded, night after night, maiden after maiden, beheading after beheading, until the king seemed to be performing these rituals out of force of habit.

It is at this point that I enter the story.

I was but a young maiden at this time, some months prior to today. And I lived with my sister, Dunyazad, within the fine apartments of my father, the grand vizier, who was that same Aziz who I have mentioned earlier within my tale.

So it was that one morning I chanced upon my father in a state of great worry, for as I approached he wrung his hands repeatedly, only pausing in these actions to pull upon his beard, and further did he seem to take no notice of me when I entered the room, although in the normal course of events my arrival would always be rewarded with a word or a smile.

'Father,' I therefore asked, 'what vexes you so?'

My question caused him to look upon me at last, and he

14

attempted a smile which his worry would not allow. 'Oh my daughter!' he replied. 'I am faced with the most perplexing of difficulties. Three hundred days and nights have passed since our king returned from his travels and decided to change his habits. Alas! Every marriageable and even some not-so-marriageable woman in the kingdom has fallen to our ruler's curse! And now, if I can find no one to occupy the great king's bed this evening, I fear I shall fall beneath his head-shearing blade myself!'

To this worried exclamation, I could but smile and gently remark, 'But, Father, you have two fine daughters yourself.'

'Scheherazade?' he whispered, as if the thought had never occurred to so protective a father. 'Dunyazad? No, never shall I expose either of my daughters to such a fate. It is better that I be beheaded!'

'Nonsense,' I replied. 'There may be a certainty that I shall enter the king's chambers, but I am not certain in the least that I shall lose my head.'

Still did my father protest, giving me many fine examples and stories of the difficulties that I might endure, for it was always the custom within my family to illustrate our concerns with the telling of tales. But still was I adamant in my goal, for I felt that someone should show our good king that certain small errors had crept into his behavior, and that he should be far happier should he abandon these errors; much as women have responded over the years to those many modest errors of their near-to-perfect husbands. And, should I succeed in this task, I should then spare all those other marriageable women who had recently fled or were in hiding within the city walls.

This did I insist to my father, until he at last said, 'It is beyond me! If you insist upon this thing, it is in the hands of Allah!' But he did add, if I was to have union with the king, it would be a legal union, in accordance with his position as a grand vizier. Therefore would there be the first royal wedding in some 298 days.

Having made his decision, my father left to make all necessary preparations for that evening's wedding. And I had preparations to make as well, if I was to ensure my survival beyond the wedding night. So it was that I spoke to my younger sister, Dunyazad, and insisted that she find her way to a certain place at a certain time and, at the first indication of difficulty, I told her the proper things to say and do, most specifically that she should mention loudly, and repeatedly if necessary, that Scheherazade was especially noted for her tales of marvel.

15

Soon my father returned with my wedding garments, and they were fine indeed, fully suited to a vizier's daughter who was about to be married to a king. So did I ready myself for my wedding and the hour came when my transportation arrived to bring me and my family to the palace.

So it was that I began my journey to the king's chambers, on what all surmised would be the last night of my existence.

## Chapter the Third,
### in which our heroine acts before she speaks.

This begins the true tale of Scheherazade.

For the wedding proceeded in the way of all weddings, except that perhaps the great wailing of the women was fraught with an extra edge, due to the certain possibility of the bride's very short life expectancy. And, once the festivities were at an end, Scheherazade and Shahryar, wife and husband, queen and king, retired to their chambers with a suitable retinue to attend to their needs.

So was it that the king took Scheherazade into his strong arms and said to her, 'Come, my queen, and give me pleasure, as is a wife's duty, but do not speak of cushions, or lances, or riding, or seal rings, nor should you laugh to excess, nor pretend to be humble when you are in actuality bewitched, nor make any oblique references to *djinn* or magic in any form!' And as the king spoke, his manner became ever more agitated, and he pulled his hands away from his betrothed and, with a great twitching and moaning, found his gaze evermore drawn to the sword at his belt.

Now Scheherazade, who had received much learning and had heard many stories at the feet of her enlightened father, could surmise what might next transpire. Therefore, she did remark with all speed and clarity, 'No, my king, I should not think to mention any thing that you do not wish. Still, before you take overmuch time admiring your sword, might I mention that I was looking forward to your ravishing my virginity?'

'A sword?' the king replied in a voice that was exceedingly strange. 'A sword is rather like a lance, isn't it? What did I say about lances?'

'I was speaking of my soon-to-be-lost virginity,' Scheherazade reminded him gently.

'What?' the king remarked, as if awaking from a trance. 'Oh, yes. Most certainly. Virginity. And ravishing. Yes, very much indeed.'

'Is there some problem that I should be aware of?' the new queen asked most sweetly.

'No, not particularly,' the king replied, surprised that a woman whose life was probably now measured in minutes would sound so concerned for his welfare. So it was that he found himself speaking thoughts that he had shared with no one before. 'Well,' he therefore began, 'you have no doubt heard of my many marriages and trysts and what-not. And I'm sure that rumor has it that I ravished every one of these women, and then beheaded them in turn.' He paused to sigh deeply. 'In actuality, not all of this is true. Some of the marriages and trysts have not gone as well as planned. Yes, yes, and a large number of the ravishings have not been given sufficient time to be entirely successful either. Alas,' and here he paused to sigh again, 'only the beheadings seem to have been a total success.'

'That is the saddest of stories,' Scheherazade commiserated as she undid the sash about her garments, 'but perhaps a bit of ravishing will put you in a better mood.'

'Ravishing?' The king began to shift his garments as well. 'Well, yes. Now that you mention it, I suppose things could be looking up a little here.' He fumbled with his robes, which seemed to have become entangled with his scabbard. 'I seem to be a bit out of practice.'

'Perhaps,' Scheherazade remarked softly, 'it would be easier if you first removed your sword?'

'My – sword?' the king sputtered. 'My lance, don't you mean? Or what about my *cushions*? My *riding*? *My seal ring*?'

He freed his scabbard from his robes only to draw his sword. 'All this talk of ravishing almost had me beguiled! As if I would knowingly want to ravish a demon!' And so did he raise his sword to strike.

This, then, was the terrible moment that the young queen had been preparing for. 'Wait, Oh great king!' Scheherazade therefore called in her most pitiful tone, making certain that her remarks were accompanied by copious tears. 'If you must kill me, I pray that you grant me one final boon.'

And the king, shaken by her weeping, hesitated in his terrible judgement. 'Well, yes,' he remarked, 'I suppose, before this talk of swords, you had shown great concern for my difficulties. Therefore, I shall listen to your final request before I end your life. But I warn you, a single mention of cushions or seal rings, and my sword shall strike!'

'Very well, Oh master of my fate,' Scheherazade replied, and

18

she was most careful in the words she chose next, so that nothing might lead the king's thoughts back to those things that directed his sword arm. 'I have but one final wish. Before I die, I would like to see my beloved younger sister, Dunyazad, one last time.'

The king frowned at that. 'Well, I suppose that is not so unreasonable a request, save that it might take some time to fetch this beloved sister.'

'On the contrary, my king, she may join us immediately.' And with that, Scheherazade called out her sister's name. Immediately, the door to the king's chamber opened, and the fair young Dunyazad entered the room.

The king's frown only deepened. 'There are things here that I do not understand.'

'Oh, sister,' Dunyazad called out upon seeing Scheherazade. 'It is so good to see you again. Pray, tell me one of your tales of marvel, that I do so admire!'

With that, the king called out in great consternation, 'I cannot even ravish this young woman, and now I have to listen to her stories?'

But Scheherazade smiled most sweetly at that remark, and replied that she had mentioned nothing about not being ravished.

Dunyazad, for her part, decided this was a good time to examine the woodworking in the other nearby chambers of the king's quarters. Scheherazade, however, did anything but move the other way. Before he could think further upon it, Shahryar found his outer garments removed, and then his inner garments.

When Dunyazad had determined that a sufficient time had elapsed, and also when the loud cries had ceased to emanate from the adjacent room, she once again visited her sister and the king, who lounged together beneath great squares of silk and the cured skins of exotic animals.

'Ah, most assuredly,' Shahryar said from behind half-closed eyelids. 'Ravishing. I shall have to partake more often. Now, what have I done with my sword?'

But instead of giving him a most direct answer, Scheherazade remarked, 'Regard, Oh king! My sister, Dunyazad, has returned.'

And Dunyazad, for her part, replied, 'Pray, Oh sister, tell me one of your tales of marvel, that I do so admire!'

With that, the king raised his eyebrows in interest. 'Oh, yes, yes, I suppose the sword might wait for a bit. Let us have a story by all means!'

Dunyazad and Scheherazade then exchanged a secret smile, in

the way that sisters sometimes do. And Dunyazad found a place to sit among the cushions, being careful not to mention those objects by name since, when she had been outside the chamber door, she had heard all that had transpired within.

'Perhaps,' Scheherazade said, 'I might think of a suitable story.' And with those words, she firmly laid the path of her Destiny.

*Chapter the Fourth,*
*in which a story is left hanging,*
*rather than a head.*

And Scheherazade told the following story:

THE TALE OF THE MERCHANT AND THE *DJINNI*

'I have heard, Oh auspicious king, that once there was a great merchant, revered among all of his kind, and known to market-places great and small throughout all the civilized world. Great were this merchant's travels, for he roamed the world looking for new items to trade and new wonders to explore.

'So it was that this merchant found himself in a distant place upon the passing of the old year unto the new, far from his family and acquaintances. And further did he go for a walk in this strange land, which was built on the edge of a beautiful but arid waste, and in the course of this walk he did find himself traversing that space where arable land gave way to desert. Truly the merchant had come to a magnificent vista, for in this spot where he now found himself, the two spaces were separated by a great ravine, so that all was green upon one side, and all was barren rock upon the other.

'What better place, the merchant thought, to contemplate his life and the nature of existence upon the new year, than in this spot where life and death dwelt side-by-side. So it was that he found a suitable spot to rest where he could observe both these realms, and, having gained a certain degree of comfort, he reached within his food bag and began to chew reflectively upon a series of dates, eating one after another, as is the manner of a lonely man and a bag of dried fruit. And, within the midst of this chewing and great reflection upon life, the merchant did further amuse himself by tossing the pits down within the ravine.

'This last action, alas, was not among the most fortuitous decisions made by the merchant. For, after he had thrown three pits within the ravine, he heard a great commotion from down

21

below, followed by a tremendous roaring that rapidly approached that point upon which the merchant sat, until who should jump from the ravine but a powerful *djinni* of fearsome appearance—'

## SCHEHERAZADE INTERRUPTS HER TALE
## WITHIN A TALE

It is here that I paused in my storytelling to mention:

'—although I do have it on good authority that this *djinni* was nowhere near so powerful, and barely even half as fearsome, as our own Ozzie.'

'WELL SAID,' spoke the head of the great green *djinni* from that point where it watched the three storytellers and their audience. 'ARE YOU THEREFORE AN EXPERT IN SUCH MATTERS?'

'I humbly submit that I am, Oh great *djinni*,' was my measured reply. 'A storyteller, to be convincing in her art, must be an expert in a great many things.'

Ozzie nodded at this. 'YOU HAVE INDEED HELD YOUR OWN AGAINST THE STORIES TOLD BY SINBAD AND ALI BABA, AT LEAST IN THE MATTER OF BEGINNINGS. I HAVE DECIDED, THEREFORE, NOT TO KILL ALL OF YOU IN SOME HORRIBLE, PERHAPS EVEN UNSPEAK-ABLE FASHION, AT LEAST FOR THE TIME BEING. PRAY CONTINUE.'

## THE TALE OF THE MERCHANT AND THE *DJINNI*,
## CONTINUED

'You are most gracious,' I allowed as I returned to my tale. 'Now this fearful *djinni* pointed to the merchant and said, "Stand, so I may kill you as you have killed my son!"

'The merchant trembled at this accusation, and was further at a loss for a suitable reply.

'"It happened as my son was streamlining his magic carpet," the *djinni* further bemoaned. "You know that things never go fast enough for the young. He looked up at the precise moment that one of the date stones fell and hit him in – well – that fatal spot that all *djinn* have and that I would not even mention to you if I was not shortly to murder you."

'But, with that most recent mention of murder, the merchant's wits once again reacquainted themselves with his head and he rediscovered his voice. "That is a tragic tale," he said to the *djinni*. "But I ask for a boon."

'"A boon?" the *djinni* replied in a tone that indicated his displeasure.

'"While I have no doubt caused the death of your son," the merchant quickly explained, "I submit to you that I had no knowledge of this act until it was done. Therefore will I tell you that I am an honorable man, and always fulfill my obligations. But, to go to my death with a clear heart, there are certain debts and obligations that I must discharge. Therefore, I ask you for one week's time to put my affairs in order. At the end of this time, we shall meet here again, and you shall do as you will."

'The *djinni* pondered this request. The merchant certainly spoke with great sincerity and, while this human was also responsible for the death of his son, the *djinni* did not wish to appear to be an unreasonable entity. Therefore did he grant the merchant the week to finish his affairs. But, at week's end, the merchant had to swear that he would return so that the *djinni* could wreak his terrible revenge.

'And with that, the *djinni* returned to his ravine, and the merchant swiftly traveled back to his home city and discharged all that he considered fair and equitable among those to whom he owed monies, and those who owed monies to him. And so it was that the merchant bid a final farewell to all his friends and family and then returned, as promised, to that spot where his death awaited him.'

## THE TALE IS INTERRUPTED,
## THIS TIME BY THE BIRDS

At this point, Scheherazade paused to take a breath. And her younger sister, the fair Dunyazad, spoke to say, 'Listen! It is almost morning! I hear the calling of the birds!'

'Indeed, you are correct,' Scheherazade replied humbly. 'I have most assuredly spoken for far too long. It is the greatest of shames that I have had a chance to tell but a mere portion of my tale, and those great marvels, miracles, and reversals of fortune that were to happen later in the story will have to remain unsaid.'

'Yes, it is a pity,' the king agreed. 'And after all that nice ravishing, too.'

'Well, you are the king,' Scheherazade replied, ever so sweetly. 'And if you feel that it is important to dispense with any further ravishing, not to mention hearing the end of my ever-more-dramatic tale, I shall understand, even though such a decision shall cost me my head!'

'No, no!' the king declared. 'I cannot have you face such a sacrifice! My swift and terrible sword can surely wait until tomorrow night!'

'As you wish,' Scheherazade replied with the contented smile of a woman in the presence of such a decisive king.

'Come,' the king called to his slaves, who had been waiting discreetly nearby. 'Scheherazade and Dunyazad shall wait for me within my harem while I attend to my daily affairs of state. And, then, tonight—' The king paused, as though even one as great as he had difficulty deciding what to say next.

'Tonight,' Scheherazade offered for him, 'shall be even more fantastic than the night before.'

'So be it!' the king agreed, and clapped his hands in that way that instructed his staff and servants to make his wishes so.

Therefore was Scheherazade escorted to her new home, a place suitable in other times for a queen. But this harem had been affected by the king's penchant for separating pretty heads from lovely shoulders, so that certain dark forces had entered even these inner confines of the palace.

But Scheherezade, along with her sister Dunyazad, entered this place with a light heart. For how were either of them to know that it was not the nights, but the days, that would offer them both far more opportunities for death?

*Chapter the Fifth,*
*in which there is some discussion of matters of life*
*and of death, as well as certain individuals who*
*may exist somewhere in between.*

So it was that Scheherazade and Dunyazad were shown to the great harem of King Shahryar. And it was truly a magnificent edifice, with five times a hundred separate cubicles for the lesser wives and concubines, and another dozen or two more finely appointed apartments for the more favored among the king's familiars, not to mention common areas of substantial size, including a bathing pool the length and width of a marketplace, and a garden larger than many villages. Furthermore, the many rooms were graced with great, high-domed ceilings, the numerous walls were covered with a thousand different colorful tapestries, and even the hundreds upon hundreds of pillars all showed fantastic designs of flowers and birds painted there in gold.

But, while this harem was in the first place huge, and in the second place well appointed, it also struck the sisters in the third place as being empty in the extreme. Scheherazade asked their guide if this sense of emptiness held any basis in truth. And at that, the elderly servant who showed them their way nodded sagely and replied, 'Once, this place boasted a thousand servants for the many wives and concubines. Alas, after all this beheading business began, the wife and concubine population experienced a precipitous drop. After that occurrence, there seemed no need to keep together such a staff, since hardly anyone remained to be served.' The elder coughed delicately. 'There has also been a certain tendency for some of the unfettered servants to quietly disappear, as if they believed that this propensity for sudden death among their mistresses might be contagious!' At this, the elderly servant laughed but he also rubbed at his neck, as if to assure himself that all his parts were still in their proper places.

'Ah, but as underpopulated as these quarters are,' he added

hurriedly, 'they are still far from empty. Omar! Where are you, you scoundrel?'

'Always at your service,' a high voice said from immediately behind them. Scheherazade and her sister spun about to find a man of enormous height and girth towering above them, his plentiful flesh exposed, layer after layer of glistening fat, save for a small, discreet loincloth of golden fabric that covered his privates, and a number of golden bangles that encircled his arms, his neck, and large hoops that dangled from either ear.

The elderly servant turned about at a more leisurely rate. 'Ah,' he said genially. 'Good of you to be so prompt. These two young women have need of apartments.'

'Really?' the large man replied in a beautiful soprano. 'You have no idea how long it has been since I've heard those words!' He laughed merrily. 'And who might these women be, so that I can be assured of finding them suitable accommodations?'

The elder servant first introduced Scheherazade.

'The new queen?' Omar proclaimed in wonder. 'I always knew that someday, *someone* would survive that first night! Ah, I shall have to show you our very best accommodation.' He clapped his hands. Somehow, his immensely pudgy palms made hardly any sound at all when they came together. 'And believe me, you may do whatever you want with the apartment during your stay. We'll simply clean it up after you're dead.' He giggled softly. 'This leads me to recall a poem:

> 'Once these rooms were full of sunlight,
> Rich with sweet laughter and flowers gay
> But a cloud covered the sun, the laughter died,
> Should you pick a flower, you'll find decay.'

Oh, thought Scheherazade. This had been a somber poem, but not without a certain poignancy.

'Second verse!' Omar announced:

> 'Once these rooms were filled with life
> And sweet perfume that's long forgot,
> But the floor is now bathed with woman's blood,
> And fair smells have been lost to rot.'

'Yes,' Scheherazade stated, 'a most excellent poem. Now if we might get on—'

'It becomes even more dramatic in verse number three!' Omar announced as he once again resorted to rhyme:

> 'Blood and death and rot and sorrow
> Make up this spot's exigency,
> And all who step within this place
> Are covered with malignancy.

'So ends my humble offering.' Omar bowed slightly and smiled. 'Sometimes I think it makes us all feel better if I can put something in rhyme.'

The elder servant, who seemed to pay no attention to the poem whatsoever, further introduced Dunyazad.

'A relative?' Omar said, with considerably less enthusiasm. 'Well, there must be some out-of-the-way place where we might put her. Ah, I know the very room; well, it is little more than a closet, really, but it is in the same quarter of the harem as the queen's chambers, and little more than a five-minute walk from those apartments.'

Scheherazade decided it was at last time to make a modest request. 'Are not my quarters large enough to accommodate more than one?'

'In actuality,' Omar answered, 'your quarters are large enough to accommodate a modest army. Why do you ask?'

'I wish that my sister might stay with me,' Scheherazade said sweetly but firmly.

'Oh, dear,' Omar replied with the slightest of frowns.

'It would be such a comfort,' Scheherazade urged. Dunyazad, for her part, smiled politely, although her eyes were full of sadness for her sister.

'Comfort?' Omar sighed. 'It is highly irregular. But, I suppose, since there are so few left to judge propriety in this place, and in consideration of the short period of time you will no doubt occupy the room – well, I certainly don't see why not.'

'Very good.' Scheherazade offered her benefactor the most gracious of smiles. 'I thank you for your courtesy.'

Seeing that the formalities had been nicely taken care of, Dunyazad then sought fit to ask a question of Omar on her own. 'Are you then Chief among the Eunuchs?'

The very large fellow hesitated before answering. 'May I say that I can but aspire to that title. Were it not for certain shortcomings—' And with that, Omar's voice dropped off discreetly, as if the whole issue were far too painful to discuss.

'I will leave you ladies now,' the elderly servant announced. 'Omar will show you to your quarters. Rest well. The king shall see you again at sunset.'

Omar nodded pleasantly. Although he probably weighed twice that of Scheherazade and Dunyazad combined, his feet made no sound as they glided across the polished floors. He led them quickly through the long entry hall, which was the size of twenty houses built end to end, and across one corner of the garden, which was so large that Scheherazade could not discern the far wall. There they came to a pair of doors made of solid gold, that measured twelve feet high by twelve feet wide.

'This is your apartment,' Omar remarked as he pushed open the nearer of the doors. 'These seven rooms will be your home. I regret to inform you that, due to the lack of staff, we have closed off the other two-thirds of the apartment.'

'This will do very nicely,' Scheherazade said to the man who could only aspire to be chief among the eunuchs. She thereupon turned to her sister. 'We must get a few hours of sleep, so that we are both ready for this evening.'

Dunyazad nodded at the wisdom of that remark as she preceded her sister into the room. Yet Dunyazad had taken but a single step into the room before she cried out in fright.

Scheherazade quickly walked in after her, to find Dunyazad pointing to the far end of the very large room. There stood a woman, wearing a robe of dark silk, whose face was as pale as the ice shipped down from the great mountains. The woman, upon seeing Scheherazade, turned quickly and vanished behind a partition in the corner.

Omar crowded in behind the women. 'Do you find something amiss?'

'Who was that?' Scheherazade asked.

'Who was who?' was Omar's reply.

'That woman who was just here,' Scheherazade explained. 'The one wearing the fine, dark silk.'

'There are no other women here but the servants. And the servants do not, as a rule, wear silk.' Omar hesitated, as if he was unsure that he should continue. 'That is, there are no other living women. Oh, now, some of the women servants have said that this place is haunted with the souls of those whose lives passed too quickly from the earth.' Omar coughed with great delicacy. 'There would certainly be a lot of those souls, considering our recent circumstances. And reflecting upon the bloody, violent and thoroughly unpleasant way that they ended their lives, these departed might want to wreak a horrible vengeance upon the living when they least expect it. But what are these stories but idle and no doubt harmless gossip?' The large fellow giggled again. 'This reminds me of another poem.'

And with that, he lifted his two hands towards the ceiling with all the fingers folded save for the little one on either hand, which he pointed to the sky. And Omar further declaimed:

> 'Turn the corner, you'll find death,
> A hanging form, a bloated corpse,
> A severed head and pools of gore—'

'Yes,' Scheherazade interrupted. 'While your poetry is most finely wrought, I believe it is time for my sister and I to take our repose.'

Omar frowned at that. 'Oh, dear. I suppose that verse was not among my best work. It is so difficult to find anything that rhymes with corpse.' Omar bowed remarkably low for one of so great a girth, and walked backwards towards the door with a silence equal to that of his forward motion. 'I hear and I obey! I leave you now so that you might gain your much needed repose.'

Scheherazade turned to ask her sister what she thought might be the best course of action. But Dunyazad had already crossed the room to that point where the mysterious lady had disappeared.

'She vanished behind this screen,' she declared as she also moved behind the partition. 'But there is nothing here but two bare walls!'

'Ah, now I do not want you two worrying about vengeful spirits,' Omar said from his position at the doorway. 'No doubt, if there was indeed another woman present within this room, we can also find a reason for her disappearance. Rumor has it that this harem is riddled with secret passageways and hidden doors. Back in those days when these quarters were more crowded, it was said that these hidden corridors were used with some frequency for purposes of court intrigue, especially assassination.' Omar's cough was the height of discretion. 'Let me assure you that there was very little bloodshed involved! Yes, death within the harem has almost exclusively been through poisoning. Which reminds me of another verse.'

'Were we not so fatigued!' Scheherazade exclaimed.

'Of course,' Omar agreed. 'I hear and I obey.' He grabbed the handles of the door and began to swing them shut. 'Give no thought to poisoning! Some food will be brought to you presently. I trust that the two of you will have the most restful day.' The doors slammed into place, and Omar was gone.

'What is happening here?' asked Dunyazad with some consternation.

Her sister paused a moment before giving her considered reply. 'The corner of the palace which contains the harem is immense and empty, and the more frightening because of that. But I feel there is more than emptiness here, and that this harem has a certain history that is with us still. I fear there are other forces at work within these walls that may be contributing to the king's problems.'

Dunyazad attempted to smile at Scheherazade's response. 'As always, sister, you speak with the sweet light of reason. Although our surroundings are troubled, I am doubly glad that we are together.'

'So am I, dear sister,' Scheherazade agreed. 'Now I truly think it is best that we sleep, so that we might have our wits about us.'

But Dunyazad would not relax so easily. 'You expect to sleep after what Omar told us?'

Scheherazade smiled gently at her sister's concern. 'I doubt that anyone should bother to kill us today when I am due to die by the king's hand this night. And once I am gone, you are no doubt the next in line for the king's attention.'

Dunyazad would still not be reassured. 'That is small reason to have an untroubled mind.'

At that, Scheherazade remarked: 'The plans of man and the actuality of events are often two different paths. No one may predict his Destiny. Of course, one would be foolish not to occasionally nudge Destiny in the proper direction.'

This caused Dunyazad to smile at last. 'Is that the sort of thing the wise men say?'

'No,' Scheherazade replied, with an answering smile. 'That is the sort of thing one learns as a storyteller.'

So it was that they both selected couches from the ten plus one that were scattered among this first room of the queen's apartment, and soon both had fallen into a deep and untroubled sleep that lasted through the morning. And, after the two of them had been roused for the midday prayers, half a dozen female servants arrived to take care of their needs, and both Scheherazade and Dunyazad were bathed in the great bagnio of the harem. There were they both anointed with precious oils and fine perfumes, and brought garments of delicate silk which contained threads of spun silver and gold. And when this was done, the two sisters were presented with a fine meal of fruits and meats and breads. And the servants sought to pass the time with palace gossip, which was almost nonexistent, since there were no longer any women of note within the palace.

Now, thought Scheherazade, this would be the proper time to ask about the strangely pale woman they had encountered within the queen's quarters. So did she ask the servants if there was some other occupant of the harem.

'There is, of course, the king's mother,' one of the servants replied. 'Some secretly speak of her encouraging all these beheadings. She has never thought that any woman was good enough for her son. But she is old and infirm, and seldom leaves her apartments.'

This, thought Scheherazade, did not sound like a promising line of inquiry. The woman they had seen was not in the least old nor infirm.

'Omar mentioned that there might be ghosts,' Dunyazad said.

At this, the servants nodded in unison.

'We have all heard rumors of spirits,' one of the servants agreed.

'There are shadows that move in every corner,' a second servant agreed.

'The night is often filled with strange noises,' added a third.

'But no one can say if any of these things are truly among us,' the first servant cautioned, 'or if it is only the wind.'

'No one has definitively witnessed any of these events,' the second servant agreed more cautiously.

'Well,' the third servant amended, 'no one has witnessed such events and then remained among the living for a long enough period to discuss them.'

Scheherazade and Dunyazad found all these remarks not quite so consoling as they might have wished.

'If it is not the returning dead,' fretted Dunyazad, 'what might it be?'

Scheherazade decided that it was the proper occasion to ask another question of the harem's more permanent occupants. 'Is there, then, no other woman who might be found somewhere within this vast harem?'

The servants looked to one another for a moment before the second of the three spoke up. 'There are also rumors that one woman has missed the king's sword.'

The third servant added, 'And that she lives in the back apartments and hidden corners of this vast place, fearful lest she be discovered and finally put to death!'

The first among the servants glanced at her two companions. 'If such a woman exists, maybe that was who you saw. The queen's apartments, after all, had not been used for the three hundred days before your arrival.'

All paused as, in the distance, they heard the deep ringing of a gong.

'The king is done with the duties of the day,' the first servant remarked. 'It is time for you to present yourself before his royal highness.'

Scheherazade looked to the doorway of the bathhouse, where she could already see Omar gliding silently across the floor to collect her and her sister.

Dunyazad gathered her elaborate skirts close about her body and leaned near to her sister.

'I am uncertain,' she said to Scheherazade. 'Have we learned any truths this day from our talk with the handmaidens?'

'Surely,' Scheherazade replied quietly, 'I feel this strangeness has something to do with the king. More than that, I cannot say.'

She did not add aloud that she felt both she and her sister were now unavoidably involved in whatever strange Destiny enveloped this palace. Why else should she have that feeling, for all of the afternoon, that there was something near, within the harem shadows, watching all that transpired?

## Chapter the Sixth,
### in which are discovered stories within stories, and mysteries within mysteries.

So it was that evening once again came to the great city, and Scheherazade was once again called before the king. And once again did Dunyazad accompany her sister, for her part in this drama was a crucial one.

On this occasion they were accompanied by Omar, who was silent in all his movements save for the occasional whisper, barely audible, of words like 'Such a shame. Such a waste. So young. So lovely'. He looked upon the two women and said in a somewhat louder voice, 'I believe this calls for a poem.'

Scheherazade thought to object, perhaps even to order this servant not to continue, for, after all, was she not queen? But then she considered, perhaps she should seek to make this man who could only aspire to be chief among the eunuchs into her ally, for she might need friends within the harem in the days ahead.

So she did not choose to speak as Omar began again:

> 'The harem is a lonely place,
> And you might become forlorn;
> For if the king desires you not
> You can do naught but mourn.'

Then again, Scheherazade was uncertain if she was willing to befriend someone who was so prone to poetry.

As if to strengthen her resolve, Omar began upon a second verse:

> 'You are torn by palace politics,
> The cares of the harem will have no rest,
> But your spirits still can be renewed
> By the solace of a pudgy breast.'

'Perhaps Omar is not so sinister as he first appears,' Dunyazad whispered to her sister. 'He seems to be offering us his friendship.'

'Is he?' Scheherazade replied. Perhaps she was reacting to his high voice, or the way he let his little fingers lift skywards whenever he recited. Or perhaps she was simply reserving judgement until Omar completed his next verse.

Omar, of course, obliged:

> 'There is someone to whom you may turn
> When the king says you don't deserve us;
> For as a child, I was snipped too late
> So that Omar is at your service!'

'Do I clearly understand—?' Scheherazade replied, with a certain astonishment.

'How might I put it delicately?' Omar bowed his head most humbly. 'While I have no seed, I can fulfill the need.'

It was now Dunyazad's turn to object. 'Omar, how dare—'

'I dare nothing,' replied most meekly the large man who now revealed why he could only aspire to the higher ranks of his kind. 'I only relate certain poems to raise the cares from your brow. I am here but to respond to the orders of my queen. I hear and I obey!'

But there could be no more discussion or poetry today, for they had reached their destination. The elite guardsmen of the king met the three at the door to Shahryar's apartments, and instructed Omar to depart and the two women to enter. Omar therefore glided silently away. Scheherazade watched his large form retreat and decided that there could indeed be something worse than Omar reciting his poetry. And that something would be Omar reciting his poetry while naked.

So it was that Scheherazade and Dunyazad once again entered that place in which one of them, at least, had some belief that she might never leave again. And when they were ushered again into the king's presence, they found him moodily reflecting upon the sword at his belt.

'It is amazing,' he mused, without glancing at either of the women, 'with all this beheading business, how many swords that I go through. Well,' he paused, being especially careful not to look directly at Scheherazade, 'not that you will have to worry about this blade for more than a second or two. I assure you that I have become quite proficient with practice.' He sighed deeply. 'Why do I brood so?' His hand tightened upon the hilt of his sword. 'Perhaps I have been too long without the proper action!'

It was at this point that Dunyazad received a look of great meaning from her sister.

34

---

'Oh, Scheherazade!' Dunyazad therefore declared, as the two sisters had prearranged. 'Pray, continue with your great tale of marvels, that I do so admire!'

With that, the king looked up in astonishment, as if he had only awoken from a mystical trance. 'Well, yes,' he remarked, in a far less mournful tone, 'I suppose I would like to hear the continuation of that story as well. But, I must admit, I was rather hoping there would be some ravishing this evening as well.'

'Did I say anything about there being no ravishing, Oh husband and master?' was Scheherazade's reply.

And Dunyazad once again thought it prudent to examine those furnishings and fixtures that were so important to the other rooms within the king's chambers for a sufficient period of time. But, when things were again adequately peaceful within that certain room, Dunyazad once again considered it fit to return, and found the two others once again beneath their bedclothes upon the couch.

'Ah,' the king said with a contented sigh, 'this ravishing could become a thing of habit. It makes a man glad that he knows how to ride.' He blinked in astonishment. 'Did someone mention riding? Hey?' His beatific smile was replaced by the most fearsome of grimaces. '*Could a mighty lance be far behind?*' He reached convulsively for his sword which, fortunately for all concerned, remained in the midst of a pile of clothes upon the floor.

It was at this point that Dunyazad received another look of great meaning from her sister.

'Oh, Scheherazade!' Dunyazad therefore declared, true to her training. 'Pray, now is certainly the time to continue with your great tale of marvels, that I do so admire!'

King Shahryar blinked again, as if recovering one more time from another of his periodic trances. 'Oh, yes, there is that, isn't there?' His smile returned to his face. 'And, perhaps after the story, and certainly before the blade, we might have time for a bit more ravishing.'

'Most assuredly, Oh most honored husband,' Scheherazade answered most prudently. 'So it is that I shall continue with my tale.'

And so did Scheherazade begin to speak:

## THE TALE OF THE MERCHANT AND THE *DJINNI*, CONTINUED FURTHER

'So it was that this honest merchant, having completed all those

35

obligations that awaited him in his homeland, returned to that spot where he should meet his final obligation, which was death at the hands of the *djinni*. And so he sat upon that very spot where, a week before, he had so imprudently eaten those dates and tossed those pits and so secured his doom.

'At the moment, however, the *djinni* was nowhere in evidence. Instead, the merchant saw three men approach him from those three directions other than the ravine before him, and each man was accompanied by an animal or two. And further, as these men approached, the merchant realized that each of them was a venerable sheikh.

'Now, the first of these sheikhs led behind him a graceful gazelle upon a golden chain. And this sheikh called out to the merchant, and asked him why he waited in this spot, for it was surely cursed by the most vengeful of *djinn*. So it was that the merchant quickly told his story, which we have already heard.

'When the merchant was done with his tale, the second sheikh came within hailing distance. This sheikh was followed by two great black greyhounds, tethered by leashes of finest leather, inset with bits of ruby and diamond. And this second sheikh called to both men before him, warning them that this was not the best of places to rest, since it was haunted by a *djinni* of evil disposition. As the subject had again arisen, the merchant quickly told his story once more, but we here know it well and it would serve no further purpose to repeat it now.

'So it was that the last of the three sheikhs, who himself led a she-mule whose bridle was inlaid with gold and silver and tied with ribbons of fine Chinese silk, came close to the gathering of men and animals. He hailed all those before him, further mentioning that perhaps it would be more fortuitous to meet elsewhere, since this particular spot was not only *djinni* infested but lately seemed to be filled with the refuse of passing travelers' meals.

'The merchant, after wondering for a moment where all three of these noble individuals had been a week before when he might have better heeded their advice, told his grim tale once again, but it would serve no good end to further study this earlier story, for, by this point, even the merchant had grown weary of the details.

'No sooner had the merchant finished this third and, he hoped, final telling of his tale, than there came a great commotion from the ravine, followed by a whirlwind that leapt up from the precipice and swept across the plain to but a short distance from those gathered there.

'It should come as no surprise to those listening to this story that in an instant the whirlwind disappeared, and in its place was the vengeful *djinni*, and on this occasion this *djinni* carried a great sword with the keenest of blades. The *djinni*'s eyes, which seemed to be lit by fires within, looked straight at the merchant, and the creature said, "Come, you have killed my child, and I shall give you a horrible and no doubt extremely messy death in return!"

'So did the merchant fall to his knees and await his fate with copious wailing and beating upon the earth. But the three sheikhs took pity on this poor man, and the first among them gathered his courage and spoke to the *djinni* saying, "Oh finest among all magical creatures, I myself have a story of marvels that concerns my own person and this gazelle. Should you find favor with this story, I beg you to spare one-third of the blood of this merchant!"

'"Very well," the *djinni* remarked after a moment's hesitation, "since, should I endeavor yet to take two-thirds of the man's blood, he is still sure to be dead three times over."

'"You are among the most merciful of *djinn*!" the first sheikh declared. "Here, therefore, is my story:

## THE TALE OF THE FIRST SHEIKH

'"Know ye, Oh great *djinni*, and all you others present, that this gazelle that you see before you was once my uncle's daughter, and blood of my own blood. Now I married this woman when she was but a girl and we lived together for thirty years, though Allah never saw fit to grace us with a child. So it was that, in time, I took a concubine, and in this case had the great good fortune to produce a strapping son. All seemed well until, at the time when the boy had aged to fifteen summers, I was obliged to leave the city on matters of business.

'"But dark things occurred in my absence. For little did I know that my wife had been well schooled in the witching arts when she was but a child. So it was that she used this sorcery to change both my son and his mother; the boy into a calf, the concubine into a cow, and then put them in charge of my herdsman with the rest of the cows. And, when I returned from my journey, my wife came to me and declared, 'Your slave has died, and your son, in his grief, has fled to I know not where!'

'"Great were my tears at this occurrence, and so did I suffer for the better portion of a year, until our annual Day of Atonement came upon us; that day when all of us must give up something of value to help feed us all. So it was that I instructed the keeper of my herd to locate a particularly fat cow that we might use for this purpose. When the herdsman brought this cow into my presence, I was taken by its face, for its eyes seemed to contain all the sadness upon this earth, as if this beast knew a suffering a hundredfold greater than my own. And when I lifted my knife to sacrifice this beast, the cow moaned deeply and began to cry great tears.

'"It was more than I could bear to kill this beast, despite the protestations of my wife, who observed all this close by my side and reminded me that the sacrifice had to be made. Therefore, I gave my knife to my herdsman and ordered him to kill the cow in my stead. This he did but, as we cut open the cow, we found no fat or flesh within, but only skin and bone.

'"Truly, this was most strange, and would not do as a sacrifice. So it was that I told the herdsman to pick a fatted calf from the herd while I pondered the meaning of this slaughtered cow who was cow no more.

'"The herdsman brought the calf and, when this calf saw me, he let out with a great cry and broke the tether that held him, and he ran towards me. And, as he approached, I saw that this calf's eyes contained the same sadness as the cow we had so recently slaughtered, and further did this calf begin to cry great tears as well.

'"I decided then that I could not sacrifice two such creatures and, patting the calf atop the head, instructed the herdsman to find another among the herd to serve as our sacrifice. But at that moment, my wife, who remained nearby, said, 'Why do you seek another calf when that one is so fatted to perfection?' And, indeed, I did wonder that myself, but the hand of Providence kept me still from this sacrifice.

'"So did that day end and the next begin, and on that second day my herdsman came to me with a tale of wonder.

'" 'Master,' he said to me, 'this calf was so sad and strange that I brought him to my daughter, who, like many women in this time and locality, has dabbled somewhat in the mystical arts. And when she saw this calf, she wept and laughed and covered her face with a veil, and further said, "Do you think so little of your daughter as to bring a strange man into her presence?"

'" 'I was quite astounded and asked my daughter what she meant. She responded quickly that this calf was truly not what he seemed, but was instead the bewitched son of our master the sheikh. Further, she had laughed at the bewildered expression upon his face, but she had wept that his mother had been sacrificed to the knife upon the day before.

' " " "Could this truly be?" I wondered aloud. And, in answer, she made certain signs in the air and said to the calf, "Assume your true form, whatever that may be." In an instant, there was a calf before us no more, but a strong young man of sixteen years.'

' "So did the herdsman once again present me with my son. And, so overjoyed was I at this event, that I insisted that my son and the herdsman's daughter be married as soon as possible, the only other business being the proper punishment of my wife. Upon hearing this, the herdsman's daughter said, 'Would not the most fitting punishment be to visit upon her what she has brought to others?' And, with that, the daughter turned my wife into the gazelle which you see before you now.

' "This is my story. What say you, Oh wondrous *djinni*?" '

### THE STORY OF THE MERCHANT AND THE *DJINNI*, CONTINUED FURTHER STILL

'At that,' Scheherazade continued, 'the *djinni* rose up to his full height, which was very high indeed, and raised his sword to an even greater height above his head, and all before him, merchant, sheikhs, and animals, cowered before his wrath.'

### THE TALE IS INTERRUPTED BY CERTAIN PINK TINGES

But at that very moment, as Scheherazade paused to take a breath, Dunyazad detected the first pink tinges of dawn through the shutters that enclosed the room. So did she say, 'Look! Your tale has been so involving that you have spoken until morning, and we can see the first welcoming rays of the sun!'

'My younger sister is again among the most observant,' Scheherazade remarked. 'Therefore shall I pause so that my husband may pursue his duties, even though I was only at this very moment coming to that part of the tale where surprise follows upon surprise, and the drama increases ten-fold. So come, Oh lord and master, and do what you must!'

'What I must?' the king asked with dawning comprehension. 'Ah. You must be talking about the sword. But how could I use that instrument upon your lovely neck when you are only now approaching the heart of your tale? Plus, there is all that ravishing to consider.'

'As my master wishes,' Scheherazade replied.

'Now where has that sword got to?' Shahryar remarked. 'Ah. Here it is beneath the sheepskin. No, for now the sword stays firmly within its scabbard. And we shall meet to enjoy another evening. Oops!'

And with that last remark, the sword fell from between the king's fingers, and clattered free of its scabbard on its own account, its momentum appearing to carry it twirling across the floor towards the storyteller at such a speed that Scheherazade, who was as quick of foot as she was of tongue, was forced to leap out of its path.

'Most clumsy,' the king remarked. 'One of these evenings, however, I will have to get some sleep.'

Scheherazade could not so easily be reassured. To her, the sword's movement did not seem like an accident. Rather the sword, or whatever invisible force guided the sword, moved with a will of its own.

And the object of that will was the death of Scheherazade.

## Chapter the Seventh,
### *in which life becomes less predictable than the tales of the storyteller.*

'What troubles you, Oh sister?' Dunyazad asked Scheherazade when the two of them were again alone within their apartments in the harem.

'I have been gifted with a supple imagination,' was Scheherazade's considered reply, 'and it is a gift that has served me well on this last pair of days. Yet, because of this boon, I find it sometimes difficult to discern the true nature of certain happenings and what precisely they portend. So it is with my surroundings here. I am troubled by various circumstances. Think upon the mysterious woman who appeared to vanish, the king's accident with the sword, even the uncanny silence of Omar.' The storyteller could not help but shiver. 'While perhaps it would be premature to associate these occurrences one to another, I surmise that none of these point to the healthiest of futures for the two of us.'

'Surely, things cannot be as bad as you suggest,' Dunyazad replied with what reassurance she could muster. 'You are the wife of the king, after all, and thus the most important woman in all of the kingdom. Your attentions are reserved for the monarch, and his subjects should beware anything that might interfere with that.'

Scheherazade gave the sort of small laugh that might have benefited from containing more humor. She asked, 'Such as a sword that might interfere with the connection of my head and body?'

'Well, there is that,' Dunyazad replied with a frown. 'But surely that is a special case.'

'So others will not kill me for fear that the king will instead?' Scheherazade further reasoned.

Dunyazad opened her mouth to comment, then closed it in thought. Her mouth opened a second time, but no words emerged. She took a deep breath, and remarked at last, 'It cannot be as bleak

41

as it first appears.' She shook her head. 'None of us is receiving sufficient sleep.'

'Perhaps that is indeed the reason that sweet understanding eludes us all,' Scheherazade agreed. 'I suggest that we proceed to that sleep as quickly as possible, before some other situation arises to confound us even farther.'

But, even as the sisters spoke, they both heard a deep gong sound three times in the distant recesses of the palace.

'Make yourself ready!' a high-pitched voice announced behind them. 'The Sultana approaches!'

Both the sisters jumped from their couches at the same time, for neither had heard Omar approach, nor had they heard him open the door.

'The Sultana?' Dunyazad inquired as she made some attempt to regain her breath.

'The mother of our noble king,' Omar explained for those not familiar with that particular honorarium. 'It is a great honor to be visited by the Sultana, for she has not graced any of those three hundred that preceded you with her presence. Of course, the fact that those three hundred did not remain within these quarters long enough to even plan for a royal visit might have something to do with that. At least—' He coughed politely. '—they did not remain among the living. Still, no matter. The Sultana's visit is the highest honor one may receive within the harem, and, after it is over, one might easily give up one's life and be fulfilled!'

Scheherazade, who had managed to regain her own breath during Omar's long summary, assured the fellow that his information was most reassuring, being careful not to mention that portion concerning the giving up of one's life. Instead, she prepared to ask Omar some questions about the Sultana's nature, so that she might better greet her. But, before she could firmly compose a sentence, the fellow who aspired towards the chiefdom of all the harem's eunuchs suddenly stepped aside and announced, 'It is our most holy Sultana! All lesser beings grovel at her feet!'

Scheherazade wondered for an instant if that remark concerning groveling was an honorarium bestowed upon the old woman, or a thinly veiled instruction as to how Scheherazade and Dunyazad were supposed to behave. Before she could consider this issue further, however, a woman of a girth equal to Omar, and moreover dressed all in deepest blue, swept into the room.

'Greetings, Sultana,' Scheherazade began, 'your most serene high—'

'You dare to stand in my presence?' the Sultana demanded. 'I have had many beheaded for far less than that. Of course, why should I bother with such an order when you shall surely lose your head tomorrow? A Sultana does not waste effort.'

Ah, Scheherazade considered. Omar's words had been an instruction for behavior, then. Scheherazade was most surprised that the Sultana, while a full head shorter than either of the two sisters, still managed somehow to look at both of them down the length of her nose.

Scheherazade affected a slight bow, and her younger sister mimicked her action. 'I am sorry for any misunderstanding.' She turned to her sister so that Dunyazad might also understand. 'The Sultana is, of course, the second most important woman in the kingdom, after the queen.'

The Sultana made a noise more common among certain breeds of livestock, but that in this case surely indicated surprise rather than an unbalanced diet. In the meantime, the new queen considered her own somewhat surprising actions. Why had Scheherazade, who had been well trained to remain gracious in all things, allow her speech this time to betray the slightest tinge of anger? Indeed, she further wondered, why was the Sultana among the most annoying women Scheherazade had ever set her eyes upon? She surmised at last that such things were beyond thought, and rather were in the hands of Destiny.

'How dare you?' the Sultana spluttered at last. 'I should surely have you beheaded now, except, as I mentioned before, I should not wish to waste the effort. It is important, after all, for my son to be able to pursue his whims without parental interference.'

Scheherazade swallowed those next words that came to mind, which were quite explicit upon the subject of interference. Instead, perhaps she should put aside her poor first impression and give this older woman the benefit of her counsel. 'Has it not ever occurred to you,' she therefore said, 'that your son is cursed?'

'Cursed?' the Sultana demanded. 'How dare you! I must say, my opinion of you is certainly changing. I believe that beheading you would sweeten the air within these quarters.'

This latest statement was too much even for Dunyazad. 'But the king has killed three hundred women. Surely, someone is cursed?'

'Exactly!' the Sultana cried. 'Think of the ill fortune that has befallen my son, to meet three hundred women so afflicted.' She paused to look meaningfully at Scheherazade. 'Or, should I say, three hundred and one?'

But Scheherazade was adamant upon this point. 'I do not agree. My purpose here, if any, is to lift this yoke of sorrow from around the neck of your son.'

'I see.' The Sultana nodded thoughtfully. 'I had heard that you had a tongue of gold, and could deceive even the most righteous among us. For a moment even I, the protector of my son's honor, imagined that you might be speaking reason. Truly, you are dangerous not only to the king, but to the entire realm!'

Scheherazade could do naught but stare at this woman and her amazing leaps of logic.

'Still,' the Sultana continued, pleased at last that she faced no contradictions from her audience, 'I do not wish to interfere, for I feel my Shahryar is far happier when he feels he has a free hand. However, should you continue to avoid your well-deserved beheading, I will have to reconsider my position. As unfortunate as it may seem, deadly accidents have been known to occur within this harem.'

With that, the Sultana smiled, and swiveled her extraordinary bulk back through the twin doors that connected the apartments with the courtyard beyond.

'Oh,' cried Omar aloud as she departed, 'what an honor it is to be visited by the glorious Sultana! I believe it is time for a poem!'

And so he began, even though his recitation seemed to make the Sultana hurry her steps, rather than slow her pace to hear this adulation.

> 'So does your visit raise up this place
> From the miserable level of hovel!
> In your grand presence all men and maids
> Would be honored to submit and grovel!'

Numerous other verses followed, rhyming impinge with cringe, dictate with prostrate, divine with whine, and marketplace with debase. The length of Omar's poem, in fact, meant the Sultana would not only have time to leave the harem, but the entire palace and city beyond.

And, having so cried, and recited, and further, somehow, managed to bow, Omar took his leave as well with a final recitation of 'I hear and I obey!', closing the great double doors behind him.

There was, at last, a moment of silence within their quarters. Dunyazad, who seemed as flustered as her sister by all that had so far occurred, gazed at Scheherazade with a face that seemed beyond emotion. 'What do we now?'

Scheherazade sighed, and turned to smooth the cushions upon her couch. 'I suggest we pursue what sleep we can, and take small comfort in the fact that our lives cannot become more uncertain.'

So it was that the two women attempted to claim some repose in the midst of chaos. But so difficult were their surroundings that even their dreams were troubled. And no matter what monsters and horrors confronted them in the world of sleep, they were not half so frightful as what was soon to happen in their waking lives.

## Chapter the Eighth,
### in which the story sharpens considerably due to a certain outside edge.

So it was that the two sisters managed a few fitful hours of repose, after which they were again fed and bathed and perfumed, and brought to the rooms of the king when his day's work was done. And, as they entered these chambers, Dunyazad exclaimed, 'Oh sister! I worry so for your welfare!'

And Scheherazade said in return, 'Do not fear, for I have reflected upon this very problem as I drifted in and out of slumber. Tonight, I shall tell a story that will make the king forget all about swords.'

But, when they stepped within that room which contained the king, Scheherazade found her husband preoccupied with other matters. For he stood proudly before three great scimitars spread upon the rug before him, each scimitar encased in a scabbard of gold, with one sheath covered in rubies, one in sapphires, and one with diamonds.

'Look at what my dear mother, the Sultana, has given me as a gift,' the king announced. 'They are three fine swords, each one sharper than the next, and all begging to be drawn and tested.' The king rubbed the palm of one hand against the palm of the other. 'Such fine swords. How do I long for the feel of naked steel!'

So it was that Scheherazade realized the Sultana had already been at work on providing certain inducements to the king while the sisters slept. Before this moment, the queen had not realized the cunning of her adversary. Scheherazade looked down at the three exceedingly sharp swords, and knew that her task would now be three times as difficult.

Still, it would not do to show her concern. 'So you might, Oh master,' she said sweetly instead. 'I was considering how much you might like to see something else naked.' As if to clarify her meaning, she allowed a dainty foot to show from beneath her robes.

47

But Shahryar's attention was still focused upon the three weapons displayed upon the floor. 'Eh? What could compete with swords?' His fingers flexed, as if they could not wait until they gripped one of the weapons before him. 'Sharp, virgin swords, ready to be whetted with the fruits of battle!' He paused to mop his brow, which was becoming damp with perspiration.

Scheherazade decided that the time had come for her to be a bit more direct. 'Perhaps, something naked that you might find worthy of ravishing.' With that, she allowed her entire leg to break free of its covering.

'Oh, my.' The king's gaze left his swords to travel up towards Scheherazade's thigh. 'Well, there is that, isn't there?'

Dunyazad made ready to begin her nightly exploration of other portions of the king's private quarters when Shahryar abruptly clapped his hands. 'No. It has been too long since I have cut! I must hold a sword! I slice, therefore I am!'

Without further thought, both Scheherazade and Dunyazad placed protective hands over their all-too-delicate throats. But, at that same instant, one of those servants who were always lurking about appeared from behind a curtain. 'What do you wish, Oh king?' the servant inquired.

'Cut!' Shahryar announced between clenched teeth. He also seemed to be developing a spasm in the muscles about his right eye. 'I need to cut!'

With that, the servant bowed low and vanished behind the curtain. Scheherazade swallowed while she still retained those parts that allowed such action. Had the attendant disappeared so he would not witness the twin murders of the sisters?

Shahryar fell to his knees before the central one of the three swords, whose hilt and sheath were covered with diamonds. He stroked the scabbard as one might the arm of a loved one. 'Cut,' he whispered. 'Swords. Hatchets. Knives. Lances.' He blinked, or perhaps it was another spasm. *'What did I say about lances?'*

The servant reappeared as the king made to draw the sword. The king frowned, but paused in his precipitous action.

'I have brought you something to cut, Oh master,' he announced. In his hands, the servant held a melon as large as a human head.

'Cut?' the king murmured. 'Yes, cut!' With remarkable speed, the king was upon his feet, the sword was free of its sheath, and the melon was sliced completely through, not once, but twice, so that the globe had been divided into four quarters of near equal size.

'Forgive me,' the king announced as he regarded his handiwork.

48

# CHAPTER THE EIGHTH

'My actions are careless. Were I not so tired and worn, I could have been more precise in the melon's equal division.'

'Oh,' was all the queen at first could say. Yet Scheherazade recovered from her surprise to a sufficient degree to smile and even move her robes around so that she might expose a bit of shoulder. 'Perhaps, Oh husband, I might ease those cares.'

'Ravishing?' the king asked, as he regarded her. 'Well, I imagine so.' He paused to wipe clean his blade with his kingly robes. 'It might have to be a little quicker than that of nights past. There is, after all, something else that must be done.' He closed one eye and peered down the length of the sword.

After a moment he glanced up at the unusually silent Scheherazade. 'We have to eat the melon.' He paused to resheath his sword. 'You also must continue your tale.'

'Most assuredly, Oh master,' Scheherazade most readily agreed. And so did the night proceed, with melon eating, ravishing, and at last to that part of the evening in which Scheherazade wove her verbal spell. On this night, Scheherazade prayed that she would be particularly inspired, for only now was she realizing the depths of the forces gathering against her.

'Now where have we left our tale?' the king inquired. 'Our unfortunate merchant is about to be killed by a *djinni*. Yes, but three sheikhs happen by leading four animals, and one promises to tell his story to the horrible creature for some sort of boon?'

'One third of the merchant's blood,' Dunyazad amended demurely.

'So he will only lose two-thirds of his blood to the *djinni*?' Shahryar again clapped his hands. 'A most excellent problem!'

'Indeed it was, my king,' Scheherazade agreed, almost as impressed by the king's memory for detail as she was with the speed of his sword. Apparently, the king craved particulars. Therefore, she would give him particular particulars. She announced, 'I will now resume my tale.'

### THE TALE OF THE MERCHANT AND THE *DJINNI*, RESUMED

'So had the first merchant concluded his amazing tale, and then did the *djinni* raise his sword in great agitation. And, making the strangest of faces, the *djinni* placed the sword behind his shoulder blade so that its tip delicately touched a point close to his spine, and

49

he further rubbed that point of the sword back and forth for a long moment before issuing a sigh of surprising contentment.

'"Excuse me," the *djinni* remarked when he was done, "I had a bit of an itch back there." He laughed in a tone that might even contain a hint of apology. "Your story was so fascinating that I chose to wait to its end before I tended to this annoyance."

'The merchant was astonished at this turn of events. Perhaps he would not be struck down instantaneously after all.

'"I have to admit that it has taken some getting used to my home, now that I no longer have my son about: life of my life, blood of my blood. I can't seem quite to get comfortable. The place seems far too spacious. I will have further to admit, however, that it is much quieter around the old ravine. And I have been able to use the sanitary facilities whenever I desired. It is amazing how long those youngsters take within those walls, is it not?"

'The *djinni* paused, and pointed his sword again at the offending party. "But he was life of my life, blood of my blood! And, speaking of blood, there is a merchant present who owes me two thirds of his own!"

'Ah, the merchant thought with a certain fatalism. Here came his fate at last. But before he could even extend his neck for the benefit of a quick and clean finish, the second sheikh stepped forward with his two greyhounds in tow. And this sheikh spoke to the *djinni*, saying, "Forgive my impudence, Oh being who might crush me as I might crush a fly, but I believe I have a story of such merit that you should find it even more wondrous than that first story shared by my fellow!"

'"Is this so?" asked the *djinni*, who seemed to be in no hurry to get on with this execution so long as there was the promise of free entertainment.

'"I believe it to be," the second sheikh replied. He cleared his throat, for talking to a *djinni* in such a manner was not the easiest of tasks. "When I am done with my tale, if you do agree, I would then ask you to grant me a second third of this merchant's blood."

'"A second third?" the fearsome creature replied with a frown. "Ah, I can see where this is going. We *djinn* weren't born yesterday, you know. Why, my son was already two hundred and twelve years old. Can you imagine how much of a trial a child can be if he doesn't leave home for three hundred years? But, never mind. If your story is more fantastic than the first, I will indeed grant you a third of this man's blood. I warn you, however, that, even should your story meet with my unusually high expectations,

50

# CHAPTER THE EIGHTH

I get to choose what part of the merchant loses that final, bloody third."

With a remark such as that, the merchant did not know whether to be relieved or doubly troubled. Still, he could do naught but listen as the second sheikh began his story:

## THE TALE OF THE SECOND SHEIKH

'"Know, Oh most magical of mystical beings, that these two hounds are my brothers. But how did this transformation come to pass?

'"Many years past, upon the death of our father, we three found that we shared a modest inheritance that allowed each of us to open our own separate shops. And all went well for some months, until one of my brothers endeavored to take a voyage further to increase his worldly goods. So did he leave our city, and so did he travel for a year and a day, but when he returned to my presence, he confessed that he had met with great disaster, that all his goods had been lost to him, and that he was destitute.

'"It so happened that this occurred at that time of year when I totalled my accounts, and so, when I balanced all my debts and payments, I discovered that I had made a profit of a thousand dinars. This I then split equally between my brother and myself, so that we might both continue in business.

'"So it was that all three of us continued to pursue the mercantile arts with some success. But, while being a merchant is often profitable, it is seldom exciting. It therefore occurred that my brothers decided it was time for another voyage of profit and discovery.

'"At first I resisted this suggestion, for my first brother's voyage of a year and a day had turned out so badly. And, at my reminder, both my brothers lost some of their enthusiasm for the journey as well, but after a couple of additional months of doling out dried beans and lengths of cloth, they had again quite forgotten their reservations. And, to be honest as to my own motivations, I had seen enough of the inner four walls of my shop as well. So it was that, despite my brother's earlier experience, and the further knowledge of how these stories always end when related by storytellers, I agreed to join my siblings on their journey.

'"I did, however, insist upon one precaution before we ventured forth. And this precaution was that all three of us should combine our worldly goods, and bury half of that sum in some

51

secret place in case our journey should turn out as badly as had our brother's in the past. After some thought, my brothers agreed to this plan and, with what money remained, we hired a stout ship and stocked it with goods of great variety.

' "So did we venture forth and we met with great success upon the early part of our journey, buying and selling and trading until the worth of our goods had increased ten dinars for every coin we had originally spent.

' "But, as these voyages always do, this was the point at which our journey became stranger than strange. For, when we returned from the city to the seaport, I was approached by a woman dressed in rags, who spoke to me in a voice ragged from sorrow and said, 'Be kind to me, master, and deliver me from my misery!'

' "I was astonished at this woman's boldness, not to mention the incredible distress of her appearance. So did I say to her, 'I have met with good fortune this day. What would you wish of me?'

' " 'You must save me from my poverty!' was her reply as she clawed at my sleeve with filthy fingers capped by broken nails. The breath from her upturned face, even covered by her veils, held the air of fish parts left too long in the sun.

' " 'How can I do that,' I asked in concern, 'who am only passing from this island to the next?'

' "Her suggestion, after she had paused to emit a hacking cough and rid herself of a large gob of phlegm, was a simple one: 'Then marry me, so that I might pass with you.'

' "Marry her? This proposal, while startling at first, appealed to me after I had thought upon it, for, when you are keeping a shop all day, there is very little opportunity to go out and meet good women and further, underneath the layers of grime and rotting clothes and nagging illness, I could detect a woman of some interest. So it was that a merchant often may detect a bargain that the common man might miss entirely. And so it was then that I agreed to her request, to her delight and the astonishment of my brothers.

' "Then were the nuptials immediately performed and we set sail again soon thereafter. I bade my new bride to clean herself with the copious rainwater stored in large tanks upon the ship's deck, and added that she should further adorn herself in whichever of the rich robes from my merchant's store that struck her fancy. So it was that she re-emerged, properly cleaned and clothed, and all could tell she surely was a woman of comely appearance, or at least as much as anyone could tell that sort of thing under all those layers of robes and veils. And my brothers no longer scoffed at my folly but instead became overwhelmed with jealousy at my good fortune.

'"Who knows what made my brothers so? Perhaps it was the work of Satan. Or perhaps it was the gentle love play of my wife and myself upon the ship's deck when my beautiful wife would sidle up to me and exclaim:

> '"'Hey there, big boy,
> Whatcha wanna do?
> Come on up and see me
> Hootchy hootchy coo!'

'"Although, how anyone could take offense at such a charming rhyme is totally beyond me.

'"Or perhaps my brothers took umbrage at the odd habit of my possessions always to shine, so that it looked as if the gold in my keeping was equal to twice that of my brothers' hoards. Or perhaps they became disgruntled at those odd circumstances when, no matter how foul the weather, the moment my wife and I were upon the deck, all rain would cease, the wind would abate, the clouds would part and rays of sun would shine down to bathe the two of us in golden light. Even I must admit that this last happenstance seemed to be a remarkable bit of serendipity, especially upon those occasions when it occurred in the middle of the night.

'"Whatever the cause of my brothers' ill will, both my bride and I were blissfully unaware of it, so lost were we in each other's presence. So it was on one particular day, when the rain had ceased and the sun quite abruptly began to shine, that I looked at my most beauteous wife across the deck and she called to me:

> '"'Hey there, hey there,
> Keeper of my shop.
> Why don't we go down below,
> And do a belly flop?'

'"Surely, you might say, this was not the most decorous of behavior, and perhaps I should have taken more notice of the way my brothers watched my wife and me, or perhaps listened more closely to my siblings' dark mutterings. But my eyes were filled with my wife's beauty, and my ears were full of her song as she further remarked:

' " 'Hi there, merchant man,
I'm a customer for love.
Why don't we go someplace
We can give these goods a shove?'

' "Her hands rose above her head, and the baubles that she wore upon her wrists dazzled in the sunlight. And, although these baubles had been quite common when I had given them to my bride, they now somehow appeared to be encrusted with fabulous gems that matched every color of the rainbow, so that the baubles now looked to be three times more valuable than anything my brothers had ever touched.

' "But still did I not think overmuch about the cries that issued from my brothers' throats, thinking them to be more the results of wonder rather than anger.

' "Now did my bride approach me, and in a voice both low and sultry, although not so low that those about us could not hear, she further sang:

' " 'Hey there, you there,
With beard and manly stare,
What say we find some privacy
And try to split some hairs?'

' "I surely do not need to tell you that no mere mortal could resist such an advance. But as I moved toward my beloved, my brothers were both acting as well.

' " 'Flaunting wealth! Flaunting love! Hootchy coo songs! It is more than we can bear!' my brothers called in unison, and tossed us both over the side.

' "I thought in that instant that a moment of foolish bliss had cost both my wife and me our lives. But, before we even hit the waves at the ship's side, the appearance of my wife changed before us and she took on the semblance of an ifritah, her countenance grown terrifying with a mystic anger.

' " 'Do not be surprised, Oh my husband,' my wife turned ifritah counseled as she snatched me from the waves. 'For I have accepted the mercy of Allah into my life, and have decided to live a righteous life. So it was that I appeared to you as a poor woman in rags, for I sought a man of true mercy to be my husband. Now you must excuse me for a moment, for I will find a dry spot for you to rest while I go and kill your brothers.'

' "But, as soon as I recovered from my surprise, I bade my wife

54

to wait and consider her actions, for does not the wise man say, 'The wicked man shall be punished for his own wickedness, for he shall never find inner peace and will very seldom be given the truly good tables at tearooms.'

' "'I must do what I must do!' was my wife's only reply as she instantly transported me back to my homeland and my shop. But before I could caution her further, she had disappeared, and I fell into an exhausted sleep.

' "Upon the following morning, I awoke to see my wife standing at my bedside, accompanied by these two hounds you see before you now. And the hounds, regarding me, began to whine piteously, and to hang their heads in the manner common to their kind.

' "Then did my wife announce to me, 'Do you not know these beasts?' I told her no, I had never seen them before. 'Do you not recognize your brothers?' she further asked. And, upon closer inspection, I saw a certain shiftiness of gaze and deficiency of posture that these dogs did indeed share with my siblings.

' "'I thought upon what you had said,' my wife continued, 'and decided that rather than kill these curs, it was better to change them in such a way that they might regard their folly. So it was that I consulted my sister, who specializes in this sort of thing, and she turned them into dogs, and as dogs they shall remain for a full ten years.'

' "Those ten years have now gone, and I was on my way to visit my sister-in-law and return my brothers to human form when I came upon this scene. Thus, this is my story, and it has come to an end."

## THE TALE OF THE MERCHANT AND THE *DJINNI*, RESUMED ONCE MORE

'The merchant was doubly astonished by this tale from the mouth of the second sheikh, as was the vengeful *djinni*.

' "This sister-in-law of yours," the *djinni* asked. "Her name isn't Eunice, is it?"

' "Why, it is the very same!" the second sheikh cried in astonishment.

' "You and I are related – why, by marriage, of course – but still, we are family!" the *djinni* exclaimed. "Most certainly will I grant you a third of this man's blood." The *djinni* paused once again to heft his sword. "Now, you will excuse me, while I take that final third which is due me from this merchant, which I intend to extract from between the chest and the knees."

'So did the merchant once again find himself confronting his fate, until that moment when the third sheikh, leading his mule, came between the merchant and the *djinni*'s sword.

' "Oh," the *djinni* remarked before the third sheikh could even utter a word, "I most undoubtedly should have seen this coming."

' "Come, oh most noble of extremely large and unusually fearsome creatures," the last sheikh replied. "You have listened to the stories of both my compatriots. Can you do no less for me? And further, you have granted one third of this man's blood if their tales were to contain sufficient wonder. Is it not only fair that you allow me those same terms?"

' "Well, I suppose so," the *djinni* replied in a voice that was at first more sullen than gracious. "And I must admit, however reluctantly, that I am gaining some enjoyment out of these tales. Now that I no longer have the life of my life, blood of my blood around underfoot, I realize I need to get out more often. Life in a ravine can be so confining!"

' "Very well," the third sheikh replied. "I will therefore tell my tale, which is so filled with spectacle, novelty and amazement that it might put both those stories related by my honored companions to shame."

## THE TALE OF THE THIRD SHEIKH

' "Know you, Oh most excellent *djinni* who knows a top notch tale when he can listen to one, that this mule you see with me was once my wife. Now it so happened that I had to be away from my home for a considerable period of time and, upon my return, I found the woman in the arms of another man. A common story, you may say? Alas, what happened next was anything but common!

' "My wife leapt from her divan and grabbed a pitcher of water. She thereupon threw this water full in my face, and, uttering certain phrases in an unknown tongue, finished with these words in our own language: 'By the mystic powers, you will become a dog!'

' "This, then, was the beginning of my misfortune. Yes, not only was I wet, but I had indeed been turned into a hound!

' " 'What?' my wife then cried in outrage. 'Whoever has let a dog into this place? My husband would never stand for such a thing! Out! Out of here, this minute!' With that, she opened the door and forcefully ejected me with the toe of her shoe. And, as the door

56

closed upon my startled and recently altered countenance, I could hear the woman say, 'Come now, Hassan. We shall no longer be interrupted by beasts. Now you are free to discuss the curative powers of love nibbles.' But, as she emitted a final squeal, the door was closed and I could hear no more.

'"What could I do in my sorry not-to-mention-canine state? Certainly I could expect no handouts from the woman for whom I had provided everything! So it was that I wandered to the neighborhood butcher shop, for, while I had been turned into a dog, I still had to eat."

'"I entered the environs of the butcher with some trepidation, for he might have no patience with animals who sought handouts. But to my surprise, upon seeing me, he called out most pleasantly, saying, 'We have a new dog in the neighborhood! And a scrawny specimen he is! Perhaps we can find you some sustenance to better your lot!'

'"So did he locate some scraps upon his cutting board and toss them to me, saying, 'No one who ever enters my shop, man or beast, shall go hungry.'

'"I looked down at the bits of fat and gristle that had been placed before me. This, then, was my lot as a dog, and the most that I could expect.

'"'What is the matter, there?' the butcher called. 'Do you find something wrong with my wares?'

'"I decided that I had better eat what I was offered before it was taken away from me. So I attempted to chew the food, except that the scraps fell from my mouth and I slobbered most piteously, for, only recently having been turned into a dog, I did not yet have the proper working knowledge of my jaw.

'"'That is truly the most pitiful thing that I have ever seen,' the butcher remarked at my lack of coordination. 'No wonder you are scrawny, for you have no knowledge of how to eat. I cannot help but take pity on such a poor creature. I shall take you home and allow my daughter to care for you.'

'"So was the butcher good to his word, and, upon the close of his working day, he closed up his shop and led me to his home down the road, where he presented me to his daughter with the words, 'See? I have brought you a companion!'

'"But his daughter, rather than seeming pleased at being given such a gift, instead gathered her veils about her most hurriedly, saying, 'How dare you bring a man into my presence?'

'"The butcher frowned at that. 'What do you mean, Oh daughter of mine?'

'"'Only what I say,' his daughter replied most petulantly. 'Father, can you not even listen? Once he was a man, and now he is a dog. What could be more simple?'

'"Her father then muttered something about not being able to understand the ways of the young. But his daughter would not be deterred. She thrust her hand into a pitcher of water on the table beside her and, withdrawing that hand, proceeded to sprinkle my brow with three drops of water.

'"'Speak with your own true voice!' she declared.

'"At that instant, I felt the muscles within my throat stretch and bend, and I further discovered that, instead of bow wow and woof woof, I could once again form words and coherent sentences.

'"'Mistress,' I pleaded with the return of my voice. 'Might you turn me back into my true form?'

'"'I do have those arts,' the maiden readily agreed, 'and further can I teach you how to turn your wife into any animal you wish as a retribution. But first, I should ask a boon of you.'

'"'Anything you desire,' I replied, as I was most eager to regain the shape of a man.

'"'It becomes so tiresome sitting in this place all day. Not, of course, that my sweet father does not provide for me, except that, being an only child with a mother who has passed from this earth has limited the development of my social knowledge. Perhaps, before I change you back to what you were and you exact your just retribution, you could first tell me a story of the outside world.'

'"What could I do but oblige?

'"'Oh,' she added quickly, 'and make it a story filled with liveliness and amazement.'

'"But isn't any story worth telling filled with such attributes? This, then, was the narrative that I told her.

## THE TALE OF THE FISHERMAN
## AND THAT WHICH HE CAUGHT

'"'So it was,' I therefore related, 'in a time not so long ago, in a kingdom not that far from here, there resided a fisherman who would always cast his net upon the water three times in the morning, no more and no less, and three times after he had performed his midday prayers.

'"'Now had this man of very regular habits already spent a

morning on this day in casting his net with no luck whatsoever. But still did he have that time after noon, and surely his luck would change and he would be rewarded for his diligence.

' " 'The fisherman returned to one of his favored spots upon the shore, and again cast his net upon the waters, wading out to make sure the net was well spread as it sank below the surface. When the net had had sufficient time to sink to the bottom, the fisherman tugged upon it, but found that it would not budge.

' " 'Surely, he must have netted a great fish at last! So it was that he lowered himself into the water, tugging upon his net this way and that, until he managed to gather the net around a large object that must truly be the king of fishes. Then did the fisherman exert a great effort to drag this large prize from the water, only to discover, when he had brought his burden upon the shore, that it was not a fish after all, but a dead ass instead.

' " 'Was this his fate? he thought, to seek sustenance and receive only refuse? So it was that, as he freed his net, he made up little songs to keep him company, as do many people in stories. And this was the song that he sang:

> ' " ' "The hard job of fishing
> Will cost you most dear.
> You'll look for the foremost,
> Yet receive the rear."

' " 'So it followed that he freed his net at last, and further wrung the net free of excess water and ass portions. After this was done at last, he cast his net a second time, thinking that surely he would have better fortune upon this occasion.

' " 'He waited a time for the net properly to submerge once more. And, upon tugging on this net for a second time, he discovered it again contained a great weight, although on this occasion that weight could be moved, albeit with some difficulty. Perhaps, he mused, this time I have caught a whole school of fish, and can not only feed my family but the families of all within the village. So did he steadily yet carefully pull up the net from the water.

' " 'It was to his double dismay that he regarded what his net had snared this second time, for the webbing was filled with naught but broken glass and bits of pottery covered by that deep silt that coated the water's bottom.

' " 'The fisherman thereupon resolved again to free his net of the large mass of debris gathered there, and he further decided to sing

59

to give himself solace. This, then, were the words that issued from his lips:

> ' " ' "What is wrong with my net?'
> I'm compelled to ask.
> I search long for treasure
> But find only trash."

' " 'The fisherman had to admit it. Even his songs were becoming depressing. But eventually he rid his net of every piece of glass and shard of pottery, and prepared to cast it again out over the water.

' " 'So did he pray to providence to grant him good fortune in this, his last cast of the day. And then he flung the net and watched it again sink beneath the surface.

' " 'When a sufficient time had again elapsed, he pulled upon his net and discovered it was ensnared for a third time this afternoon. On this occasion, however, the fisherman discovered, with judicious labor, he was able to pull the net from the water without the excessive labors of either of his previous attempts. Still did the net pull against him with such a weight that he knew it was not empty and, as hope is the most immortal of emotions, he once again envisioned a great fish trapped within the weave.

' " 'So he pulled the net from the water, and opened the net to examine what prize it held within. At first sight, his hopes diminished, for the object he had caught was certainly not a fish but some sort of jar covered with mud. Still did the fisherman console himself that this was better than either a dead ass or a bunch of broken glass, so he set about cleaning his newest catch. And, indeed, once he had judiciously removed the mud, he discovered a vase of fine workmanship made of purest copper.

' " 'The fisherman became truly happy for the first time that day, for this was a vase which would surely gain him ten golden dinars should he sell it at the marketplace. But perhaps his good fortune might extend even farther, for the vase was still sealed with a mark that looked as if it might come from the court of the great prophet Solomon. Surely, the fisherman thought, he must be truly ill educated to read this seal in such a way, for Solomon had lived a thousand years and more before the fisherman was born. He would therefore pry off the lid to look inside, and determine the true worth and origins of the contents as well.

' " 'The fisherman then picked up one of those knives he always kept about to aid in the cutting and scaling of fish and stuck its point in the soft wax of the seal. After a moment's prying and working the knife point back and forth, the lid of the jar exploded upward to the height of the tallest palm, and great dark smoke issued from the jar below.

' " 'Perhaps, the fisherman considered, his recent course of action was not the most judicious possible, for that sort of smoke could only be associated with a being of great power or some item that had fermented in the extreme.

' " 'The worst of his fears were realized when the smoke resolved itself into a gigantic ifrit, who looked down upon the fisherman and cried, "Oh, great lord Solomon, truly I was only joshing when I told you that I would kill you and all your troops most horribly! Cannot you detect a simple jest from an ifrit who does not know his station?"

' " ' "Pardon," the fisherman replied when he had at last found his voice, "but there is no Solomon here."

' " ' "Solomon isn't here?" the ifrit repeated with a frown. "Perhaps he is off hunting, then, slaying others of my kind?"

' " ' "If you refer to the great King Solomon," the fisherman answered most honestly, "he has not been here in quite some time."

' " 'The ifrit's eyes shifted back and forth upon the waterfront, looking no doubt for lurking Solomons upon the length of beach. "Nowhere about at all?"

' " ' "No, he has been dead for quite some time."

' " ' "Dead, did you say?" The large fellow narrowed his eyes in the most cunning of expressions. "You wouldn't fool a poor ifrit, would you?"

' " 'The fisherman decided to tell this magical creature the whole truth and be done with it. "Solomon's time was over a thousand years before our own."

' " ' "Dead a thousand years and more, do you say?" The ifrit smiled at last, and it was an expression that the fisherman did not find in the least pleasant. The creature laughed, a sound surprising in its malignancy, as the ifrit grew to ten times his original size.

' " ' "In that case, fisherman," he next announced, "I shall give you a gift. And that gift will be your death!"

' " 'Somehow, the fisherman realized, this conversation had gone badly. Further reflection on this issue was impossible, however, for he detected a great hand the size of a house that now reached for him, no doubt to crush the very life from his trusting form.' " '

\* \* \*

## SCHEHERAZADE AND THE KING, RESUMED RATHER LATER THAN ANTICIPATED

Scheherazade blinked as the gong rang announcing the commencement of the courtly day.

'Oh, dear,' remarked Dunyazad, every bit as startled as her sister, 'I entirely forgot to remind you of the coming of morning.'

'Um, yes,' Scheherazade managed, 'well, the ifrit and the fisherman, I suppose it can wait.' She found that, once she had established a certain storytelling pace, she was reluctant to let it go.

'And I have entirely forgotten about sleeping,' the king remarked with the most prodigious of yawns. 'Perhaps I can catch a bit of a nap during one of the longer cases. And I would like to work in a bit of practice with these swords. It seems such a shame to leave them here completely untested.'

Then, the storyteller thought, as the evening began with swords, so it ended with swords. Scheherazade had successfully navigated another night. But would the chopping block be waiting for her when evening came again?

And what other surprises might the king's mother have in store?

## Chapter the Ninth,
## in which we learn that a harem
## is not a home.

Scheherazade now knew such exhaustion that she was quite certain she would be able to sleep, no matter what confronted her upon her return to her apartments. But, as the wise woman says, there is no certainty greater than demise and tariffs, and at least one of these waited for her at the harem.

So it next occurred that Dunyazad and Scheherazade were again escorted back to their quarters. Omar was waiting there for them, and in his hands he held a silver tray.

'Look what I have here,' he said most cheerfully, his high voice like that of a singing bird. 'It is the gift of a friend who wishes to remain unnamed.'

A friend? Scheherazade was suspicious at once. Within the confines of this palace, she knew a father, a sister, and a husband, but had yet to develop friends.

'What is this gift?' she therefore asked the man who could but aspire to be the chief among the eunuchs.

'It is here, upon this silver tray,' Omar further explained. 'It is a silver goblet, and within this goblet is a very special wine.' And yet the servant frowned ever-so-slightly when he looked down at the wine before him. 'Perhaps,' he added, 'it might be time for a poem.'

'Or perhaps it is not time for a poem,' Scheherazade said sternly, attempting with all her being to act like a queen. Unfortunately, even being a queen did not seem to help her understand what now transpired. Again, Scheherazade felt that Omar was attempting to communicate something in a manner that was rather indirect. But should not a queen be able to clarify such situations?

'In what way is this wine special?' she therefore asked.

'Well, it does have an extremely pungent aroma,' Omar answered, 'the like of which one might never encounter within one's life.'

63

'Within one's life,' Scheherazade repeated. What an interesting way to describe this vintage. Perhaps, if she pried again, Omar might be willing to reveal more. 'Does this wine have any other characteristics?'

Omar pointed a pudgy finger at the rim of the goblet. 'Well, there is this spot along the edge of the cup where the liquid appears to be corroding the metal.' He glanced quickly to his right and then his left, as if he had spoken an indiscretion. 'But I am sure this is a very old goblet! It is a shame that the wine had to be served in such an unworthy vessel!'

'And you say that this wine is a gift from an unspecified friend?' Scheherazade asked. 'You cannot offer further information, even for the queen of the realm?'

'For the queen?' Omar paused to glance about the room before he added, in a somewhat lower tone, 'The friend is very highly placed, and may be a close personal relative, except only by marriage. But I can say no more!'

Then this servant was telling her this was a gift from the Sultana? That same Sultana who had given Scheherazade's husband the gift of three extremely sharp swords, all primed for cutting?

Scheherazade had to use all her composure as a storyteller not to back away as Omar approached with the goblet, especially since she could now hear the goblet, or the liquid within, making a high hissing sound that seemed more suited to snakes than wine. And, upon closer inspection, the whole upper edge of the goblet appeared ragged and pitted where the wine spilled over the side. The liquid smoked as it made contact with the silver tray. Scheherazade did not wish even to smell this offering, much less drink it, for fear that the aroma might corrode her nose hairs in much the same way that it now ate at the rim of the cup.

Still, it would not do to show someone in the palace her distress. 'We must thank whoever gave us this gift,' Scheherazade therefore replied in her best queenly manner. 'However, it is time that my sister and myself gained some repose, and I fear such a drink would interfere.'

'It would be inexcusable for you not to accept such a gift,' Omar remarked sternly. He glided forward, his body a full three hundred pounds of quivering grace. 'Take but a single sip, and your repose will be as never before.'

The servant took a final step forward, a look of great reassurance upon his countenance, when that look was replaced by a great surprise.

'Oops!' Omar exclaimed as the tray shifted left and the goblet flew to the right, away from Scheherazade. The servant ended upon his knees, while the goblet followed its contents to the floor.

'The greatest of pardons, Oh most merciful queen!' Omar exclaimed at the accident before him. 'I did not know that I could be so clumsy!'

Scheherazade realized that she held a very similar opinion to that of her servant. Until but a moment before, with the way that Omar glided from place to place, she had not thought the large man to have a single clumsy bone in his body.

'I will quickly clean my mistake,' Omar declared as a great, sizzling cloud rose from where the liquid had spilled upon the thick carpets. The servant waved away the smoke. 'Oh, dear. I shall have to replace those rugs. They seem to have developed a large hole. I suppose it is simply the shoddy workmanship one can expect in this modern world. But no one could excuse my clumsiness.' He rolled up the affected rugs with a remarkable dexterity. Scheherazade could still hear a muffled sizzling come from deep within the pile.

'I should undoubtedly be whipped,' Omar continued as he backed from the room, the rugs tucked beneath his arm. 'Thank you so much for ordering it. I shall see to it immediately.'

But with that, the large servant stopped quite abruptly and stared across the room. 'Oh, dear,' was all he said.

Both Scheherazade and Dunyazad turned to see what had startled Omar to such an extent. There, disappearing behind one of the room's many screens, was the edge of a black robe and perhaps a black-clad foot. Or perhaps it all was naught but a very deep shadow, shifting in the early morning light. It was over so quickly that the exact nature of the event was difficult to discern.

However, Omar seemed to be greatly affected.

'Sulima,' he whispered.

'What did you say?' Scheherazade asked.

'Say?' Omar replied, blinking as if he had only recently awoken from a deep slumber. 'Why, nothing whatsoever. It was simply the out-take of breath flowing past my tongue and teeth.' He laughed nervously. 'There really is nothing to worry about on supernatural beings. Who, after all, do we know who has seen such things? Or, at least, who has seen them and lived to tell about it?'

He laughed again, a sound remarkably even higher than his earlier titters. 'I mean, one should not fret about supernatural things, especially those you are uncertain whether or not you have seen, for, if you have not seen them, there is nothing to worry about, is there?' His laugh this time held a hint of the hysterical. 'Surely, I am upset for I have had an accident, and the two of you have gone for a very long time upon very little sleep. It is no wonder then that we are seeing things! Therefore, I would totally discount harem legends about the deadly nature of certain visitations, and have a most welcome rest!' Omar sighed. 'I suppose I could end with a poem, but I no longer feel inspired!'

The door slammed shut and he was gone.

Scheherazade was not certain of the precise meaning of what had so recently occurred, or, indeed, of the exact nature of some of the occurrences. Perhaps she should have allowed for Omar's poetry after all, for he appeared to say in rhyme what he could not say in prose.

However, poetry or no poetry, she determined she must ascertain certain facts for her own wellbeing.

'Pardon me, sister,' she therefore said, 'but I must investigate this screen.'

She walked briskly over to that point in the room where she could have sworn she saw a disappearing robe and foot. She gazed behind the screen. As she suspected, the other side of the partition held nothing behind it whatsoever. She ran her hand upon the screen itself, but there seemed to be nothing unusual about its construction.

'Pardon me,' Dunyazad said most sweetly but directly, as was the manner of all women in her family, 'but might you comprehend what has ensued since we returned from the palace?'

Scheherazade considered the succinctness of her little sister's remark. It seemed to her that they had recently witnessed two very separate events.

The first, which had to do with a goblet and whatever had rested within, had had a most curious conclusion, with the ever graceful Omar's accident. Perhaps their servant was unable or unwilling to speak in an uncomplimentary fashion about the gift from someone in power, even if that gift might be poison. Yet, he might be able to indicate the true nature of the gift in other ways, or devise a method by which that deadly gift would never reach the person for whom it was intended.

She thought of his offer of the night before, concerning a certain physical solace. The thought of such a union brought a cold chill to her stomach, but still, Omar had been, in his way, very discreet concerning this suggestion. Perhaps he could not help but be

66

discreet, no more than he could help groveling before the Sultana. But that sort of discretion did very little to answer the storyteller's questions.

And then there was that further incident, when Omar, who had hardly seemed flustered at all by the incident of the spilled wine and ruined rug, seemed entirely undone by his sighting of the woman in black. And what was the name he had whispered? Sulima? Scheherazade had heard that name before, but she was now so tired, she could not remember whether the woman was a part of this palace or simply the character in one of her stories.

Scheherazade frowned at this dilemma. At the very least, she still had much to learn about royal harem etiquette.

'We must sleep,' was the only answer Scheherazade could give to her worried sister.

So it was that both the sisters reclined upon their couches, and both fell into a fitful sleep, and, while Scheherazade could not speak with authority for Dunyazad, she could say with great conviction that her dreams were filled with mysterious women in black, always barely out of sight. And further were these women always watching her, and always waiting.

But what were the women waiting for? And why was Scheherazade convinced the the dark-clad women were smiling, but that the smiles revealed nothing but evil?

She awoke three times over the course of the morning, but there was nothing else in the room.

That is, there was nothing but shadows.

## Chapter the Tenth,
## in which our heroine has
## the opportunity to call fowl.

The time came at last for the two sisters to be bathed and fed and prepared for another evening. On this occasion, however, rather than being attended by the six handmaidens as was their due upon the previous occasion, their servants now numbered only five.

Dunyazad remarked upon this fact as she and her sister were prepared for their bath. She thereupon added with some concern, 'Is one of your number ill?'

The remaining five servants looked nervously from one to the other until at last one woman, who seemed to be the senior among them, turned to the two sisters and spoke.

'Alas! We do not know what happened to her,' was her response. 'All seemed well last night when we left the garden to retire to our cubicles. However, when we awakened at dawn, only five of us congregated in the common area.'

'And the other woman?' Dunyazad asked.

'We went to seek her out,' the senior among the servants replied, 'but she was gone.'

'And that is not the worst of it,' another of the servants urged. 'Tell her what you found!'

'What you found?' Scheherazade now prompted.

'Yes,' the second servant encouraged, 'within her clothes!'

'Well, it probably has nothing to do with our missing sister's whereabouts,' another of the servants remarked. 'But still—'

'Very well,' their elder interrupted. 'As senior among the staff, it is my duty to wake and perhaps discipline those of our number who are tardy. But when I came upon her couch, there was no woman there.'

'But her clothes did move!' a third servant insisted.

'Indeed,' their senior agreed a bit abruptly, 'that is true. There was something beneath those robes that jerked one way and then another, as if struggling to be free.'

The servant looked from Scheherazade to Dunyazad before she continued her tale. 'So there was a shape upon that couch, but that shape was by no means as large as the woman who was gone, but seemed rather small and quick. You can imagine what thoughts came upon me as I witnessed this surprise. What demon might have taken her place? As afraid as I was in that instance, I grabbed the corners of her dress farthest away from the moving shape, and pulled.'

'And what do you think she revealed?' the second servant demanded.

'Please,' her senior remarked soberly, 'I am telling the story.' She glanced again at the queen and her sister before continuing, with great portent, 'What was there beneath those robes but – a chicken.'

'A chicken?' Dunyazad cried in astonishment.

'Do you have many chickens in the harem?' Scheherazade added in like fascination.

'Generally,' the senior servant replied, 'only after they are cooked.'

'Where could that chicken have come from?' Scheherazade asked pointedly.

'That is the mystery,' the senior among the servants agreed. 'One of many that have occurred in this harem of late.'

Ah, Scheherazade thought. This was the very sort of information she desired.

'Mysteries?' she asked. 'What do you mean?'

But the older woman frowned at the question. 'Some things are perhaps best left unexplained.' The senior pushed the other servants before her so they were once again all marching down the corrridor. 'Here we are,' she explained, 'chattering like a group of old women, when you have not even had your bath. Omar will be very upset if we do not have you ready in time.'

'It does not do to get Omar upset,' another of the servants agreed.

'He is very fond of whipping,' a third agreed.

'That,' yet another servant added, 'and other things.'

Certain of the younger servants giggled after that last remark, and Scheherazade remembered that strangest of poems.

'Enough!' their senior announced, and began to assign the others their tasks. In short order, Dunyazad and Scheherazade were bathed, perfumed and fed with amazing efficiency. But the senior servant would no more address the mysteries she had alluded to before, saying that, no matter what the others saw in the shadows, she had no time for such foolishness.

So busy were they in their preparations that Scheherazade almost forgot the earlier story, until a telling remark from her sister brought all those details back.

Dunyazad stared at the plate before her. 'Are we not eating chicken?' she inquired.

With that reminder, Scheherazade looked soberly upon her meal and wondered if they were eating that mysterious visitor to the harem. Perhaps the servants would allow that question, if not during the meal, then after they had all experienced some degree of digestion.

She resolved to ask her question as soon as they had a moment of repose. But the gong that announced the end of the king's day arrived before they had even finished dressing in their finest silks.

'Quickly!' the eldest among servants called. 'Omar will be here at any moment!'

'I am already waiting,' Omar announced from a shadowed alcove beyond the bath. He stepped forward to regard the seven women. 'And while I am but a poor fellow who can but aspire to the heights of my craft, and thus am of no personal importance, it does not do to keep the king, whose orders I obey, waiting.'

'Dear Omar,' Scheherazade replied in a voice that was both quick and yet reassuring. 'We know you are among the most loyal of my husband's servants. We would never think to do anything that might reflect badly upon you.'

'Very well,' replied Omar, somewhat mollified. 'Perhaps I am still ruffled by my accident of this morning. Or perhaps I have overstated my desire to please with one so devoted to her king. And then, of course, there was that vision of the woman—' He paused to shiver. '—but I shall talk no more about that which I certainly could not have seen!'

He clapped his enormous hands, which once again produced only a very muffled sound. 'But come. Your king awaits. And, from what I hear from my friends in the palace, he is most agitated.'

'Agitated?' Dunyazad whispered to Scheherazade as the two women followed Omar to the king's apartments.

'No doubt his mother's doing,' Scheherazade whispered back. 'But I know a way to ease his fevered condition.'

Dunyazad laughed softly in relief. It was a relief that Scheherazade wished she, too, could share.

And while relief has been mentioned, that seemed to be the very emotion exhibited upon the faces of the guards as Omar and the two women approached.

'Greetings, Oh Queen,' said one of the guards, who had never spoken to her before. 'The king is most anxious to have you in his presence.'

Scheherazade and Dunyazad had time for but a single shared glance before they were ushered before the monarch.

'Swords!' King Shahryar screamed, and he held one of the very same in his hands, and it was with that same sword that he repeatedly slashed at what must have once been a pillow but was now little more than a collection of fabric scraps and feathers.

'*Sharp, sharp, sharp!*' the king declared. 'Swords! *Slice, mince, rend, rip!* Swords!' He blinked, as if realizing there was something in his apartment beyond that sharp object which he held in his hands. 'Pardon? Has someone else come into my presence?'

'Pardon me, Oh king,' the guard remarked softly, 'but the queen, Scheherazade, and her sister, Dunyazad, have come to join you in your apartments, as is your nightly command.'

'You dare?' the king demanded. 'The impudence!' He raised his sword as if the blade would divide his guard in two. In that instant, his gaze fell upon the two women and the anger fell from his face. 'But it is my beloved Scheherazade, and her charming sister, Dunyazad! Why did you not warn me that they were coming?'

'It is my fault entirely,' the guard replied quickly, his eyes still upon the sword above the monarch's head. 'Does the king wish to reprimand me?'

'Only if you do not leave the royal presence immediately!' the king rejoined. The guard obligingly bowed and backed from the room at remarkable speed.

'Good. I am glad that we are at last alone. Now I might be able to welcome you properly.'

Scheherazade decided that she would feel more welcome if Shahryar were to lower his sword. She very gently mentioned this possibility.

'Sword?' the king asked. 'What sword?' He glanced above his head. 'Oh, that sword. I seem to be getting a bit forgetful lately.' He lowered the sword and placed it upon the couch beside him. 'Perhaps if I were to receive a little rest.'

'Perhaps,' Scheherazade remarked helpfully, 'you may rest upon certain parts of my anatomy.'

But, rather than a look of delight, the king's countenance took upon it a certain doubtful, ashen quality. 'Rav – ravishing?' He wiped his damp brow with a silken sheet. 'Well, perhaps, I could – after I get a little rest.'

There was now no doubt for Scheherazade. The king was definitely not himself.

'Why, look at what I have found!' the king cried in surprise. There was the sword again in his hand, almost as if it had slithered into his grip of its own volition. 'Yes, my friend. We know the needs of a sword.' His smile was most unpleasant. '*Tatter, tear, cut, carve, cleave!*'

Scheherazade and Dunyazad both again found their hands in protective positions before their throats. That movement drew the king's attention.

'But what am I doing?' Shahryar remarked as he again stared at his bride. 'Playing with swords when I have guests to entertain?' His fingers sprang away from the hilt, and the sword clattered to the floor. 'I have no desire to brandish weapons about my beloved. Especially when she has a story to finish.'

Scheherazade smiled at that. Perhaps her presence could have some good effect after all, if it would get the king's mind away from swords.

The king frowned at his feet. 'But I cannot have a beautiful weapon like this laying about on the floor. They were a gift, you know.' He looked rather apologetic as he reached down to the floor. 'What would my mother say?'

'Let us not talk about your mother,' Scheherazade suggested. 'Let us talk about ourselves and the rich evening we have before us.'

The expression of apology disappeared the moment he touched the sword. '*Dissect, hack, hew, mangle, mutilate, pulverize, gash!*' his voice rose once more in triumph. The king shook his head. 'Pardon me, Oh queen. I was distracted. Did you speak?'

'Only to remind you that I was about to resume my story.'

'*Shred, saw, shear, sever, sunder!*' the king screamed as he replaced the weapon within its scabbard. 'There. Much better.' He took a deep breath in an attempt to calm his quivering form. 'That sword does seem to distract me. Now, what did you say about that story?'

Scheherazade smiled most sweetly and decided to redouble her efforts to make her tale fantastic and complicated. While this might capture the king's attention, she hoped there might be some way she could further remove that sword as well.

For the king did not appear to be entirely under his own control when he touched that blade. And she had no idea how she might continue her tale, if her body no longer sported a head.

## Chapter the Eleventh,
### in which the tale takes some unexpected turns, and perhaps the teller does as well.

This, then, was Scheherazade's story upon that night:

### THE TALE OF THE MERCHANT AND THE *DJINNI*, RESUMED DURING THE TALE OF THE THIRD SHEIKH AS HE IS TELLING THE TALE OF THE FISHERMAN AND WHAT HE CAUGHT

' " 'So it was that the fisherman had unleashed a large and fearsome ifrit and, in telling this creature that they were no longer in the time of the great King Solomon, had unleashed the ifrit's anger as well. And the fisherman had further committed this less-than-intelligent act upon a wide and empty beach from which there was no escape or hiding place, unless, of course, he might somehow be able to reach yonder bushes, which seemed quite impossible when he considered the ifrit's height and quickness, so that the fisherman's only destiny now appeared to be death.

' " 'But still was the fisherman not going to go to his death silently.

' " ' "Why," he therefore asked, "Oh great and fearsome creature, would you wish to kill someone as insignificant as myself, especially since it was I who freed you from your prison?"

' " ' "It is true that you did free me from my bondage," the ifrit said after a moment's consideration. "And even the most fearsome of creatures may show mercy. I will therefore allow you to choose your manner of death. But I warn you, I will only accept a choice that is sufficiently horrible, so that your cries of terror might be heard all up and down this shore."

' " 'So, the fisherman thought, now not only did he have to die, but he had to choose a death of sufficient agony to please this monster? And he could still think of no conceivable manner in

75

which to reach those bushes. It was too much for a simple man such as himself to bear.

""""But what is my fault?" he therefore asked. "*What is my fault? Or, to put it another way, what fault have I? Or, perhaps, what fault led me to do that which you fault me for? Or, further, whose fault is it that I faulted you? Or, to put it in another manner entirely—*"

""""I would rather you would not," the ifrit interrupted. "Very well. Perhaps you do not deserve this shock of sudden death. I will therefore tell you my story before I kill you most horribly. In this way, not only will I inform you as to the emotional reasoning for your death, but my telling will further allow me to relive those injustices thrust upon me by the race of humanity, and thus increase my anger one hundred fold, so that I may dispatch you with an even greater cruelty."

""""Oh," the fisherman replied. If the ifrit put it that way, perhaps they shouldn't talk about fault at all. "Actually," the fisherman further remarked, "perhaps we could pick a more neutral topic. Tell me, what do you think about net fishing?"

""""No!" the ifrit disagreed in the loud manner of one used to abusing authority. "Once I have begun my story, I will not rest until that story is fully told. I am simply that sort of ifrit!"

""""I was only asking," the fisherman said defensively. His gaze wandered of its own accord in the direction of the shrubbery.

""""And now I am telling," the ifrit replied. "And you shall listen."

""""Well, I suppose I must," the fisherman agreed with great pragmatism. He shifted about, as if he was in some discomfort. "You wouldn't mind, if, while you spoke, I wandered about in those bushes over there, would you?"

""""And thereby experience an even earlier and more terrible demise?" the ifrit considered. "I suppose it would not bother me, although you would not hear the end of my story."

""""On the other hand," the fisherman amended, "I now feel no desire to visit those bushes whatsoever. And I further have a sudden compulsion to hear your tale to the end, including whatever further explanatory remarks you may have upon that story's conclusion. It is truly strange how those urges come and go."

""""I have noticed that sort of thing in humans," the ifrit agreed. "Very well. Then listen to my tale as I prepare to murder you most malodorously."

"""Malodorously? the fisherman thought. He had a most

76

unpleasant sensation as he wondered if his demise would have something to do with dead fish.

' " 'But then he could wonder no more, for the ifrit began to talk.

## THE TALE OF THE IFRIT AND HIS ANGER

' " " "Many years ago, there was a great battle between ifrits and men, to see who would truly rule this earth. And among the many rebels of my kind, I was the king. But the man who led your kind was named Solomon, the son of David, and he was a king also, and even greater than I.

' " " "There came a final battle, as there did in every war, when I fought against Solomon's forces, led by his vizier. Many men and many ifrits were lost in that great struggle, which lasted a hundred days and one day beyond, and on that last day I knew the rebellion was over, for we had no strength remaining to fight again. The vizier had defeated me, and he brought me before Solomon, and so was I humbled before your kind.

' " " "Still, though, did I hold a great anger in my heart. And Solomon looked down upon me as I huddled upon my knees and said:

' " " " 'Repent! If you shall take the true faith to be your own, and learn the ways of men, I shall pardon you.'

' " " " 'Never!' I cried in my anger. 'Though my body might be broken before you, my spirit shall be free!'

' " " "King Solomon nodded his head at that, and replied, 'As you wish.' Then did he have his vizier through his magics place me within that jar that still lies yonder, and Solomon further caused a most holy seal to be placed upon that jar, and on that seal was engraved the name of King Solomon himself, so that I might never escape. After this was done, the king commanded certain other ifrits who had accepted his conditions to take the jar that now contained me and throw that container into the middle of the sea.

' " " "There did I wait for one hundred years, and in all those hundred years I did say, 'Oh, would that some man should free me from bondage! I will then give whatever treasure this man desires.'

' " " "But that hundred years passed, and then two hundred more. And, in that time, I resolved, 'What am I talking about, giving but a single treasure? That is far too simple a boon! I will show the one who frees me all the treasures of this world, so that he may pick the very finest among them all.'

' " " "But then those years had passed as well and I began to panic, thinking that I should be lost beneath the sea forever. Therefore, did I wait for the next three hundred years, saying, 'The world's greatest treasure is still not enough! I will give the one who frees me the three dearest wishes of his heart!'

'"'"So I had waited, for one hundred years, and then two hundred years after that, and then still three hundred years more, which you must admit is a very long time indeed to loiter about in a bottle. And still no one came.

'"'"What was an ifrit to do? Especially when he had been trapped for all those years in such a small space, a condition which, among other things, can produce some of the worst cramps man or ifrit has ever felt. The isolation, alas, was too much for me, so that, upon year six hundred and forty-six of my imprisonment, a Tuesday, at 2:17 in the afternoon, I screamed at last, 'All right! So no one's going to find me? So that's the way it is going to be? Very well, I shall show all of you! Now I will kill the man who frees me, and my only gift will be his choice of death!'

'"'"So it was that I waited yet another four hundred years to fulfill my vow. And that is what I offer you now!"

## THE TALE OF THE FISHERMAN
## AND WHAT HE CAUGHT RESUMED,
## EVEN THOUGH THE FISHERMAN WOULD AT THE
## PRESENT MOMENT
## RATHER BE HIDING IN THE BUSHES

'"'With this statement, the ifrit again fell silent.

'"'"That, then, is my only option?" the fisherman summarized. "That I get to choose the manner of my death?"

'"'"No more and no less," the ifrit agreed. "Now I suggest that we get on with it. I have to subjugate the human race and lay the world to waste, besides which I haven't had a thing to eat in over a thousand years."

'"'But while the ifrit was telling his story, the fisherman was reviewing his options beyond that unattainable goal of reaching the bushes, and he thought perhaps he might be able to match his wits with this supernatural creature.

'"'"Very well," he therefore answered the creature. "I have but one condition that must be met before I die, and that is that I must know the truth."

'"'"Pardon?" the ifrit said with a frown. "I am a creature of such great power that I am virtually all knowing and all seeing, yet I can make no sense of your question."

' " 'The fisherman was greatly encouraged by this confusion, for he hoped that he had presented the ifrit with the very best bait.

' " ' "I have but a single question myself," he therefore explained, "which must be answered before I die."

' " ' "Well then, speak up," said the ifrit with growing impatience. "What is that question?"

' " 'The fisherman pointed at that receptacle from which the ifrit had originated. "Let us be quite frank here. Look at you: large, imposing, perhaps overwhelming. Now look at this pitifully inadequate vessel. How can I believe you truly came out of this tiny jar? Now we should be lucky if we were to enclose only a hand or foot of yours in so confined a space!"

' " 'The ifrit looked down upon the fisherman in astonishment. "Why should you even ask this question? Did not you see me arise from this vessel but minutes ago?"

' " 'But at that, the fisherman nodded his head most skeptically. "I did see you arrive, but some of the events around that event are hazy in the extreme. The arrival of an ifrit is an excellent condition for the inducement of shock, not to mention surprised awe and bewilderment."

' " ' "As it should be, I suppose," the ifrit replied after some consideration. "When you have a reputation for terror, you have to expect that sort of thing. But I assure you that I did come out of that jar."

' " ' "Never would I believe such a thing unless I could see it happen with my own eyes!" the fisherman declared with a remarkable stubbornness. "If you are so all-knowing and all-seeing, why don't you show me?"

' " ' "Oh, very well," the ifrit replied with a notable reluctance, "I suppose I must. But, as soon as I demonstrate, it's the graveyard for you, my man, and I'm off about my business."

' " ' "I would expect no more," the fisherman agreed. "But I shall be fulfilled, for I shall die knowing the truth."

' " ' "Humans!" the ifrit remarked as he rolled his bloodshot eyes towards the heavens. "Watch carefully now. Here goes. One moment I am huge and imposing—"

' " 'The creature paused as he was instantly transformed from a huge monster into an equal portion of smoke. It took but mere seconds from that moment when the smoke located and entered the jar, until the last wisps disappeared within.

‘“‘“—and the next,” a voice echoed from deep within the recesses of the earthenware, “I am compact and easy to carry from place to place. What could be simpler? Now allow me—”

‘“‘But before the ifrit could be allowed to do anything, the fisherman slammed the lid back atop the jar and further reattached the seal as best he could, using some length of hemp that he retained to repair his nets.

‘“‘“What?” the ifrit called out in surprise. “What are you doing? I warn you, this will not win you an honorable death!”

‘“‘“This will win me no death at all, at least at the hands of an arrogant ifrit!” the fisherman replied in triumph. “First shall I return you to the sea from where I caught you. Then will I build my house upon this very shore and warn all who pass this way not to fish here, for an ifrit awaits below the water, and he will kill any unfortunate who rescues him!”

‘“‘“Kill?” the ifrit replied in a tone of astonishment. “Why would I want to do such a thing? Can’t you humans recognize a little ifrit humor? After all, spending a thousand years and more in the jar, an ifrit can use a little levity. Now let me out of this jar, and I will give you those many and wondrous benefits that you have always deserved!”

‘“‘“You lie, Oh creature of vile sorcery!” the fisherman retorted. “This conversation between us reminds me of nothing so much as what passed between the vizier of King Yunan and Rayyan the Doctor!”

‘“‘“What passed between the vizier of King Yunan and Rayyan the Doctor?” the ifrit called out in astonishment. “I have never heard of this incident before. What tale of marvel is that?”

‘“‘And this is what the fisherman replied:

### THE TALE OF WHAT PASSED BETWEEN
### THE VIZIER OF KING YUNAN
### AND RAYYAN THE DOCTOR

‘“‘“Know you, Oh creature of deceit, that there was, in another place and at another time of man, a king named Yunan who lived in the great city of Farr in the land of Roam. Now Yunan was a powerful ruler, beloved by his people and feared by his enemies, but he had one difficulty that kept him from achieving complete happiness. And this difficulty had to do with his skin. Ah, you might say, I have known many of the rich and famous whose skin was not among the best.

'"'"But this did not begin to address the problems of Yunan. For the skin of his hands was extremely dry, and great flakes would fall whenever he would touch any person or any object with his fingers. And these flakes were only matched by those large white particles that would descend from his hair to rest upon the shoulders of his robes of office, as well as the floor immediately below. And yet, despite this extreme dryness, his face would sport great oily areas of red, which might often sprout great, corpulent pustules that would grow so rapidly that you might actually see them spring from nothing to their final oozing state in the space of a short conversation.

'"'"Truly did this horrible condition confound all the doctors of the land, and many were the words used in an attempt to describe this incurable ailment. Even that most dreaded term 'leprosy' might have been mentioned, were we not here speaking of royal blood, and that the nature of the king's ailment might further be considered insulting to certain lepers.

'"'"But one day, this city was visited by a doctor both old and wise, and the name of this doctor was Rayyan. And Rayyan had read widely in Greek, Persian, Latin, Arabic and Syriac. He knew both the craft of medicine and the rule of the stars. He further had studied the uses and effects of all plants and of herbs, whether fresh or dry. And he had furthermore studied the art of philosophy, as well as dabbling in woodworking on the side.

'"'"Now Rayyan the doctor came to hear of the king's skin condition. And since Rayyan was well renowned as a man of great compassion, and further, like us all, he had some accounts that needed to be settled, he decided to pay a call upon the monarch to see if Yunan could use his consultation. So it was that the doctor dressed himself in his richest clothes and proceeded to the palace, and, in due time, the physician was announced and presented before the king. Rayyan stepped forward and, bowing low before the monarch, kissed that space between his hands, which was certainly a more appealing prospect than kissing those hands themselves.

'"'"'Sire,' the doctor remarked after offering a suitable blessing. 'I have heard that you suffer from an unfortunate and exceedingly depressing skin condition, which all the physicians in this land have been unable to cure.'

'"'"'Indeed this is so,' the king replied in the most morose of tones. 'I have been given every sort of drug and pellet and ointment for my malady, but all to no avail.'

""""'I am not surprised at this news,' Rayyan replied, 'for I know of only one cure for a malady such as yours, and it is not delivered through potion or salve.'

""""'You know of a cure?' the king replied, his voice half filled with wonder and half with disbelief.

""""'I most certainly do,' Rayyan replied, 'and further will the cure be free of both weariness and pain.'

""""'If this is the case,' said the king, 'I shall make you a rich man, and your sons shall be rich as well. Now tell me, good doctor. How long will it take you to prepare such a cure?'

""""'The doctor paused for a moment to reflect before he responded, 'I think that the treatment should be ready at the end of one full day.'

""""'Very well! Prepare your cure for tomorrow!' the king declared, for he was sore wearied by the constant itch.

""""'Rayyan therefore left the palace and immediately hired a fine house suitable to his needs. And into this house he placed his books, and cures, and aromatic plants. When he had completed this task, he set about making extracts of those drugs and herbs that were necessary to the cure, and further fashioned a hollow mallet into which to pour these extracts, and a handle which would plug that hollow and trap the extracts within. And he finally fashioned a ball to accompany the mallet.

""""'When the doctor's labors were completed, the sun had set and then risen once again, so that he proceeded directly to the palace. There he presented the king with those objects that he had fashioned, after again kissing the air between the king's hands. Then did he give the king the following prescription: that the monarch should mount his horse, and ride to the polo-ground, and there hit the ball with the mallet repeatedly.

""""'That is the entire cure?' the king called in disbelief.

""""'No,' Rayyan replied in the most kindly of manners, for his methods often produced this sort of skepticism. 'It is only the process through which the cure is effected. All will become apparent to you once you have completed the task.'

""""'And so winning and sincere was the physician's courtside manner that the king then proceeded immediately to the polo ground, accompanied by numerous members of his court. And there the doctor met them once again, so that he might give this further instruction:

""""'Take this mallet and grip it in the way I show you now. Ride your horse upon the field and strike the ball as many times as it may take for your hand and arm and body to be covered by perspiration. In this way will my cure enter through your palm and travel the length of your body. When you have had sufficient time to sweat, then you should return to your palace and bathe. At the conclusion of this bath, you will be cured. Until such a time, peace be with you!'

'"'"With that, the doctor left the polo ground and the king proceeded to perform his task in the way the physician described. And, when he was done with his exercise and fully covered with perspiration, he retired to the bath. And when the bath was done, he looked upon his skin and found it smooth and whole, with not a single sign of flaking or itching upon his body, and nary a pustule to pop upon his face.

'"'"The king then summoned the doctor to return to the palace and, when he arrived, the monarch gave Rayyan the sum of two thousand dinars, as well as fine robes and many other gifts of honor. And, much honored by this attention, Rayyan further discussed his cures for headaches, which involved a great number of birds and a period of time playing upon the flute; and also his cure for the common cold, this last taking some two weeks and including an ocean voyage.

'"'"But all was not well within the palace of Yunan, for the grand vizier witnessed the manner in which his king exalted this doctor, and further honored this man in a way in which not even the vizier himself had previously been so valued. Two thousand dinars? he considered. For but a single task? And for giving the king a polo mallet?

So did this grand vizier, who was a man of honor and a great attendant in all other ways, become jealous of the doctor Rayyan (after all, two thousand dinars?), and could not help but voice certain suspicions to the king.

'"'"'Oh most honored among monarchs, who may reign for a hundred years and all the years beyond,' the vizier began, thinking upon all that gold, 'I fear I must give you serious counsel, for there is he among us whom you exalt, but who wishes to do you nothing but harm.'

'"'"The king, greatly concerned by the direness of this warning, urged the vizier to continue.

'"'"'I speak of none other than that upstart doctor, Rayyan,' the vizier proceeded (and all those dinars all at once!), 'for I am convinced that he plans to do you ill.' (It was the part about the polo mallet that really sealed his opinion.)

' " ' " "But the king could not believe the vizier's accusations. 'How can you say such a thing?' he cried in astonishment. 'This doctor has cured me. I no longer flake, nor do I sport a single pustule! He is truly my friend, and you are speaking from jealousy, much as occurs in the ancient and venerable tale of King Sindbad!'

' " ' " "King Sindbad?' the vizier remarked, but he did not think it fit to raise any further objection. Besides the fact that there might be a certain amount of truth in the king's words concerning jealousy, the vizier was well trained to honor the wishes of his monarch, foremost among these being the knowledge of when to ask the ruler a question properly to further the conversation. So it was that the vizier dutifully announced, 'How then did this thing happen?'

' " ' " "And this was the story that King Yunan told:

## THE TALE OF KING SINDBAD AND THE FALCON

' " ' " "Know you,' the king began, 'that in an ancient time in this very kingdom there lived a great monarch named Sindbad, whose glories were such that my own accomplishments resemble but a few meager seedlings while his would fill a full-grown tree—' " ' " '

## ALL THESE TALES ARE TEMPORARILY INTERRUPTED BY AN IMPATIENT OZZIE

'WAIT A MOMENT!' the large and less-than-courteous green head of Ozzie the *djinni* interrupted. 'WE HAVE ALREADY HEARD THE STORY OF SINBAD!'

'That is my name!' the thin man named Sinbad spoke quickly and, it appeared from his expression, not entirely voluntarily.

'Yes,' Scheherazade replied most courteously, as she had learned in her time in the harem, 'but Sinbad is an ancient name of honor, and this is another great man of whom I speak.'

'VERY WELL,' Ozzie replied in the most dubious of tones. 'SIMPLY REMEMBER THAT IT DOES NOT DO TO FOOL-ISHLY HOAX A *DJINNI*!'

'You must beware of the power of magic!' agreed a jar that now retained the still-mortal remains of Kassim, brother to Ali Baba, a man of evil past who, despite being torn into six-times-six pieces, still, through sorcery, retained the ability to speak for these many days since his accident, although the various pieces were beginning to be a bit the worse for wear, and it was now best if you remained upwind of the jar.

'QUIET!' Ozzie called. 'OR I SHALL SCATTER YOUR REMAINS ABOUT THE CAVERN!' The *djinni* paused to laugh heartily at his bullying.

'Very well,' was Scheherazade's only response, for she had resolved, when she did trick the *djinni*, she would do it in any way possible – except foolishly.

She therefore resumed her tale:

## WE RETURN TO SCHEHERAZADE, AND HER TALE WITHIN ANY NUMBER OF TALES

'"'"'Now Sindbad, whose name continues down through the generations, and is so great that it is given to all classes of men, was a great lover of sport. And foremost among these sports was hunting, and fondest was he of hunting with his falcon. And, on this certain day, his chief falconer approached him, addressing him most humbly, and said that the weather and all other conditions were ideal for hunting.

'"'"'Hearing this greatly pleased the king, and he quickly made ready. Taking his falcon, the king was then accompanied by a great company, and that party at length came to a valley which the monarch deemed suitable, and he further instructed that the nets should be spread below. And, with the suddenness of frightened animals, a gazelle fell into the nets.

'"'"'"I will kill the man who lets her pass!" the king shouted in great excitement, for he was indeed very serious about his hunting. So did the others pull the nets forward in such a way that the gazelle was drawn towards the monarch, and the beast did rise up upon its hind legs, as if in salute to the king.

'"'"'The king applauded to see such a show before him, but when he clapped his hands, he frightened the gazelle, and it leapt above the nets and straight beyond the king's shoulder.

'"'"'At this remarkable occurrence, he looked back to his subjects and could not help but detect a certain amount of winking, snickering and prodding with elbows among their number. He turned to his grand vizier and asked what might be amiss.

'"'"'"I most humbly beg your pardon, Oh light of the kingdom," was the vizier's most considered reply, "but I cannot help but suspect that the men are thinking of your earlier order, that you would kill any man who let the gazelle pass."

'""""At this, the king seemed the slightest bit discomfited. "I did? Well, I suppose I certainly—" He paused to think. The gazelle had certainly leapt directly past him, hadn't it? And he definitely would have stopped the animal had he not been so surprised. Surely, he could somehow explain this to his subjects, couldn't he?

'""""Well," he continued somewhat hesitantly, "a king's edict is certainly not to be disobeyed, is it? Unless, of course, there's – death, did I say?" The monarch paused to clear his throat. "Quickly, my followers! We must not let the gazelle get away!"

'""""So did the king and all his huntsmen ride their horses with all their speed, until they again came upon the gazelle. And the king's falcon flew before them with a mighty squawking (for the bird did call out so much, the king sometimes almost thought it could talk), and struck the gazelle upon the brow with its beak, so that the beast was both blinded and confused. Then the king raised his mace and felled the gazelle with one blow, and the now dead beast was properly disemboweled and flayed, and the carcass was mounted upon the king's saddle-bow.

'""""When this was done, the king declared that he was thirsty, for the day was hot, and the hills over which they had run bordered upon the desert. But there before them the king saw a great tree, and down the sides of this tree water flowed as thick as butter.

'""""The king was delighted, and took the small cup that hung about the falcon's neck so that he might sample the liquid. But at the moment that he raised the cup to his lips, the falcon flew forward and announced, "Squawk! Seware! Sanger! Squawk!" And then the falcon knocked the cup from King Sindbad's hand.

'""""The king was greatly startled by this action and looked to his bird as the falcon once again settled upon his gloved hand. "Oho," the king stated. "So you are thirsty, too? Well, you have done good work today, and so I shall give you the honor of the first drink."

'""""The king filled the cup a second time and offered it to his bird. But the falcon reached forward with its beak; and further remarked, "Squawk! Son't Srink! Squawk!" And with that, the falcon again knocked the cup away.

'"""""So that is the way of it?" the king remarked in some annoyance. And he again had the sense that this bird was trying to tell him something. But he felt it necessary quite quickly to fill the cup once more, for he could sense that the hunters about him had once again begun to wink, snicker and prod each other with their

86

elbows. Therefore, he would show the falcon who was king here, and he offered the first drink to his horse.

‘ “ ‘ “ ‘But the falcon once again took flight, and this time knocked over the cup with an outstretched wing. Then did the falcon fly before the king, so that the bird's eyes looked directly into that of the monarch, and the falcon further called, "Squawk! Seadly! Soison! Sunderstand?"

‘ “ ‘ “ ‘This was too great an affront to the king who became enraged, calling the falcon an ill-omened bird, and, quickly, drawing his sword, he struck off both the falcon's wings.

‘ “ ‘ “ ‘The falcon did nothing in return but move its head towards the upper reaches of the tree and say, "Soison sourself. See swaht si sare! Squawk!"

‘ “ ‘ “ ‘The king, so astonished by this behavior, let his gaze follow that of the falcon, and there, in the upper branches of the tree, he saw a vast nest of serpents, a hundred or more all coiled one upon the other, and all these many snakes had opened mouths, with venom flowing out from their fangs. And the king realized that it was this venom that he found flowing down the tree, which he had taken for the pure water of a spring.

‘ “ ‘ “ ‘ “What have I done?" the king then called out to Heaven, but at that instant the falcon, after a final death rattle of "Squawk!" and "Stupid sit!", expired from its wounds. Only then did the king realize that he had killed the one who had saved him from a frightful death.

### THE TALE OF WHAT PASSED BETWEEN. THE VIZIER OF KING YUNAN AND RAYYAN THE DOCTOR, RESUMED EVER SO BRIEFLY

‘ “ ‘ “When the vizier had finished hearing the story that his monarch had to relate, he spoke in turn, 'Oh most generous and benevolent of kings, I do not know why you relate a story with such a sad ending. For I am only concerned with your own welfare, and I pray that you shall see the truth of my words, for I fear that you shall perish as did a certain treacherous vizier who wished to bring harm to the son of a king.'

‘ “ ‘ “ ‘I believe that you are prepared to begin another story,' the king remarked, for he was well versed in these things.

‘ “ ‘ “ ‘Not only powerful but wise beyond his years!' the grand vizier exclaimed, for, the more he spoke with the king, the more he could sense the disappearance of his retirement income. 'Truly is he a king for all the ages!' And with that, and before the king could make any further interjection, he began his tale:

## THE TALE OF THE PRINCE AND THE OGRESS

'"'"'Once was there this king,' the vizier began, 'who had a son who was very fond of hunting. But the king, who worried for his son since he was still quite young, had also ordered one of his lesser viziers always to accompany the boy upon his excursions. So it was that the king's son and the lesser vizier traveled upon one of their many hunting expeditions, taking with them the prince's golden saddle and his jeweled quiver and arrows, for the prince's father never gave him anything but the very best.

'"'"'But this expedition was unlike all the others, for, as they explored the wild, the prince and the vizier saw a truly miraculous beast rise up before them, with great tusks and a hide as rough as an elephant, but matching in color the first rosy hues of dawn. And furthermore did this beast have a great mane of what looked like nothing so much as feathers, with half those feathers being a deep green in color, and the other half the brilliant yellow of wild flowers in spring.

'"'"'Now the lesser vizier, who knew what form of beast this was, shouted to his young ward, crying, "After her, for she is truly a prize worth possession!" So did the prince run for his horse, but the vizier further stated, "Take my mount, for it is closer!"

'"'"'And so did the prince jump upon the vizier's horse, which was a fine steed if somewhat less well appointed than his own mount, and he further spurred this horse forward and gave chase to this strangest of creatures. But the creature was fast and soon out of sight, so the prince had to follow the beast's tracks which seemed to be fashioned from an odd combination of hoof and foot. But after a time, even those tracks disappeared.

'"'"'The prince was at a loss as to what he should do next when he heard a prodigious weeping from the other side of the hill he now climbed. He rode forward and discovered a beautiful and finely dressed young woman crying by the side of the road. She looked up in great astonishment as he approached, crying, "Here is someone to rescue me! I was a traveler on a caravan from the city of Hind, which moved during the night when this region is cooler. I foolishly fell asleep and was lost from my mount but, because it was dark, no one had missed me and the caravan went on. I was left behind, and I thought surely I would die!"

'"'"'Now the prince, being a man of compassion, as his father had taught him, took pity on the girl and said "Fear not, fair maiden, for I shall take you to your home."

'"'"'With that, the girl clapped her hands most loudly and joyfully and allowed the prince to place her upon his saddle-bow, so that she might direct him upon the proper route. And, as they rode, the prince did his best to begin a conversation so that he might discover more about the maiden.

'"'"'"So you were upon a caravan?" he thereupon asked most politely.

'"'"'"Yes," she answered most demurely, "from the city of Hind."

'"'"'"And where were you bound?" he further solicited.

'"'"'"We came from Hind," the young woman replied brightly.

'"'"'The young man frowned at that. Perhaps, he thought, they spoke a slightly different language in this other city. Still, if he was not successful in his first line of inquiry, perhaps he would attempt another. He therefore asked, "And you fell from your horse?"

'"'"'The young woman looked blankly at him for a moment before brightening and replying, "Was I lost from my mount? Oh, yes. Because it was dark, no one had missed me and the caravan went on."

'"'"'"And have you been waiting here for a long period of time?" the prince further encouraged a reply.

'"'"'The young lady nodded most eagerly. "Since I fell from my mount. Did I mention that I was sleeping? I was left behind, and I thought surely I would die!"

'"'"'The prince had to admit that this conversation was not all that he hoped it would be. Perhaps, like many women, this girl had not been out much in the world. Or, conversely, perhaps she simply wasn't very bright.

'"'"'It was at this time that they happened to pass a ruined home by the side of the road. And, at the same moment, the young woman smiled most sweetly at the prince and requested, "Pardon me, Oh my benefactor, but I believe I should have a more pleasant time upon the rest of my journey if I paused a moment now to answer the call of nature."

'"'"'To this, the prince most readily agreed, for he had been in many similar situations himself, and, furthermore, this was the first statement the young woman had made that did not have to do with falling asleep and plummeting from her mount. So he helped the young woman from his horse and waited there for a respectable period of time while she performed her necessities within the ruins.

' " ' " 'But a sufficient amount of time did at last go by, and then twice a sufficient amount of time, and the prince began to worry, for these were not the most innocent of environments for one to answer the call of nature. The prince therefore decided that it was time discreetly to explore his surroundings to see if there was anything amiss. He therefore very quietly approached the ruins and was surprised to hear what sounded like the maiden's voice, although the tone of that voice seemed much coarser than before.

' " ' " ' "Ah, all my nice young pretties," that voice said, "you will be well fed tonight, for I have brought a fat young prince for your meal!" And this voice was further answered by a chorus of laughter that was of such a timbre that it chilled the young man's blood.

' " ' " 'Terrified, the prince located a crack in the crumbling wall and, peering through, saw that the young woman he had rescued had been transformed into an ogress, and she was further surrounded by a dozen or more ogre children, or, as they are known in those more learned circles, ogre-ettes.

' " ' " 'This was why he could get no further conversation from the young lady, for ogres are considered to be by far the most stupid of those supernatural creatures whose habit it is to eat people. But then, upon reflection, it was he who was in danger of becoming dinner. Perhaps there was a certain prince in this matter who had been acting even more foolishly.

' " ' " 'Still, one wise decision was better than none, and the prince determined that, at that moment, it would be very wise to leave.

' " ' " 'It was extremely unfortunate that, at that very moment, a hand smashed through the rotting mortar and grabbed him around the collar.

' " ' " ' "Bring him in, mother!" the ogre-ettes chanted. "Bring him in so that we may gnaw on his bones!"

But the prince, who was, even he had to admit, a bit on the portly side, would not fit through the crack.

' " ' " ' "I shall have to go around and fetch him," the ogress announced. "Quiet now, so that he shall not suspect."

' " ' " 'And with that, the hand released his throat. Now that he was free, the prince considered that he should run as fast as he was able, but his legs were shaking so much that they refused to move in any way. He looked up as he heard someone's feet coming down the gravel path around the corner, and prepared for the worse. But when she appeared, it was not the ogress he saw, but that same young woman he had rescued.

' " ' " 'The young woman frowned as she approached, for she could see how distressed the prince appeared.

' " ' " ' "Why are you afraid?" she therefore asked.

' " ' " 'He supposed, since he could not run, that he might as well play this game as well. "I am afraid for I have discovered that I have an enemy."

' " ' " ' "Perhaps you would feel better if we went for a little walk," the young woman suggested with the most seductive of smiles. "I have found some very interesting things to show you."

' " ' " 'At that remark, the prince's quivering doubled.

' " ' " ' "But why do you let your fear rule you?" asked the young woman who was actually an ogress. "Did you not say that you were a prince?"

' " ' " 'The son of the king could but nod his head.

' " ' " ' "Well, then, princes are rich," the young woman reasoned, which was a great leap of logic for an ogress. "Should you not have enough money to pay this enemy so that he should never bother you again?"

' " ' " 'The prince could see no reason why he should not answer honestly. "I fear that money would not satisfy him, and that he would be pleased only with my death."

' " ' " ' "Then, from what I understand, you have only to call upon the mercy of the Almighty, and you will be saved," the young woman mused, "especially if that creature is full of malice, or so I have heard." She smiled, and the prince could have sworn that expression had more of the ogress about it than the young maiden. "But come, surely you have regained your strength and are able to walk. I have many hungry mouths – I mean fascinating things to show you."

' " ' " 'But the prince in that instant realized that, even though the ogress probably had no conception what she was talking about, she had put forth a worthy idea. So it was that he called upon the Almighty in that instant to show him His mercy. "Save me please," he further implored, "from the dire appetites of this ogress and her brood."

' " ' " ' "Oh," said the ogress who appeared to be a young maiden, "you mean I was your enemy? I assure you, I was going to eat you in the most friendly manner possible." She frowned as she looked down upon her form. "Oh, drat," she mentioned, because she had noticed that she was fading away and would soon vanish altogether. And vanish she did.

'"""'With the ogress gone, the prince discovered that his legs did once again work beneath him. So it was that he remounted his horse and galloped back to that place where he had first seen the beast. And, when he had returned to that spot, what should he discover but the lesser vizier contemplating a pile of riches that had formerly belonged to the prince, including his golden saddle, his bejeweled bow and arrows, and many other weapons of great value.

'"""'And as this villain regarded his treasure trove, the vizier did muse to himself, "What a lovely bunch of riches. Now where shall I bury it? And I further have to practice." And with that he put on the most sorrowful face imaginable. "Oh woe, sire, an ogress has stolen your son, and she has taken his horse and weapons as well!" Tears streamed down his face for a full minute as he lamented upon his knees. Then he stood again, wiped the moisture from his cheeks, and returned to admire the hoard. "Yes," he said, "that shall do quite nicely."

'"""'The prince became outraged, and rushed forward to confront the villain. "You have encouraged me to chase an ogress, who would surely be the cause of my death! And, once I had departed, you have gathered all my possessions into your own personal golden hoard!"

'""""Why, my prince!" the lesser vizier replied. "What a pleasant surprise!" He stepped quickly before the pile of amassed riches. "But, hoard, did you say?" He glanced behind and saw that his robes of office did not quite hide the pile. "What golden hoard?" Perhaps, he must have thought, if he took a step backwards and spread his skirts . . . "Surely you are mistaken."

'"""'It was at that moment that the vizier tripped and fell backwards, impaling himself on a golden sword whose hilt was inlaid with rubies the color of his now flowing blood.

'"""'So fall the wicked. And so ends my tale.

## WHAT PASSED BETWEEN
## THE VIZIER OF KING YUNAN
## AND RAYYAN THE DOCTOR,
## CONTINUED AT SOMEWHAT GREATER LENGTH

'""""But I fear, Oh my king,' the grand vizier continued, 'that if you continue to listen to this doctor, you will die the most horrible of deaths.'

'""""Perhaps this may be so,' the king repeated doubtfully, 'although I am still not convinced, and further, you perhaps do not perform a service for yourself if you are to tell me stories of dishonest viziers.'""'"'

## A SUDDEN INTERRUPTION OF THESE TALES BY A PRUDENT DUNYAZAD

'Pardon, me, Oh sister,' Dunyazad interjected into Scheherazade's protracted narrative, 'but if you wish to pause in your story-telling, I think you might do so now.'

But Scheherazade would not think of such a thing, for her story-telling was the one pursuit that would guarantee that both she and her sister would still have necks attached to bodies once morning had arrived.

'Surely, you jest, my precious sister,' she therefore replied. 'But, as I was relating my tale concerning the king and the grand vizier—'

'Certainly,' Dunyazad interrupted again, 'you may continue your tale if you wish, but I am afraid it is lost upon your audience.'

Would Dunyazad now say something against the king? Scheherazade reacted quickly and in a panic. 'Forgive her, Oh my husband, for she is young and the hour is late. Besides, you do not wish to miss the next part of my tale which is so fascinating that—'

'It is no use telling the story to your husband,' Dunyazad stubbornly interrupted once more. 'He has been asleep for quite some time.'

As if in agreement, the king snorted loudly from his position reclining among the cushions.

'Asleep?' Scheherazade repeated in disbelief.

'I believe he has been in such a state for some little while,' Dunyazad further remarked, 'at least through some portion of the ogress story, and perhaps even before.'

Scheherazade then allowed herself to pause and study the king. The king, for his part, snored quite softly but regularly. Scheherazade had been so dedicated to her storytelling art that she had not paid sufficient attention to her audience. Of course, matters were further accentuated by the fact that the king, when he was not busy ravishing or playing with swords, did seem to be a rather passive individual. In other words, his position while listening and his position while sleeping appeared to be virtually identical.

Shahryar's head lolled back, his mouth opened, and his snores became prodigious indeed.

'He is falling into an even deeper sleep than before,' Scheherazade observed.

'Perhaps this is an opportunity for us to sleep as well,' Dunyazad suggested.

'I do not know if that is the best of ideas,' Scheherazade replied in a doubtful tone, 'for what if we were to sleep and he was to awake. Those swords are still far too close, and I fear that the king still seems to be influenced by outside forces.'

'Again, sister,' Dunyazad said agreeably, 'you are most wise. Still, might we not sleep one at a time? In that way, she who watches could wake—' She paused and pointed at the king. 'But wait, he stirs!'

And indeed her sister was correct, for the king's arms and legs began to thrash back and forth as he continued to snore.

'Perhaps he is having a dream,' Dunyazad mused.

'I fear it is more than a dream,' Scheherazade replied in the darkest of tones, for she could see that he had managed to roll over upon his stomach and had now risen to a crouch upon his cushions, even though his eyes were still closed and his breathing very deep and regular. The snores continued to come from deep within as he managed to stand.

'He walks in his sleep!' Scheherazade exclaimed.

But the king was not finished with his somnambulant surprises, for he bent down to the couch beside him and picked up one of his newly acquired swords.

'Behold!' Dunyazad agreed. 'He will cut in his sleep as well!'

In this instance, Scheherazade feared that her sister was all too correct. For, sleeping or no, the king had freed the sword from its scabbard and now approached the two women with sword held high.

'Sire!' she called out to the king. 'Awake!'

'But, sister,' Dunyazad reprimanded, 'I have heard that it is most dangerous to wake one who walks so in his slumbers.'

'Pardon me, sister, for contradicting you so,' Scheherazade replied, 'but do you not think that our present situation is more dangerous still?'

She ducked as the king's scimitar whistled through the air overhead. He had actually missed her by quite some distance. The fact that his eyes were closed seemed to be affecting his aim. She hoped this might work to their advantage.

Dunyazad had snuck up behind the king, and now tugged upon his night clothes. 'Oh, Sire!'

Shahryar responded by swinging his free hand about to grab Dunyazad's hair.

'Oh, sister!' Dunyazad called. 'He has me!'

And with that, the king pulled upon her head so that Dunyazad was forced to lift her head and expose her most delicate neck. The hand that held the sword raised itself too, as if to deliver the killing stroke.

And, through it all, King Shahryar snored.

Would there be no way to wake him before he had murdered Dunyazad?

## Chapter the Twelfth,
## in which a chicken
## crosses to the other side.

'Sister!' Dunyazad called out in great fright and consternation. 'There must be some way to prevent the king from using his sword!'

Scheherazade called out to Shahryar again, but his only response was to deepen his snore. The sword wavered about his head, as if the king, not being able to see the proper way to cut Dunyazad's throat, wished to sense it instead.

But Scheherazade would not allow such a thing to pass. Yet what could she do against a man who was strong in muscle, powerful in office, and currently unconscious? She could think of but one possible solution, which, since it had worked when the king was awake, might function again while the king was asleep. She therefore once again began to tell her tale:

THE TALE OF THE MERCHANT AND THE *DJINNI*,
RESUMED DURING THE TALE OF THE THIRD SHEIKH
AS HE IS RELATING THE STORY OF
THE FISHERMAN AND WHAT HE CAUGHT
AND THE FISHERMAN IS FURTHER EXPLAINING
WHAT PASSED BETWEEN THE VIZIER OF KING YUNAN
AND RAYYAN THE DOCTOR

But Scheherazade paused before she could truly resume her tale, for the king snorted most loudly and violently. What, she thought with more than a trace of fear, could such a violent snort portend?

But then the king simultaneously growled and shook, as if instead of cutting something with his weapon, he now fought a battle within himself. It was a most frightening sight, but at least in his tremors he did not move his sword. Apparently, hearing the title alone of Scheherazade's tale had caused the king to hesitate in the midst of his killing stroke.

97

Dunyazad must have come to the same conclusion as Scheherazade, for the younger sister called out, 'Quickly! Pray continue, before I lose my head.'

So Scheherazade took a breath to begin anew. But, at that very moment, the gong resounded that announced the beginning of another day.

That clanging sound seemed to have an immediate effect upon the king, who ceased to quiver violently as his sword slipped from his slack fingers and clattered to the ground. The king's eyes fluttered open and he smiled upon both Scheherazade and Dunyazad.

'A most excellent story,' Shahryar announced most heartily. 'Again, I am sorry to hear it end, if only until tonight. My, I seem to have stood up. I must be even more tired than I thought. But come! You must retire to your harem, while I proceed with my day's business.' He yawned and stretched, further remarking, 'Oddly enough, I do not feel quite so fatigued as I have on nights past. That only shows you the rejuvenating power of a good story, I suppose.' He waved as the women hastily made ready to leave. 'Until tonight, then.'

He took a step forward and almost stumbled across the blade upon the floor. He looked down at the weapon with some astonishment, and then spoke with a great wistfulness. 'I wonder if I might be able to get away from court for a bit today and practice with my swords?'

So were Scheherazade and Dunyazad escorted from the king's chambers and returned to their own.

After they were a sufficient distance from the hearing of the king, Dunyazad remarked, 'It appeared that he remembered his sleepwalking not at all.'

'I have heard of such things happening before,' Scheherazade agreed. 'When you walk in your sleep, it is as if you are acting out your dreams. I feel, however, in this instance, there is another element at work. I do not believe the king walked under his own power, but was instead subject to a trance. He was not acting out his own dreams, but the dreams of another.'

'A trance?' Dunyazad wondered with a shiver. 'But how can you tell he is being controlled by another's dreams?'

'It occurred to me,' Scheherazade replied most thoughtfully, 'in the way that he was drawn to pick up the sword. And I have sworn that I have seen the swords move of their own volition. I believe the weapons to be enchanted!'

98

Dunyazad despaired at this revelation. 'How might we hope to overcome enchantments?'

'So far,' Scheherazade said most humbly, 'I have been fortunate enough to weave an enchantment of my own.'

This greatly reassured the younger sister, so that they walked in silence for the remainder of the distance to the harem.

All was silence as well when they had returned to their apartments and there were no signs of mysterious women in black, nor were there any gifts of sinister purpose.

'Do you suppose whosoever controls the enchantment of the swords is also responsible for these other difficulties?' Dunyazad asked as the two women prepared to sleep.

'There is no way yet to know,' Scheherazade replied, 'although I expect the hands against us will become more apparent as the days go by. Now, ask no more questions. If we are to be at our best, we must get our repose.'

So saying, the two women reclined upon their individual couches.

And, upon that morning, Scheherazade dreamed of chickens.

Scheherazade opened her eyes. She was not simply dreaming of chickens. She had heard a chicken, in that very room.

'Is there someone here?' she called out to the dimly lit room.

A call came from a far corner of the apartment: 'Bawwwk!'

The younger woman stirred in her sleep. 'Did you say something, sister?'

'Be still, Dunyazad,' Scheherazade whispered in return. 'There is someone in the room with us.'

'Someone with us?' Dunyazad came fully awake. 'What horrible creature is it now?'

'Actually,' Scheherazade replied calmly, 'I believe it to be a chicken.'

As if in answer, the mournful call once again wafted from some far corner of their quarters.

'Bawwk!' And again. 'Bawwk!'

'A chicken?' Dunyazad asked. 'Could it be?'

'I most certainly think it could,' Scheherazade agreed. 'I believe we are being visited by *the* chicken.'

The cries that came to them were far more excited than before. 'Bawwk! Bawwk! Bawwk bawwk!'

'It is almost as if this chicken understands us,' Dunyazad said in astonishment.

'Little wonder,' Scheherazade agreed, 'since I believe that chicken was once a lady-in-waiting.'

Dunyazad rose from her couch and went to seek the bird. 'Do you mean she was transformed by sorcery?'

'The same as those people who were turned to animals in the tale of the merchant and the *djinni*,' Scheherazade explained. 'Many of my stories, after all, contain a considerable element of truth.'

'I never doubted that for an instant,' Dunyazad said most admiringly. 'Now, where is that bird? Or should I say lady servant?'

But oddly enough, as Dunyazad crossed the room, the chicken's voice seemed to retreat as well.

'Bawwk!' came the cry again, now barely louder than a whisper. 'Bawwk bawwk bawwwwwww—' And then the clucks faded to nothingness.

Dunyazad turned back to her sister, a look of consternation crossing her brow. 'There is no chicken here! The bird has disappeared as surely as that mysterious woman in black.'

'Really?' Scheherazade ruminated. 'Perhaps there is more sorcery about here than a simple transformation spell.'

Dunyazad hugged her arms to her chest and shivered delicately. 'I do not care for these complications.'

'There is nothing for us but to persevere,' Scheherazade replied simply. 'Our father raised us to practice gentleness and to respect truth, and I have faith that these two qualities can overcome whatever forces rally against us.'

As if waiting for that very moment, there was a knock upon the door. Dunyazad went to open it, and discovered the servant women. But they were anything but their formerly cheerful selves, and they now numbered only four.

Scheherazade thereupon asked the following questions: 'Then did one of your number disappear during the night? And, when you went to search for her in the morning, was there an animal in her place?'

'How did you know?' the first among the servants called out in astonishment. 'We were again missing one of our number when we gathered this morning. And, when we went to explore the room, we found nothing but a goat.'

'And now, I imagine, the goat has disappeared as well,' Scheherazade further remarked.

'How did you know?' all four servants called together.

'Yes,' Dunyazad echoed. 'How precisely did you know?'

But Scheherazade's answer was simplicity itself. 'It seemed to me that the pattern set the night before would be repeated again, for, after all, both women are victims of the same sorcery.'

'Sorcery?' one of the servants cried in alarm.

'Then the rumors are true!' another added.

'Sulima has returned!' called a third.

'Quiet!' their superior called in a most forceful tone. 'This gossip does nothing but upset our mistresses and ourselves. If there is sorcery, well, we will learn to cope with it, as we have learned to accept those other things that happen within this palace.'

'But cannot you do something to counteract this sorcery?' Dunyazad insisted. 'Could not Omar protect you?'

'Perhaps,' one of the servants replied. 'If he would choose to listen to us, rather than recite his poetry and press us with his favors.'

'Omar keeps his own counsel,' a second agreed grimly.

'He would, on the other hand, be most glad to behead us if we try to escape,' the third remarked.

'He often mentions beheading as a cure for the boredom of harem life,' the first servant continued. 'He speaks of it most wistfully.'

'Better to be a chicken than to be without a head,' the elder summarized for all.

'The king's mother is rumored to have dabbled in sorcery,' one of the juniors suggested.

'She could be an ally,' a second agreed, 'if she were not so passionately jealous of every woman in the city.'

'Perhaps,' Dunyazad suggested, 'she is the one who is producing these spells.'

'It is possible,' the eldest of the servants agreed. 'She does, after all, expect us all to take away her son.'

'She expects every woman to take her son,' her subordinate agreed.

'He *is* such a handsome man,' another commented with a sigh.

'If only he didn't have this habit with heads,' one of the others agreed.

All four servants paused at that, and looked at Scheherazade as if this might be one fact it would have been better not to recall.

'Oh, sorry,' they all said in unison.

'What are you doing standing about here?' an unnaturally high voice said from behind them. 'These women must be ready in a matter of hours!'

Scheherazade looked past the servants to an extremely distraught Omar, who had once again silently arrived.

But, Scheherazade realized, this fellow had to realize who was really ruler of the harem. It was time to act as a queen. If anyone was going to be distraught here, it would be Scheherazade.

'I am sorry,' she therefore replied in a voice that did not sound sorry in the least, 'but the women are concerned. There have been rumors of sorcery.'

Omar giggled derisively. 'There are always rumors within a harem.'

Still did Scheherazade persist. 'But these rumors have to do with Sulima.'

With that, Omar's already pale face drained of what little color it contained. 'Sulima? I won't hear of it. It can't be! It mustn't be! I was assured – well, that is neither here nor there.' He clapped his hands. 'But I won't have you servants spreading rumors! Now, hurry and prepare the women for their nightly audience with the king.' He looked critically at the group of women before him. 'I see, with two of you gone, that I shall have to find replacements. And I assure you, if I can find two replacements, I shall surely be able to find six.'

He spun about and marched officiously but silently away.

'Then Omar would replace you with others?' Dunyazad said, greatly worried.

Scheherazade could understand Dunyazad's concern. The sisters had come to trust the judgement of these women in their brief time in the harem. And who might guess the true purpose of any women whom Omar might now select to take their place?

But the leader of the servants was unfazed. 'Such a task would be extremely difficult. You see, there are no replacements.'

Her fellow servants quickly explained, 'Virtually every able-bodied woman in the kingdom has been beheaded.'

'Only we servants to the bride escaped.'

'If you were a servant, after all, you couldn't be a bride.'

'You'd be surprised how many women volunteered to be servants.'

'There was quite a waiting list,' the eldest agreed. 'But, after a while, well – the list got chopped off, I suppose you'd say.'

'Now there's no wait at all,' the other servants spoke one right after another.

'Nor are there any maidens.'

'However, give the kingdom a year or two, and a new crop will be old enough.'

'Yes, there are always enough maidens,' the eldest added with a certain sadness in her voice. 'What would the king do without them?'

This speech could do nothing but strengthen Scheherazade's resolve. She had stepped forward to save any other woman from being a victim of the king. And now it appeared that the king himself might be a victim, although whether the victim of the mysterious Sulima's spells or his own mother's wishes, Scheherazade was still unsure.

So she would do her best to save the women of the kingdom, and to save the king as well.

But, she wondered for the merest instant, could she also save herself?

## Chapter the Thirteenth,
### in which some mysteries are revealed,
### and some mysteries remain.

So did the servants hurry to prepare the two sisters for their evening ahead, and further rushed them through their meal, a fact Scheherazade hardly noticed, for she found she did not at present have much of an appetite.

Therefore the time came for Dunyazad and Scheherazade once again to go before the king. But the younger sister looked upon her elder with great worry as they walked to the royal bedchamber.

'Forgive me, sister,' Dunyazad whispered, 'but I cannot help but notice how exceedingly uneasy you appear.'

Scheherazade told Dunyazad that she appreciated her concern, but spoke no further. She concentrated upon taking deep breaths and admiring the magnificence of the archways and the intricacies of the inlaid tiles as they passed through the palace, and let her thoughts roam idly through the many stories she had known. These tales had been her best friends in her childhood, for they had allowed her to see the wonders of the world while still upon her mother's knee.

So it was that the sisters came again to the king's apartments. And the same guard who had been so concerned upon the previous evening said to the two of them, 'All is quiet within tonight.'

Scheherazade looked to her sister, who still gazed upon her with some concern, so Scheherazade felt it was important to say, 'And all is quiet within me as well. I am ready for the evening's entertainment.'

The guard nodded solemnly and let them pass.

'Ah!' the king called as they entered. 'I have looked forward to your arrival!' And while he still appeared to be worn by the cares of his office, he smiled warmly at the two sisters and laughed delightedly as they bowed before him. And the look upon the king's face warmed Scheherazade's heart, so that she felt her cares fade as well.

'I felt it was time to put my affairs in better order,' the king explained as he motioned for the women to make themselves comfortable. 'So it was that I had my servants hang my new swords in the armory at the far end of the apartments. Even though they are a gift from my mother, I do not believe I should keep any such swords about unless I intend to use them.'

This last statement made Scheherazade's heart lighter still, for it sounded as if thoughts of beheading were getting to be ever farther from the mind of her king.

'But come!' Shahryar clapped his hands with great relish. 'Enough talking! Isn't it time for a little ravishment?'

At that mention, Scheherazade realized she had somewhat missed that very sort of attention when it had not occurred the night before.

So was it that Dunyazad once again absented herself from the room as Shahryar and Scheherazade took their evening's exercise. On this night the younger sister wandered to the very periphery of the apartments, briefly inspecting the servants' rooms, and the guards' quarters, and the great balcony that overlooked the interior of the palace. And she trusted it was nothing but her imagination when she passed the king's personal armory, and heard what she thought was a soft thumping sound from within.

Eventually it came to pass that the king and queen became properly reacquainted, and Dunyazad once again entered their presence. And, after another few minutes for them all to settle into their most comfortable positions, the king called to Scheherazade to continue her tale.

The storyteller smiled most sweetly when she received this request but did not resume her narrative immediately, for she was unsure exactly where the king had fallen asleep upon the night before.

'You must excuse me, O my king,' she therefore replied most sweetly, 'but we are so recently done with the ravishing that my mind cannot be entirely upon the world of tales. Therefore, could I use your help to tell me which part of my story you heard the night before?'

The king laughed most delightedly at his queen's remark and said, 'Very well.' He then paused and frowned himself. 'Indeed, this ravishing must have affected us both, for my memory is not as clear as usual on the matter of last evening. As I recall, you had recently begun a story of a king with a hideous skin condition, and the doctor who saves him with an unorthodox cure. But then there

106

is a certain grand vizier who does not trust this doctor. Certainly we were somewhere in the midst of that.'

Scheherazade clapped her hands in delight at this summary. 'What a cogent retelling!' she exclaimed. 'Truly, no storyteller could ask for a better audience. Therefore, I shall begin again.'

And this is the story that she told:

THE TALE OF WHAT PASSED BETWEEN THE
VIZIER OF KING YUNAN AND RAYYAN THE DOCTOR,
AS RELATED DURING THE TALE OF THE FISHERMAN
AND WHAT HE CAUGHT,
WHICH IS ITSELF A PORTION OF
THE THIRD SHEIKH'S TALE,
WHICH IS IN TURN INCORPORATED
WITHIN THE TALE OF
THE MERCHANT AND THE *DJINNI*

' " " "So it was that the grand vizier greatly urged the king not to trust the counsel of the doctor, for the vizier was deeply envious of the counsel that was given, not to mention those two thousand dinars. And so did the vizier continue to give his subtle counsel, saying:

' " " " 'I fear, for the very reasons I have outlined in my story, that the doctor has only gained your trust to subject you to a more horrible death, even as the ogress enticed the prince to become her dinner. For he has cured you with something that you held in your hand. Could he therefore not kill you with something you might smell, or strike you blind with something you might see, or lead you to one of a thousand other unpleasant ends?'

' " " " 'Oh, very well,' the king announced at last, although whether he was finally convinced of the rightness of the vizier's arguments, or whether he had simply grown tired of forever exchanging stories and decided it was time to get on with things, this will forever be lost to antiquity. 'We will put the doctor to death.'

' " " " 'A most excellent decision!' the vizier agreed. 'Now you must send for him at once and cut his head from his body before you are cut down by his treachery!'

' " " " 'That is certainly most excellent counsel,' the king agreed. 'I shall do so at once!'

' " " " 'You shall never regret this decision,' the vizier replied craftily. 'And, while we were on the subject of decisions, I was wondering if we might discuss my annual remuneration.'

' " " " 'And so it was that the king and the vizier spent those next moments in deep discussion until the doctor again arrived. And Doctor Rayyan, who had no suspicion as to his fate, greeted both of the other men most cordially, and asked what he might do upon this fine day.

'""""There is but one thing left for you to do,' the vizier retorted most snappishly, 'and that is to lose your head!'

'""""Surely, this a jest,' the doctor began as two burly guardsmen grabbed him and directed him towards the headsman's block. 'I know of no reason for this to occur.'

'""""My vizier has convinced me,' the king answered, 'that you would have no reason to cure me except to throw me down again once you have gained my trust. Furthermore, he suspects that you are a spy, and will kill me after you have gained the kingdom's secrets. You must die, therefore, or I shall never be secure in life!'

'""""I have been able to cure the outside,' the doctor cried out, 'but the inside is still a mystery to me!' Still were the guards relentless in their maneuvers to place the doctor's head upon the chopping block. 'Still might I call for mercy, for if you reflect upon it, you will see that I have done you no harm!'

'""""It is the harm that you could do that would worry me!' the king retorted. 'Thank Providence that I have a vizier who talked to me until I saw reason!'

'""""Still did the doctor call for mercy, and many of the king's most loyal subjects called for mercy as well, saying that the doctor had done no wrong. But the king was adamant in his goal, and said that once he had ordered a head to come off, it was already off.

'""""Oh, can there truly be no mercy?' the doctor further declared as the guards wrapped a blindfold around his eyes. 'This reminds me of nothing so much as a tale of certain crocodiles and what came to pass between them.'

'""""The king was fascinated with this remark, and asked, 'Tell us, what is that tale?'

'""""So it was that the physician began:

THE TALE OF THE THREE CROCODILES,
AND THE SEVEN HARES,
THE SIX GOATS,
THE FIVE CHICKENS,
AND THE TWENTY-SIX MELONS,
AND THE DISPUTE THAT THEREUPON AROSE

'""""But no!' the physician called from behind his blindfold, 'I cannot tell such a story in this condition!'

108

'"'"'"The king frowned. He supposed, since he was already committed to killing this doctor, that there was no way he could further compel this man to tell his story. It was a shame, the king further pondered, for that had been a truly promising title.

'"'"'"'Very well,' he agreed. 'Let us dispense with his head so that the vizier and I may continue our argument.'

'"'"'"Seeing there was no hope for himself, the doctor gave up his calls for mercy and pleaded instead that, if he was going to lose his head, the least that the king could do was to give him an hour to put his affairs in order, so that he might pay his debts, arrange his funeral, give away his library, release his servants, play a few hands of cards, spend a quiet minute or two with a close personal friend, and further bring forth the greatest of his treasures to the palace. This request the king granted for, stubborn though the monarch was, even he realized he might have acted a little hastily in giving his most recent orders.

'"'"'"So the king therefore commanded his guard to release the doctor, and further bade him go to settle his affairs. The doctor did as he was told and, an hour later, he returned to the court, for not only was he extremely speedy in his errands, but he was a man of honor. And when he came again before the king, he now carried a great book and a small kohl box filled with a ground powder. And the king commanded that both the book and the box be brought before him.

'"'"'"'It is time that I show you one final marvel,' the physician announced, 'for, once my head is cut from my body, my voice will speak to you from beyond the grave.'

'"'"'"'Truly, this is a marvel!' the king called in great excitement. 'Tell us how it is to be done!'

'"'"'"'First must the one who is to learn the greatest secrets spread a quantity of that powder upon his fingers. Then may he be ready for the mysteries of the book.'

'"'"'"The king then looked at the great tome which he now held on his lap, and asked, 'What is this book?'

'"'"'"'It holds the greatest secrets you may ever see,' the doctor explained, 'and the least of its secrets is this: If, once my head has left my shoulders, one was to turn three pages of the book, and then read those three lines from the upper left-hand corner of the third page, the mouth upon my severed head will open, and I will answer any manner of question from beyond the grave.'

'"'"'"'Then it shall be done!' the king exclaimed in great excitement.

'""''While I have no power over your decision,' the doctor further said, 'I would like to make one final request. Oh my king, you are so worried about your future that perhaps you should allow your vizier to open the book and unveil the secrets for you.'

'""''But the king would not hear of it. 'Nonsense! I will allow no one but myself to let such a wonder come to pass!'

'""''So be it,' the physician replied, and he allowed the guards to once again guide him to the chopping block. 'And, may I remind you, my king, that it is best if the book is read after my head has left my shoulders.'

'""''But the king could not wait so long for the wonders to commence. So it was that he spread the powder over a silver plate before him and opened the book before the physician could even reach the chopping block. And he did his best to turn the first page before the doctor could even kneel. But the page stuck to the next, and the king found he had to place even more powder upon his fingers to push the pages apart, and further did he put his fingers to his mouth to whet them with spittle. The second page acted in much the same way, as did the third. And each of these pages was totally blank, without writing or marking of any kind.

'"'""There is nothing here for me to read!' the king complained.

'"'"" 'Perhaps you have not gone far enough,' was the physician's suggestion. 'Now I believe I need a blindfold. And I would not mind a little quiet so that I might better enjoy my death.'

'""''But the king would not be silenced. He opened the fourth page, and then the fifth and sixth, with great difficulty, crying, 'There is nothing here! Nor here! Nor even here!'

'"'"" 'On the contrary,' the doctor said as the blindfold was finally brought. 'That book will show you the greatest secret of them all.'

'"'""What do you – urk!' the king began. 'What secret – ulp!' For he had begun to go into convulsions, since the powder and the paper, when touched one upon the other, emitted the most powerful poison.

'"'""Yes, it is true that you shall die as well,' the doctor said, 'for has not the wise man said:

> '"'""When the unjust judge judges unjustly,
> Horrible things are often done
> But more horrible still is the day
> When justice judges the unjust judge!
> She sells sea shells – oh pardon,
> that is another poem entirely.'

---

' " ' " 'Urk! Ulp!' was the king's reply. 'Not only am I dying, but I am forced to listen to moralistic poetry!'

' " ' " 'Apparently,' Rayyan the doctor remarked, 'you will no longer be able to hear my final words. Perhaps, instead, it is time for some final words of your own.'

' " ' " 'Indeed – ulp – urk,' the king remarked. 'I think it is time to kill the vizier.'

' " ' " And then the monarch expired.

' " ' " 'So it is with those who heed unwise counsel,' the fisherman concluded.

## A FURTHER RETURN TO THE FISHERMAN
## AND WHAT HE CAUGHT

' " ' " 'If you had wished me well," the fisherman further remarked to the ifrit, "I would wish you well in turn, but, since you have wished my death, I shall throw you into the sea, where you may stay until you are dead."

' " ' But the ifrit, who had thought much upon the stories he had heard, seemed to have a change within his heart, for he called out, "For the love of Providence! Please do not throw me back into that place again! Release me out of generosity, rather than blaming me for my ill temper! For does not the wise man say, 'One good turn deserves another?' No, that is not appropriate. Then what of, 'Too many cooks—' No, that does not work either. Then perhaps, 'A rolling stone gathers—' Well, I am so distraught that I cannot think of an appropriate wise man's saying, but I am sure there must be one!"

' " ' " "I have heard enough of your foul lies!" the fisherman cried. "Prepare to be submerged!"

' " ' " "Do not do so," the ifrit called in rising panic, "and repeat the fate of Ankhmar when he came into that strange land!"

' " ' " "What is this story?" the fisherman said half to himself.

' " ' But it was the ifrit who replied:

## THE TALE OF ANKHMAR,
## AND HOW HE DEALT WITH UMTECHT,
## SON OF KRASNOW,
## IN THE DISTANT LAND OF ARKANAWAH,
## WHICH IS A LITTLE TO THE WEST OF GOLLOOGALLEE
* * *

' " ' "But no!" the ifrit immediately called. "I cannot tell you such a story while I am in this position!"

' " ' "And do you expect me to believe you even now?" the fisherman retorted with a fair degree of sarcasm. "Besides which, I have already used that particular storytelling device. It is impossible to distract someone who is already a master of distraction. And, as a man who fishes for a living, I can use any distraction I may find!"

' " 'It was only then that the ifrit realized he had met his master. "Very well. I will tell you any story you wish to hear! And I will further show you items no man has ever seen, and through these items you will become among the wealthiest of men. And I will further swear any oath you require that I will not harm you. But you must let me out of this jar!"

' " 'So it was that the fisherman at last relented, after making the ifrit swear the most solemn oath imaginable before the Almighty. Then did the fisherman at last loose those ropes that held the seal firm against the stopper, and further removed the stopper as well.

' " 'As soon as the stopper had been taken out, a great quantity of thick and pungent smoke arose from the jar, and the ifrit was once again reformed, but this time he was ten times the height of the fisherman. And he looked down upon that pitifully small fisherman and laughed, long and deep.' " '

## THE KING DISRUPTS THE TALE

'Pardon me, Oh most beloved among all storytellers,' King Shahryar interrupted most politely, 'but I could swear that I hear a chicken.'

'A chicken?' Scheherazade replied rather bluntly, for it was always difficult for her to resume a conversation if she was stopped in the midst of her story. She wondered if that ghostly chicken was again trying to tell her something. If so, the phantom fowl would simply have to wait until after her present tale was done. Until then, she had no time, or inclination, to worry.

'Yes,' the king further remarked, 'and now that I think upon it, I believe I can hear the bleating of a goat as well.'

'Forgive my impertinence,' Dunyazad interjected, 'but is it so strange to hear animal noises?'

'In their proper place, not at all,' Shahryar agreed as he rose from his couch and began to stalk quietly across the room. 'Except, rather than the animal pens or the kitchens, I could swear these sounds were coming from the armory.'

Scheherazade's gaze met Dunyazad's as both of their hands again reached to protect their throats.

It was at that point that Scheherazade resumed her worrying.

## Chapter the Fourteenth,
## wherein a chicken is sought
## but all that is found is blood.

Scheherazade could hear the chicken now, and the goat as well, a distant and forlorn cluck, followed by a bleat of total despair.

But, while at one point those two noises might possibly have come from somewhere near the armory, they now seemed to retreat farther and farther into the king's apartments, as they had fled within Scheherazade's quarters earlier upon that same day.

'I must explore the armory,' the king stated decisively.

'But wait!' Scheherazade interjected as she also stood and walked to the door that led to the next room. 'I believe the noises are now arriving from back here. Dunyazad, go through that door over there, and we will entrap these strange intruders!'

But the king waved aside all such objections as he rushed to the heavily fortified door. 'No, it is the armory! I must check the armory without delay.' He rubbed his hands together in agitation. 'Whatever shall I do if something has happened to my swords?'

And perhaps the king did have some cause for concern, for, while the cries of goat and chicken seemed to fade into the distance, Scheherazade was sure something clunked and bumped ever more loudly upon the other side of the armory door. Actually, as she thought upon it, she was ever more sure that she and her sister Dunyazad were the ones who should be concerned, for she was sure that bumping sound had to do with the swords. What would happen if the king grasped one of those swords again when he was in such an agitated state?

'Pardon me, Oh my king!' a deep male voice spoke behind them. 'What is the matter?'

Scheherazade realized with relief that the voice had come from one of the two heavily armed, uniformed men who watched beyond the king's door at all times, and that both these men had now entered the room. Fortunate it was that, in guarding the king, they were never more than a few paces away!

115

'There is something amiss in the armory!' the king cried in consternation. 'I must investigate.'

'As you desire,' said the guard who had previously spoken with Scheherazade and Dunyazad. 'But I feel it my duty to remind you that you have previously ordered us, in such situations, to investigate these things before you.'

The king blinked rapidly, as if he only now considered the consequences of his actions. 'Oh, yes, certainly. But I must be advised of everything you find.'

The guards both nodded silently, as if they would never consider doing otherwise. Then the guard who had previously spoken asked the king for the loan of the royal key so that he might open the padlock that kept the armory secure. The king immediately passed the keys to the guard, and he seemed to do so with some relief.

'Do you hear that noise within?' the king inquired.

The guards both frowned, for the bumping seemed to have ceased the moment the king handed over the keys.

'I seem to hear a goat and a chicken,' the second guard remarked, 'but those sounds appear to emanate from the other room.'

'Well, never mind!' the king demanded. 'Unlock this door and let us see what lurks within!'

At this juncture, even Scheherazade could not restrain her curiosity, so, as the guards unlocked and opened the door, and the king peered through that space over both their shoulders, she glanced over the king's shoulder, too.

The guard who had spoken first pulled open the massive door, as the second guard secured a nearby torch to illuminate that space within. So did both guards stand at the entryway, their scimitars at the ready.

All appeared to be quiet within. The second guard thrust the torch forward so that they could banish any shadows that might hide an intruder.

'There is no one here,' the first guard said slowly, as if he expected to be proven wrong between the uttering of one word and the next. 'The weapons seem all to be in their proper places – but hold! Lower your torch towards the floor!'

The second guard did so.

'There!' the first guard called in triumph. 'Those three fine swords, the newest addition to your arsenal, are all upon the floor of the armory, and all three have been pulled free of their sheaths!'

'But how can this be?' the king demanded. 'I had these swords

116

placed securely upon the highest shelf. I saw it done myself before I locked this door.'

'Nevertheless,' the first guard stated with grim purpose, 'it appears that someone, or something, has been within this room. Thank Providence that they are here no longer!'

'Is it possible that there is a secret panel?' Dunyazad asked from where she watched over Scheherazade's shoulder.

'No one knows all the secret ways of this ancient palace,' the king replied. 'Still did I have a dozen men examine that room in its entirety before I transformed it into my arsenal. I doubt greatly that someone entered, or left, here through a secret entranceway.'

So it was that Scheherazade felt the need to speak. 'While I hesitate to mention such a possibility, if those swords were not moved and unsheathed through natural means, that means their portage must have in some way been unnatural.'

The king frowned at this. 'I might rebuff you for letting your storyteller's imagination run wild, save that there is no other explanation. There must be malignant forces at work in this very palace!' He took a step closer to the guards as his voice once again rose in concern. 'Perhaps I should inspect these swords personally!'

'You will excuse my impertinence, Oh majesty,' the first guard again remarked, 'but I would be more comfortable in my duty if we were to inspect the swords first. If there have been malignant forces at work here, we do not know what they have left behind, or indeed if they still may in some way be present.'

Scheherazade felt there was more truth to this guard's statement than perhaps anyone else in the room realized. In all actuality, she suspected that those unnatural forces were still within the room, and did, indeed, await them upon the arsenal floor.

It was in that instant that the first guard called out in pain.

'What is it?' the king called out in very unmajestic alarm.

'I am afraid I have cut myself in returning this sword to its scabbard,' the guard explained as he presented a ragged, bleeding scar along his finger. 'It is but a flesh wound. The swords are very sharp, and oddly slippery to the touch.'

'Is there something amiss with the swords then?' the king asked with continued concern.

'I have never seen finer steel in my life,' the second guard remarked. 'If anything is lacking, it is with our handling of these objects.'

'Yes, yes,' the king agreed feverishly. 'Perhaps I should be the only one to handle them in future.' His fingers worked as if he needed sword handles to crease his palms. 'Perhaps I should handle them now!'

Scheherazade summoned all her willpower to keep her hand away from her neck as she suggested most accommodatingly, 'Oh my king and husband. You have had a most tiresome day, at the end of a most tiresome week. The guards have told you that the swords are in good condition, and whatever danger there may have been has certainly passed. Would you not have a better experience with your swords if you were to wait until you might practice with them on the morrow, when you are suitably rested and refreshed?'

The king shook his head rapidly, as if he was attempting to shake off a blow to the skull. 'Yes. Most certainly. No doubt you are entirely correct.' He waved vaguely towards the armory. 'Guards! Place the swords back upon the highest shelf, and I shall inspect them upon the morrow. Then lock the door anew and return the keys to me.'

The guards did as they were bade without further incident, and then withdrew from the royal presence. The apartments were again quiet, for there were no further noises from within the armory, nor were there any noises that could be taken for goats or chickens.

'Very well,' Scheherazade remarked when they were gone, 'now that the apartments are again at peace, I shall resume my story.'

But the king shook his head. 'Not tonight. No more stories. And no more swords.' He staggered wearily across the room to fall wearily upon the royal couch. 'Tonight we sleep.'

Scheherazade realized she should be happy with this decision, for it gave her both a reprieve from her entertainments and another night without fear of losing her head. And yet she could not help but worry about the things that had passed in those very rooms that evening, for she felt she should fear the swords even more, now that one of them had been whetted with blood.

## Chapter the Fifteenth,
### in which it is discovered that there is not one plot, but two.

So it was that Scheherazade found her eyes opening with the dawn for the first time in what felt like months and years, even though it had only been days.

But the king appeared to be in much better spirits upon this morning. 'For the first time since I do not remember when, I feel truly refreshed,' he said in a voice so great and joyful that it echoed from the distant ceiling. 'Truly, this is a day for dispensing justice! And, Oh my queen, I expect your story this evening to be filled with twice as many marvels, for you have rested as well!' Then, with a final hearty laugh, he departed to hold his daily court.

Scheherazade was unsure whether this final remark on the part of the king was an encouragement or an ultimatum. She would hope for the best, she decided, but expect the worst. Perhaps she could use her storytelling again to restrain her husband's fascination with swords. But, from the evidence of the night before, Scheherazade feared that, once Shahryar had again gripped those cursed swords, he would never let them go again until they, and he as their instrument, had killed.

So it was that Scheherazade and Dunyazad returned to the harem, and it was there that they discovered three servant women awaiting them at the great doors to their apartments.

'Have you lost another one of your number?' Scheherazade asked before any of them could speak.

'It is far worse than the ones before,' the eldest servant wailed. 'This one has become a cow.'

Then they would soon hear phantom moos above the bleats and clucks? This was a serious situation indeed. Yet Scheherazade could think of no way to stop these disappearances, much less return these phantoms to their human form. Might there be something within those many tales of wonder she had heard where there might be described a cure for such a curse? Unfortunately,

Scheherazade decided upon reflection, while her many stories were generous in their presentation of marvels, they tended to be very meager when it came to specific explanations.

'We will have to give this situation a serious appraisal,' Scheherazade said most soberly, in that same tone that she realized her father, the grand vizier, would use when there was some problem within her family. Still, as her mother had instructed her in the art of storytelling, so her father had shown her, through his own example, many methods to solve even the most daunting problems. She realized she would need all these talents now.

She turned to the door. 'Perhaps,' she suggested to the servants, 'you should join us within the privacy of our quarters, so that we may further discuss this.'

'I fear, my queen, that there is no privacy beyond these doors,' the eldest servant said in great agitation, 'for Omar waits within.'

Omar? Scheherazade felt a surprisingly ungentle anger growing within her. What right had that mere servant to trespass within the quarters of the queen?

'Open the doors,' she said to the maid servants before her. 'I will have words with Omar.'

The doors swung open before her and she walked with great determination into the apartment beyond. Her resolution faltered, however, when she saw that Omar was not alone, but was accompanied by the Sultana.

'Ah, we have been waiting most anxiously for your return,' Omar announced in the most unctuous of tones. 'You will, of course, forgive the fact that we now recline upon a pair of your couches. My only thought was to the comfort of our beloved Sultana, to whom no man or woman could ever wish any harm!'

'Is that the case?' Scheherazade replied to the servant. She attempted valiantly to maintain her anger, but found it faltering before the unwavering gaze of the Sultana. 'And what do you wish from me this morning?'

'Only to see how you keep your apartments,' the Sultana replied in a tone of voice that indicated she did not think much of these rooms. 'My son has not previously had a wife for a sufficient period of time for me to explore such concerns.'

Scheherazade found herself for the first time at a loss for words. No matter how much she might dislike this woman, it would probably serve no useful purpose further to antagonize her.

The Sultana took Scheherazade's momentary silence as a humble consent. She looked again at her surroundings and sniffed haughtily. Before that moment, Scheherazade had not realized how much contempt could be conveyed with the simple movement of one's nostrils.

'I suppose something can be done with this place,' the Sultana remarked dismissively, then focused her gaze upon Scheherazade. 'I do trust you will remain with us for a long enough time for my efforts to be justified.'

'No one may predict her future,' said Scheherazade as she found her voice at last, and she decided to make that voice as sweet as possible. 'However, it is my humble opinion that your son had not been able to find a suitable mate in ever so long, and I am glad I have been chosen to fill that void.'

'In that particular, I agree,' the Sultana said darkly, 'only the future will be able to tell.'

The Sultana, then, would give away no secrets. Now that she was past her initial disturbance at this confrontation, perhaps Scheherazade could phrase her compliments in such a way as to elicit more information from the old woman.

'Now to these apartments,' the Sultana continued before Scheherazade could formulate another remark. She ran a finger along the edge of her couch and then regarded the residue upon it with some distaste. 'They barely look as if they have been cleaned.'

At that, Omar leapt to his feet. 'I shall have it seen to at once!' He bowed to the Sultana. 'I am afraid that these quarters have been so seldom used that certain servants have neglected their duties. I shall have them whipped!'

But Scheherazade considered the Sultana's remark a personal affront. Still did she attempt to keep her voice sweet and her face free of anger. 'I fear that my prime responsibility has been the entertainment of your son, our beloved king,' she therefore responded. 'Before his needs, all other concerns pale to insignificance.'

'That is certainly true, I suppose,' the Sultana replied in a tone of voice best suited for dismissing slaves and smaller pets that one is no longer fond of, 'for those who have only the energy to see to a king's needs, and have no care for the appearance of their surroundings. Why, look at the condition of the silks upon the cushions here, especially the rough edges upon the corners!'

'You are more than correct!' Omar cried with fervour. He rubbed his hands together so rapidly that Scheherazade was half surprised he didn't start a fire.

'Such an appearance is totally unconscionable!' Omar continued as he paced before the Sultana. 'That our servants should allow such a thing to come to pass! I shall whip them myself!'

But the Sultana was not content merely to criticize the state of the apartments. 'And you! Look at those clothes upon you! It looks as if you might have slept in them!'

Scheherazade looked down upon the fine garments in which she was dressed and realized that she had indeed slept in them. 'I am sorry that you find such concern with your surroundings,' she said, and for the first time she found the sweetness slipping from her voice. 'Perhaps, if you were to announce your intention to visit before your actual arrival, we might be able better to prepare things to your liking.'

The Sultana laughed bitterly. 'I suppose then that you would have something to occupy your time, besides having servants pamper you all day?'

Ah, thought Scheherazade. The old woman would talk of servants, then? Here at last was an opportunity to verify her suspicions concerning the Sultana. She therefore said the following:

'Alas, my most honored Sultana, there appear to be hardly any servants at all about this harem, although Dunyazad and myself do have the assistance of three able women when we prepare every evening to be presented to your son.'

At this remark, the Sultana's expression went from one of distant disapproval to one of much more immediate surprise. 'Only three servants? How can you possibly manage? I would not wish less than six servants upon my worst enemy! Omar! How derelict have you been in pursuit of your duties?'

With that, the large servant fell to his knees. 'It is truly beyond comprehension!' he agreed. 'I shall have *myself* whipped!'

'Yes,' the old woman agreed, 'you should do so until the welts ooze red.' This, Scheherazade realized, was the first time that she had seen the Sultana smile. 'I think the very least that should result from such neglect is blood.'

Omar crawled across the floor to kiss the Sultana's feet. 'Yes, Oh wisest of women, whose judgements are always above reproach! There will be rivers of blood! Thank you for your understanding!'

Scheherazade, however, was greatly surprised by the old woman's reactions. No, not the smile at the mention of blood; that seemed perfectly within the Sultana's character. Rather, the Sultana's surprise at the lack of servants within the harem suggested that perhaps she did not have some part in the creation of this situation. For the merest of instants, the storyteller thought that the old woman might have been feigning surprise to deceive the queen and her sister. But it was obvious that the old woman held Scheherazade and Dunyazad in such low opinion, that she would never stoop to such acting on their behalf.

Scheherazade knew that the Sultana was at least in some way responsible for those swords that had such a strange effect upon their king. Could someone else be responsible for the disappearances of the servants? She thought again of the mysterious woman in black. Could this woman be more than a spirit herself, and instead be the cause of the disappearing servants?

'Very well,' the Sultana said abruptly. 'I shall send one of my personal servants to oversee the renovation of these apartments. And, so as not unduly to disturb you, I shall have all the necessary work done while you are visiting the king.'

Scheherazade opened her mouth to speak, but the Sultana peremptorily waved away any comment with her imperial hand. 'There is no need to thank me for this service. I would be ashamed if others were to see the condition of this place, even if we are only related by marriage.'

With that final remark, the Sultana arose and marched past Scheherazade and Dunyazad to the still open door. Half walking, half kneeling, Omar slobbered after the Sultana, vowing repeatedly to be faithful to her forever. At the least, Scheherazade consoled herself, there had been no poetry.

Dunyazad personally closed the door when the others had retreated to a sufficient distance. She turned back to Scheherazade 'What do we do now, Oh sister?' she said.

Scheherazade spoke very softly in her reply, for she recalled those previous mentions of secret passages about the palace, and she feared there might be listening ears far closer than she would like. 'We must be concerned about that Sultana's actions, for we know she has given her son those swords. I worry what other mischief she might perform in these apartments when we are away.'

'And what of our servant women?' Dunyazad added. 'I would not wish them to spend another night in their rooms, for their very quarters seem to be cursed!'

Scheherazade blinked as if it was only now that she had opened her eyes. There were two problems here that appeared to be caused by two different sources, but both might be solved by the same solution. She took a step forward and hugged her sister close.

'Oh most clever Dunyazad!' she exclaimed. 'You may have given us the very solution that we sought! Now, let us take the shortest of naps so that our wits will be about us when it is time for us to prepare again for our evening. When we awake, I shall explain all.'

Dunyazad did as she was bid and Scheherazade retired to her couch as well, although she was so full of thoughts that she could not sleep.

Perhaps, Scheherazade thought, it did not matter if there was one woman against them, or two. Perhaps it was even the hand of Providence that had given them two enemies rather than one. Perhaps, if her plans worked, they would be able to survive them both.

## Chapter the Sixteenth,
### in which certain solutions are proposed
### which may be problematic.

So it followed, as the afternoon follows upon the morning, that
when the sisters arose Scheherazade shared her plan with
Dunyazad, for the storyteller had thought much upon it in her
repose, until she was sure that plan was without flaw.

And Dunyazad readily agreed to the worthiness of that scheme,
so they were both sure in their parts in it when the three servant
women came to fetch them.

'We need to talk about what has been happening within this
harem,' Scheherazade began, as the servant women escorted them
towards the bath. But the servant women seemed too disheartened
to talk, as if they were only waiting those few more hours until they
were turned into sheep, or dogs, or ducks.

'We have thought long upon your dilemma and I think that I may
see a possible solution,' said Scheherazade.

At this, the three servants at least glanced at the storyteller, but
there was little hope in those gazes, as one might suspect in women
whose only alternative to those transformations was to lose their
heads to an eager Omar.

'I assure you that my sister is most clever,' Dunyazad encouraged. 'You should listen carefully and consider what she says.'

The eldest servant nodded at this observation. 'You are indeed
far more clever than those earlier three hundred women who never
had the opportunity to spend any time within this harem at all.
That alone means that we will contemplate whatever you have to
say.'

'Very well,' Scheherazade replied in a voice that said she would
expect no more. 'We do not possess the art to determine what has
caused your fellow servants to change. But perhaps we may devise
a method to prevent it.'

At that, all three servants stopped and stared at the storyteller.

'Can such a thing be so?' said one.

125

'Have you learned it from your stories?' asked another.

'You give us hope,' the eldest summarized for all, 'but please tell us of this method.'

'I have indeed discovered this method through my stories,' Scheherazade agreed, 'for my tales are often how the poor but clever overcome the wealthy and powerful. So it is that I have trained myself to use my wits much as the heroes and heroines of my fables.'

All the servants were now doubly eager to hear of her solution, so Scheherazade smiled and continued, 'There is no doubt that there is a curse loose within this harem, a foul incantation that causes those of you within the servants' quarters one by one to be turned into birds and beasts. But what, I asked myself, is the nature of this curse? The spell might be directed at certain individuals, indeed it might be cast against everyone within the harem. But why would the curse be affecting women only in one quarter of the harem, while it left Dunyazad and myself, as well as Omar and his staff, the cooks, other slaves and the guards at the entranceway completely untouched?'

Scheherazade now had her audience enthralled as much as she ever had with any story. She therefore proceeded, 'How much simpler, I thought, rather than to curse a number of individuals, say, six servant women charged with the bathing and toilet of the Queen; how much simpler would it be to curse a section of this harem, say that quarter in which those six women slept at night, so that curse might come up and claim a victim night after night, until none of those servants remained?'

'What you say contains a certain logic,' the eldest servant agreed. 'But, if you will excuse the impudence, my queen, what of it? We are servants, and our place in the harem is to sleep in the servants' quarters. I am afraid that you have informed us as to the source of our doom and nothing more.'

'Yes,' Scheherazade replied, 'but if you would escape that source, you would escape that doom as well.'

'But Omar—' one of the other servants began.

'My sister does not speak of escaping the harem,' Dunyazad reassured the three women. 'No, she has simply found you a safer place to sleep within these walls.'

'Again I must speak my mind,' the eldest objected. 'How can you be sure somewhere else may be safer? We may go to sleep in one of the disused corners of this great harem, only to discover that the curse exists there as well.'

'No,' Scheherazade answered, 'I know a quarter of the harem that has been safe from the curse, and there you will stay.'

'Please tell us!' the other servants called. 'Where is this place?'

'It is within the apartments of the queen,' Scheherazade replied with a smile.

All three servants raised immediate objections.

'That is never done—'

'Omar would certainly not agree—'

'It would go against the order of things—'

'The old order of things is no more,' Scheherazade said firmly, putting an end to their objections. 'I am your queen, and thus head of your harem. This new thing will be done because I say so, and Omar must obey my orders.'

When they had heard Scheherazade's plan, the three servants smiled and laughed for the first time that day.

'Will you do this thing then?' Dunyazad asked of the servants.

'We will do it this very night!' the eldest agreed. 'After all, is this not an order from our queen?'

'I am very glad you have agreed with me on this matter,' Scheherazade replied. 'And you may share our apartments for as long as I am queen, if you so desire, or until we determine the true nature of this curse. But I would ask only one thing in return.'

'Anything that is in our power!' the eldest exclaimed. 'For, as we will not be turned into sheep, or dogs, or ducks, we will act as grateful women.'

'I am most pleased to hear that,' Scheherazade agreed. 'Now I shall tell you the thing that you must do. As you know, my sister and I attend the king every night from dusk until dawn. I wish you to remain within the apartments during those hours.'

'That is all?' the servants agreed. 'It is simple enough.'

'Oh, there is one more matter,' Scheherazade added, almost as if it was almost too trivial to mention. 'Should Omar or any other individual enter our apartments during our absence, I should like to know of it. And should they by chance leave something within the apartment, or take something away, or change my quarters in any way, I would like you to relate that to me as well. And remember, you are here upon the queen's authority, which is greater than any in this kingdom save the king's, and greatest of all within this part of the palace that is the harem, so that no one who enters this room save myself and my sister shall have authority over you.'

The three servant women looked to each other, and, although

Scheherazade could see that they shared some fear when confronted with so great a task, the fear of what had happened to their fellow women was far worse, so that all three readily agreed.

'Now,' Scheherazade further remarked, 'let us get on to the business of bathing, for we cannot keep the king waiting.'

All three servants hurried to prepare the bath and Dunyazad looked upon her sister with great admiration.

'That was indeed a wonderful idea,' the younger sister agreed, 'for, should you be correct in your assumptions, it not only saves these women from a horrible curse, but should give us forewarning should someone plot some ill end for us.'

So it was that Dunyazad began quite cheerfully to strip off her outer garments in preparation for the bath, all the time singing a little song that both she and her sister had learned in childhood.

Only Scheherazade could not share the happiness around her, for she knew that upon that very evening, she would have to confront King Shahryar after he had been practicing with his swords. And, considering the effect those cursed weapons had, perhaps the swords might be said to have practiced upon him as well. As confident as she was in her wit and in her words, she did not know if they could stand against ensorceled steel.

## Chapter The Seventeenth,
## in which both story and storyteller
## experience unforeseen complications.

Evening came, and Scheherazade and Dunyazad were again
escorted to the king's chambers, although on this occasion
Scheherazade found it difficult to think overmuch upon the story
she would tell that night.

She knew her fears were well founded when she reached the
door to the royal apartments, for neither guard stood outside and
there was the sound of a great commotion within.

'Attempt to take my swords, will you?' asked the voice of the
king, which further sounded particularly high and strained.

'No one wishes to take your swords, Oh my king,' came the
booming yet reassuring voice of that guard who had spoken to
Scheherazade upon the previous day. 'If you wish to fence all
evening, then we shall fence.'

'May we remind you, in all humility,' the voice of the other
guard added, 'that you yourself were in the midst of returning the
swords to your armory.'

'That was before I realized you would attack me!' the king
shouted.

'Attack?' the first guard answered. 'Please, my king. We only
wish to look to your welfare.'

'So you say!' the king replied in a voice as fevered as the guard's
was calm. 'But I know that you covet my swords. All men would
covet my swords!'

It was at that moment that somebody screamed.

'Oh, dear, I hadn't meant to do that,' the king added, his voice
suddenly resuming a much more reasonable tone. 'These swords
are simply so well made that they make me into a far better
swordsman.' The king's laugh held a nervous edge. 'I do hope he
survives. Then again, I suppose we always have a few extra
guardsmen.'

At that, the two guardsmen appeared within Scheherazade's

view, the guard who had spoken to her before carrying the other man in his arms. She saw as they approached that this second man had a great gash upon his side, and his robes thereabout were soaked with great quantities of blood.

The guard paused on the far side of the doorway and pulled on a great rope located there. Two other guardsmen soon arrived and the first guard gave up his wounded comrade to them with the terse words, 'Please take care of him.' The two newcomers nodded and carried their burden swiftly away without another word.

The first guard then turned to Scheherazade. 'I am very glad you have arrived,' he said, although his visage was grim in the extreme. 'I know he is our king and all powerful, but there appear to be times of late when the power seems to escape even him. I know I could be beheaded for this, but those swords—' The guard stopped himself before he could say more. 'Please see to him, my queen!'

He then stepped by Scheherazade and Dunyazad and resumed his position by the door.

Scheherazade entered the room with some trepidation. To her credit, Dunyazad followed immediately after her sister. So it was that they followed the still-moist trail of red into the inner apartments.

'There!' the king called as they arrived. 'I've returned the swords to the armory once again. That proves that I may give them up whenever I desire, no matter what certain of my guards may imply!' He blinked as he saw the two women. 'Ah,' he said, and paused for a minute. 'Oh,' he further remarked. 'It is you.' He attempted to straighten his robes but they were torn and spotted with blood in some further disarray. 'Glad I am to see you,' he managed at last, 'for my day has been full of cares.'

Remarkably, Scheherazade managed to smile, perhaps in part because she realized that the danger had passed for this night, although one of the guards had been the unfortunate recipient of a sword she believed was meant for her. 'Then we are most glad we have arrived to help ease your burdens. What will you have us do, my king?'

'Perhaps,' the king began as a frown creased his face, 'perhaps I should check again upon my swords.' But he shook his head violently as soon as he had uttered that sentence. 'No! I have locked the armory. There is no reason to unlock it again.' He attempted to take a deep breath, but coughed instead. 'Except, upon the previous evening, someone moved my swords after they were locked away! All men covet my swords!'

Scheherazade quickly walked between the king and the armory door. 'Truly, Oh husband, you appear to be greatly burdened with care. Would you allow your wife to advise you in this matter of the heart, as my father, the grand vizier, has advised you on so many matters of state?'

At Scheherazade's question, the king paused and smiled. 'That was well said. Truly, I have a queen! But what was I speaking—'

'We were speaking of the heart,' Scheherazade replied quite firmly, 'for it is evening, and time for the head to rest, and perhaps to hear a diverting story, or further amuse oneself with a bit of ravishing.'

'Story?' the king murmured. 'Ravishing? It all sounds most interesting, but wasn't there something I was supposed to do with my armory?'

Scheherazade advanced upon her husband. 'If you were to do such a thing, Oh my husband, surely you planned to do it upon the morrow.'

'I did?' the king asked as Scheherazade undid her robes. 'Oh, my. I suppose that I must have.'

And so it was that Dunyazad spent some time in the other parts of the apartments while her sister and her husband conducted their conjugal affairs. But that time passed again, and once the room was quiet Dunyazad returned to that room to sit at the feet of her sister.

'So is my body relieved of its cares,' Shahryar announced. 'Now I wish that you might continue your story, so that my head might follow.'

'With the greatest pleasure, Oh my king,' was Scheherazade's reply. And so did she resume her tale:

## THE TALE OF THE FISHERMAN AND WHAT HE CAUGHT, AS TOLD BY THE THIRD SHEIKH IN DEFENSE OF THAT MERCHANT WHO WOULD BE KILLED MOST HORRIBLY BY A CERTAIN *DJINNI*

' " "Now, as you no doubt recall, the ifrit had at last, through certain vows and promises, convinced the merchant that he should free the creature from his prison. And so did the merchant open the jar. But what should the ifrit do but grow to tremendous size and then look down upon the fisherman and laugh.

' " "Now the fisherman feared the worst, for the ifrit had nearly killed him once before. So did the fisherman call out that he would hold the ifrit to his vows, or the great creature would suffer the wrath of the Almighty. But with that the ifrit only smiled and began to walk from the beach, motioning that the fisherman should follow.

'"'So it was that they walked away from the beach, and then beyond the city in which the fisherman lived, and from there they climbed the hills beyond the city until they came to a lake nestled between the mountains beyond. Here the ifrit stopped, and he ordered the fisherman to cast his net into the lake, and the fisherman, looking down into the clear waters, could see large fish of astonishingly vivid colors that seemed to glow beneath the sun: red and yellow and white and blue swimming there in great profusion. He therefore cast his net into the lake and caught four fish, each of a different color.

'"'Before the fisherman could reflect overmuch upon his good fortune, the ifrit said to him, "Now you must take these fish to the Sultan's palace, and he will make you a rich man. I advise you to come and fish here every day, but when you come you should cast your net only once, and you should always achieve the same results. Now you must excuse me. I have been away from my kind for over a thousand years, and I have much to do. For a beginning, there is a certain female who no doubt expects an explanation for a certain Saturday night – but that is no concern of yours. I take my leave. May Providence be with you."

'"'And with that, the ifrit clicked his heels together, and the earth opened up beneath his feet and swallowed him whole.

'"'The fisherman marveled at his good fortune, and returned quickly to the city at the bottom of the hills, and there to his house, where he placed the four fish in an earthen jar that he filled with water. And the fish swam to and fro within this jar as he then proceeded to the palace, as the ifrit had instructed.

'"'Eventually then was the fisherman brought before the Sultan, and he showed his ruler the four marvelous fish, and the Sultan remarked that he had never seen such fish of that great size and such wondrous color. He therefore ordered that the four be given to his cook-maid, so that she might make a meal of them, and gave the fisherman a gift of four hundred dinars. So it was that the fisherman left the palace most joyfully and set about buying presents for his wife and children. We shall return to him presently.

'"'In the kitchens of the palace, the cook-maid proceeded to clean the fish and then fried them upon one side in a pan, waiting until they were well cooked upon that side before she flipped them over. But as soon as she had turned them one side to the other, the very wall of the kitchen split open and from that space emerged a young girl of exceeding grace and beauty, with a bright blue scarf tied about her head so that her hair hung free, and about her arms were many great gold bracelets, and around her neck gold necklaces, and great gold hoops that pierced either ear.

'"'Now, as if all this was not strange enough, the young woman proceeded to the stove where she thrust a bamboo wand that she happened to be carrying into the fire and asked, "Fish, fish, are you faithful?"

'"'And, their four voices joined as one, this is what the fish replied:

> '""'Come back and so will we,
> Keep faith and we'll keep faith,
> But should you show us treachery
> And it shall be to your scathe."

'"'At that, the cook jumped away, upsetting the frying pan in her haste. But, when she looked about, she noticed that the young woman had fled, and then she further noticed that all four fish had fallen into the fire and become burned to a crisp.

'"'Well, this was certainly a disquieting turn of events. In the first place, why would anyone attempt to rhyme anything with scathe? Indeed, though, now that she thought about it, perhaps she should not be so judgemental, for it was surprising that fish could rhyme at all.

'"'Still, there was one point that could not be argued, and that was that the fish had been lost to the fire, and so there would be nothing prepared for the sultan's dinner. She therefore sent for the grand vizier to tell him of her dilemma.

'"'Now the vizier was astonished by the cook's news, but he further knew that this woman was not often given to flights of fancy, and so what she had said must contain some element of truth. The vizier therefore sought out the fisherman, and told him to bring four more fishes from that same lake to the palace upon the morrow.

'"'This the fisherman did, again arriving with four fish in four different colors: one red, one yellow, one white and one blue. And the vizier, after consultation with his sultan, again gave the fisherman four hundred dinars, and further instructed him to come back upon the following morning in case he was further needed. So did the fisherman depart, an even wealthier and happier man, and the vizier took the fish to the cook, and informed her that he should be present while she cooked them this time, so that he personally might witness any wonders.

" " 'So did the cook again begin to prepare the fish for the sultan. And all went well as she fried the four fish upon one side. But when she went to turn the fish over to fry them further, a hole again formed in the kitchen wall, and that same attractive and well-dressed young woman with her wand of bamboo stepped through. She looked neither at the cook, nor the vizier, but instead walked straight up to the pan full of fish and asked, "Fish, fish, are you faithful?"

" " 'And the fish replied:

" " " "Come back and so will we,
Keep faith and we'll keep faith,
But should you show us treachery
And in your blood you'll bathe."

" " 'With that, the young woman flipped over the frying pan with her wand and disappeared back through that hole in the wall from which she had come, the hole, of course, immediately disappearing as soon as the young woman was gone.

" " " 'I do not believe this thing!" the vizier exclaimed as the cook rescued the fish from the fire, even though they were again burned to a crisp. And the cook could appreciate exactly what the vizier was saying. Why, that *bathe* rhyme was even worse than scathe.

" " " 'I do not know what this means," the vizier further stated, "but I believe the sultan should see this thing. I will therefore request that the fisherman catch us four more fish, and we shall attempt to cook them again tomorrow."

" " 'So it was that on the following day, when the fisherman arrived at the palace as the vizier had instructed, he was further ordered to go out and obtain four additional fish for that same reward that he had received before. This the fisherman most gladly did, for this was turning out to be a very lucrative, full time business.

" " 'The fisherman returned to the palace some hours later, with four more fish of those same four fantastic colors, and this time, when the cook-maid made to prepare them, she had both the grand vizier and the sultan as observers.

" " 'The cook dutifully prepared the fish for frying and then, heating the pan, fried all four well upon their first side. Then she did take a deep breath, for she knew what was coming next, and proceeded to flip the fish over.

' " 'At that very instant, a hole appeared in the wall but, instead of the young and beautiful maiden with a wand, a tall and burly man who might have benefited from a bath stepped through, carrying a willow branch.

' " " "Who are you?" the sultan demanded.

' " " "Agnes has the day off," the burly man explained, as he called out to the fry pan, "Fish, fish, are you faithful?"

' " 'And the fish called out to the burly man in turn:

' " " "Come back and so will we,
Keep faith and we'll keep faith,
But should you show us treachery
We will be but a wraith!"

' " 'And with that the burly man stepped forward and upset the frying pan with his branch. As soon as the fish were securely in the fire, he stepped back into his hole in the wall and the hole closed shut behind him.

' " " "That is most unusual," the sultan agreed, "but what could it mean?"

' " 'Mostly, the cook thought, it meant they had been losing a large number of perfectly good fish. However, wraith was certainly a better rhyme than scathe. Perhaps the fish were improving with practice.

' " 'But the sultan, as is the way with sultans, wished to know why this strange ritual was occurring. So the vizier once again sent for the fisherman and, when he had arrived, the sultan asked the fisherman where he had found these marvelous fish. The fisherman told them of the lake between hills and mountain, and it was a place that neither sultan nor vizier had previously heard of.

' " " "Tell us, fisherman," the sultan requested, "is this lake far?"

' " " "No, it is quite close," the fisherman replied, "less than an hour distant from this very palace."

' " 'Hearing that, the sultan decided that they should visit this place immediately. So it was that the vizier organized a party to accompany the sultan and further instructed the fisherman to show the royal party the location of the lake. And, while the fisherman had profited quite nicely from this lake so far, he secretly questioned the motives of the ifrit in this business of frying fish, for it raised such an uproar with the palace that the fisherman suspected that his days of exclusive fishing rights were over.

' " 'But the fisherman put his doubts aside and humbly directed the royal party beyond the city and up into the hills to the place where he had found the lake. And the sultan and all his men exclaimed at the clarity of the water and the great numbers of fish of all four different colors that swam therein.

' " 'Then did the sultan ask of his men if any of them had previously passed this way and seen this lake before. And among their number was a huntsman, who said that he had traversed these hills some years before but had found a desert here rather than a lake.

' " " "This is most passing strange," the sultan remarked. "There must be a wonderful story behind this surprising lake and its enchanted fish."

' " 'And there was a certain general agreement upon that point, and also the fact that it would do little good to continue fishing in this spot, for what good were fish if people were constantly popping out of walls to destroy your dinner? So did the party return to the palace, and most of the members of that party were prepared to think nothing more of the incident.

' " 'This was not, however, the case with the sultan. He became obsessed with that lake and its strange fishes, for it was the most incredible thing he had ever seen, and he decided that he would find no rest until he had learned that lake's secret. He therefore confided his feelings to the grand vizier, telling him that he would slip out that night in disguise, and that for however long he should be gone, the vizier should inform all who asked that the sultan was indisposed.

' " 'The vizier thereupon returned to the throne room to distract any and all who might wish to see their monarch, while the sultan disguised himself, and, girding on his sword, slipped out of the back entrance to the palace. He thereupon proceeded up the hills to the lake, determined to search all that area thereabouts until he could find someone who could tell him the story of the lake and the fishes.

' " "So did he walk from hill to hill and mountain to mountain, resting only in the heat of the day. But in all that night, and all the following day, he found no other habitation, and no other soul who might tell him of the lake and the fishes. Still did he walk on, across the hills and through the valleys in between, until the sun dipped low towards the horizon. It was by that last light of day that he saw a structure of black in the distance, and he hurried forward to reach this place before night might fully fall.

'"'And as he approached this great black edifice, he discovered that it was a palace, built of large black stones joined together with great clamps of steel. He hurried forward to the great double doors of this building, one of the doors being open, and knocked softly upon the wood.

'"'There was no reply.

'"'He knocked again, a bit more firmly but still in a polite manner. Still, no one answered. He knocked a third time with an authority that befitted a monarch, but was again met by silence. Finally, he pounded his fists upon the door with all his might. But, when the echo had died, there was no more response.

'"'So, thought the sultan, I should assume that I am alone in this place. Still, for the manner of form, he called out in a strong voice; "Any who reside within the castle! I am a weary traveler, and I have stopped here to seek refreshment."

'"'There was yet again no answer.

'"'Here I have come to this palace, seeking answers, thought the sultan, and I am presented with another mystery. He therefore put his hand upon his sword hilt and decided to explore within.

'"'He thenceforth proceeded down the entry corridor, all the way to the palace's inner courtyard. And the place was magnificent indeed. For the walls of this courtyard were covered with tapestries of the deepest blue, and upon these cloths were sewn myriad points of brilliant white, as if they might reproduce every star that was in the heavens. And in the middle of the courtyard was a great fountain whose feet were carved in the image of four golden lions, and the spray that fell from the fountain gleamed so in the light of the setting sun that it looked not so much like water, but rather like diamonds and pearls. And the courtyard was further filled with dozens of singing birds, of all sizes and shades of plumage, who were kept trapped within the palace by a great, golden net that stretched overhead.

'"'Yet, as magnificent as his surroundings were, still did the sultan despair, for now he doubted if he ever might find someone who could tell him the story of the lake and the fishes. So did he sit, despondent, upon one of the finely wrought benches that surrounded the fountain, to ponder what next he should do in his quest.

'"'But as the king sat there in thought, he realized that there was another sound beneath those of falling water and singing birds, and that this other sound appeared to be a human voice, quietly singing. He rose quickly to search out the source of this song and discovered a hidden door behind the nearest tapestry. And, as he pushed aside the tapestry, he could now make out the words to the quiet and sad music:

> ' " ' "I could not keep love down
> No matter how I tried,
> Now I'd wish I'd rather
> Contemplated suicide.

> ' " ' "I could not keep love down
> And now I can't recant,
> Why wasn't I in Baghdad,
> Visiting my aunt?"

' " 'And there followed numerous other verses of a similar mournful nature.

' " 'The sultan, however, was most astonished by the identity of the singer. For he was the picture of perfect youth, but he did not move at all upon the couch on which he lay. Only his mouth opened and closed to provide words to the song, and, in between verses, tears would roll from his eyes as he cried softly.

' " ' "What is amiss, young man?" the sultan asked as he entered the room.

' " ' "Only all the world," the youth replied in the dramatic manner of the young.

' " 'The sultan decided he had heard enough small talk. "I am sorry to hear this," he therefore replied. "Do you know the secret of yonder lake and those magnificent fishes?"

' " ' "That story is my story, and it is my sorrow," the youth replied. And with that he pulled off the golden robe that covered him and caused the sultan to gasp in astonishment. For, while above his waist he had the perfect muscles and flesh of youth, below that his body was made all of marble.

' " ' "Now would you like to hear my tale?" the youth asked.

## MORNING,
## AND DUNYAZAD'S INTERRUPTION,
## COME AGAIN TO THE KING'S APARTMENTS

'You will forgive me, Oh my sister,' Dunyazad interrupted. 'It is nearly morning. I thought it imprudent for us to remain awake until the beginning of the courtly day, as we have on recent evenings, for such extremes of behavior have worn upon us all. Better still that we all should receive a little sleep. As the wise woman says, one should not burn the brazier at both extremes.'

Indeed, it was her sister who was most wise in this instance, Scheherazade thought, for the more the king had his wits about him, the more he would be able to resist the spell of the swords.

'Indeed,' the king remarked. 'That is a most excellent idea. If you will pardon me.'

He almost instantly fell into a deep sleep. Truly, Scheherazade thought, the day's cares must have worn on him greatly for him to drop off so quickly.

Perhaps such a sleep on the king's part would have been more reassuring, had it not been for the king's further actions. For the way he tossed and turned upon the couch, it was obvious that his sleep was not a peaceful one, and that he was subject to bad dreams and nightmares. And in those bad dreams he spoke that one sharp word repeatedly; a word Scheherazade had already heard far too often.

Still she finally fell into a fitful sleep herself but, as she slept, her hand covered her neck.

## Chapter the Eighteenth,
### in which a curse again rears its chicken head.

But the king made no mention of swords upon the following morning. Still, Scheherazade suspected that the lure of the weapons was so great that the king would have to hold them again in his hands before the day was through. And then, once the swords were in his hands, who would remove them again? On this past night, Shahryar had only come to his senses after he had critically wounded one of his own guard. If not for that guard, Scheherazade was sure, that sword would have found her throat. For her to survive another night, would someone else have to die?

Still, the king was in excellent spirits as he made ready to go to court. And so, Scheherazade thought, she should keep her spirits high as well, for the more time she remained alive, the more opportunity she would have to overcome these vexing problems within Shahryar's court.

Therefore, she and Dunyazad returned to their apartments and there found the three maid servants awaiting them.

'Yes, it is true!' the eldest servant said with great enthusiasm. 'What you foretold has come to pass, and the curse has not followed us here! We are all every bit as human as we were the day before!'

Here at last was truly good news. Perhaps, Scheherazade thought, she might get some rest after all. First, however, she inquired as to whether there were any visitors during the night.

'None whatsoever,' one of the women said.

'Well, there was Omar,' the second amended, 'but he had barely stuck his head within the door.'

'And my, did he appear surprised when he saw the three of us!' the eldest agreed. 'He disappeared almost instantly.'

'Quicker than instantly!' another of the servants added.

All three servants laughed.

'Very well,' Scheherazade answered with a smile. 'Now, you

141

may come or you may go, but my sister and I should get some rest.'

'Ah, we do have tasks outside this room,' the eldest agreed, 'but I feel that we owe you a debt for lifting the curse from us. Therefore will one of us three always stay close by while you are sleeping, to make sure that no harm befalls you.'

So two of the servants, including the eldest, did take their leave, while the third remained discreetly behind. Therefore did Scheherazade and Dunyazad again prepare to gain a few hours of sleep.

But, as Scheherazade was on the edge of that sleep, she heard the voice of her sister.

'Did you hear a voice?' she asked.

'I believe I heard something,' the servant agreed, 'although I doubt whether it came from a human throat. I further believe it came from the balcony.'

At that, Scheherazade opened her eyes as well, and she, too, heard a distant clucking.

'That is no voice!' Dunyazad exclaimed. 'It is the cry of a chicken! I must go and investigate.'

'No,' the servant said. 'You must stay and rest. Most likely this chicken will disappear as someone approaches, as it has so many times before. But I must attempt to talk to her, for what is now a chicken was once my fellow servant and my friend.'

With that, the servant rose and ran from the room to the balcony. But the clucks, instead of vanishing, seemed to become ever louder, and the servant's voice grew louder, too, and ever more impatient. 'Where are you? I can hear you, but I cannot see you.'

Perhaps, Scheherazade thought, she should walk out to the balcony and help the servant search. She certainly knew she would get no sleep when surrounded by this racket.

The clucking renewed.

'Oh, there you are!' came the servant's voice.

And then the servant screamed.

Both Dunyazad and Scheherazade rose from their couches at once and ran barefoot to their balcony. They did not see any immediate sign of either servant or chicken, although the wooden guard was broken at the very center of the gallery.

Dunyazad stepped forward to give this broken rail a closer examination, but gasped in distress.

'Scheherazade!' she cried out. 'It cannot be!'

Scheherazade herself stepped forward to see what had upset her sister so. There, beneath them, was the servant. She had fallen to the stone courtyard some twenty cubits below and she lay down there still, her limbs splayed out at angles that did not appear natural.

Scheherazade looked most closely at where the balcony railing had given way. The part that remained appeared very ragged, almost as if the wood had been chopped apart, splinter by splinter. It appeared as though it had been pecked apart by a chicken's beak.

Now, Scheherazade thought, she had often been accused of having an overactive imagination. Surely that was what was occurring now, and there must be some other explanation of the truth. Yet, the servant's still body demonstrated one precept: There was, alas, more than one way to be followed by a curse.

One of the cooks discovered the body below, and there was a great crying and wailing as all those in the harem rushed to regard their dead sister.

Scheherazade looked away from the tragic scene below. She was suddenly aware of other banging noises emanating from the doorway behind her.

'What was that?' she asked.

'I heard it as well,' Dunyazad agreed. 'There is someone moving within our apartment.' And before Scheherazade could utter a single word of reply, her sister had left to investigate.

Scheherazade glanced a final time at the still figure upon the stones. What was in the apartment? If a phantom bird could lure a woman to her death, who might guess what evil a phantom goat or cow might bring?

'Oh, woe!' she heard from the rooms to her back.

She turned and hurried after her sister.

## Chapter the Nineteenth,
### *in which it is learned that the price of beauty may be more than beauty sleep.*

But Scheherazade found her sister with neither goat nor cow, but rather those two servant women who remained.

'She has died!' they cried. And further: 'She has fallen!' And, in unison: 'She has fallen to her death!'

Dunyazad began an observation as to how it might be for the best that they remember their sister as she was in life, rather than rushing to observe the remains. It was a shame that the still-living servants were by Dunyazad and out upon the balcony before she could finish her first sentence.

'Oh, woe!' they cried from the balcony, and 'Oh, sorrow!' 'Oh, agony!' 'Oh, travail!' 'Oh, remorse!' and onwards in their lamentations.

Dunyazad looked to Scheherazade, and the elder sister gazed back at the younger. The two sisters fell into each other's arms and cried, for this was the first time either of them had seen this sort of sudden death. Never had Scheherazade been so grateful that Dunyazad was not only her sister but also her close companion and friend, for she would never have wanted to face such a tragedy alone.

So did the two sisters calm each other. And then, after some small discussion, Scheherazade and Dunyazad decided to see if they could give some comfort to the servants who still cried out upon the balcony.

The servants' wailing quieted as the queen and her sister joined them, but it burst forth anew as Omar arrived to oversee the removal of the body. And, as the large man observed this activity before him, he patted at his brow and pulled upon his earrings in such a fashion that it appeared that even he might have been affected by this death.

So it was that morning turned into afternoon, and dead servant or no, the time had come again for Scheherazade and Dunyazad to ready themselves for the king.

'We must prepare the queen,' the elder servant said from between her tears.

'And her sister as well?' the younger servant wailed. 'Forgive me. Although this is my duty, I fear that my heart is elsewhere.'

Scheherazade wished that there was some way she might relieve them of their duties. But, alas, those duties were by order of the king, and she was powerless to change them.

'We will help as much as we are able,' Dunyazad remarked, no doubt in an attempt to cheer the servants, 'for we have been in this harem a great enough time to learn the routines.'

But Dunyazad's cheerful thought had no noticeable effect upon the servants.

Instead, the elder wailed, 'Then the queen and her sister will be forced to bathe and anoint themselves!'

And the other echoed, 'Oh, the shame!'

'We will never be able to hold up our heads within the servants' quarters,' the elder said.

'But there is no hope for it,' the younger added.

'There is always hope,' another, much higher voice said behind them. 'Or there is so long as the inestimable Omar is present.'

As soon as she had managed to still her startled heart, Scheherazade turned to the large servant and found her next speech to be rather more abrupt then her usual discourse.

'What do you mean,' she demanded, 'there is always hope?'

'I have found a replacement,' was Omar's reply, 'for all those servants that we have lost. And while those disappearances, not to mention the ensuing death, can certainly be considered tragedies, we must not keep the king waiting!'

So Omar would not allow the death to affect him overmuch. In fact, his obsequious smile seemed even broader than usual.

Scheherazade found herself becoming increasingly annoyed at this oversized manservant. 'And what makes you think that this new maidservant will be to my liking?'

'Oh, she is certain to be to everyone's liking!' Omar insisted with a surprising vehemence. 'She is so talented that she will be able to do the work of three! Her hands are as swift as hummingbirds! And who could be offended by such a gentle countenance as this?'

Such a gentle countenance as what? Scheherazade thought but had no time to say, for, between one blink of an eye and another, she noticed another woman standing by Omar's side, almost as if she had materialized from the air. Surely, Scheherazade thought, there must be some other explanation for this woman's sudden arrival. Perhaps she had been hidden by Omar's bulk, which was great enough to cover three or four women.

Still, Scheherazade did not find herself reassured. Rather, there was something about this woman's appearance that she found disquieting. Perhaps it was the fact that this woman dressed all in black. Surely, it was a common practice in that city and at that time to dress so solemnly, but Scheherazade kept thinking upon that earlier occurrence, when that mysterious woman had lurked about her apartments. That woman had dressed in this very manner! Besides this fact, there was a certain intensity about this woman's gaze, which rested unwaveringly upon Scheherazade, the woman's eyes slightly pinched into a squint of concentration, as if she were calling upon great powers. What else could call for an expression like that? Unless, of course, the woman was somewhat nearsighted.

Scheherazade sighed. She could no more discern the true nature of this newcomer than she could determine the truth behind anything else that happened within this palace. If only, she thought, real life could have the same clear plotlines and moral stance of one of her stories! But no. The woman in black was apparently not going to declare herself a sorceress. Scheherazade would therefore have to determine her true nature through other means.

'What, then, is your name?' Scheherazade asked in her most pleasant voice.

The woman in black bowed slightly. 'Whatever is your wish I will henceforth be called.'

This answer struck Scheherazade as being far more clever than it was innocent. Still, Omar smiled blissfully by her side, as if nothing in the world could possibly be amiss, now or ever before.

And, now that Scheherazade considered it, was it not Omar who was greatly disturbed by that vision of a woman in black? Indeed, the large fellow had whispered the woman's name, 'Sulima'. But now Omar stood next to this mysterious woman, and no mention of Sulima had passed his lips. Truly, there must be two different women. But why, then, did Scheherazade continue to have such disquietude? She could not help but ask another question.

'Could not your name have been Sulima?'

Omar frowned as the woman in black took a step away. A single hand emerged from her robes, and she waved at the large man before him. Omar smiled once more.

'Surely,' the woman in black said to Scheherazade, 'you are mistaken.'

But the events before her did nothing to reassure the queen. 'I think that I should ask Omar this question as well,' Scheherazade insisted. 'Have you recently seen a woman named Sulima?'

'Sulima?' the large man replied as his frown returned. 'I do not recall that name.'

But how, Scheherazade thought, could Omar have forgotten a name that inspired such terror in him before?

'But we are wasting time,' the woman in black said with a voice far too forceful for that of a common servant. 'The king awaits your presence!'

'The king?' Dunyazad called in great excitement. 'Oh, yes! We must prepare immediately!'

Scheherazade looked out beyond the latticework that covered the harem's windows, and saw that the sun had indeed traveled near the horizon. In this, the newcomer was correct, for Scheherazade had completely forgotten her duties of the night to pursue her present examination. If her suspicions were unwarranted, they could certainly make use of the newcomer's aid. Yet the thought of having this woman's hands upon her body gave Scheherazade a chill as strong as a winter wind. Perhaps, she thought, there might be a way that she could delay her decision.

'Very well,' she said to the woman in black. 'I will allow my two servants to instruct you in the proper preparations as my sister and I bathe ourselves. But, for the moment, you must sit back and watch!'

Omar made a sound in the back of his throat that resembled nothing so much as the death throes of a starling. 'No one has time to watch! You have but mere moments to prepare yourselves. Hurry! Hurry!'

'We will do what we can,' the elder servant added, 'but our hands are heavy with grief.'

'Alas,' Dunyazad agreed. 'Omar is correct. There is too much for us to do. The newcomer has to help.'

For the first time since she had appeared, the woman in black smiled. 'I am well skilled in the arts of beauty. You will be pleased and surprised by my results.'

Scheherazade thought to make some further objection. And yet their time for preparation was perilously short, and further her suspicions about this woman had not yet been proven in the least. But then her sister spoke before Scheherazade could give any opinion.

'Very well,' Dunyazad said bravely. 'Then she shall prepare me while the other two servants tend to the queen!'

So it was that, despite Scheherazade's misgivings, the three servants went to work on that extensive preparation so necessary for the sisters' presentation to the king. And, as time was short, their ministrations were hurried, but such experts were the two servants that tended to Scheherazade that when she regarded herself in the mirror it seemed that every piece of clothing and dab of kohl was properly in place, and that the jewels had been arranged within her hair in as cunning a design as she had ever received.

Scheherazade's pleasure at her own appearance was redoubled when she turned to look at Dunyazad. For her younger sister seemed to glow with such beauty that the gold and jewels that adorned her neck and wrists were put to shame. Never had Scheherazade seen her sister look so lovely. Dunyazad's smile shone with more brilliance than the light of the moon, and her eyes were highlighted so artfully that their very color might be enough to cause weak men to lose their reason.

'You have done well,' Scheherazade said to their newest servant.

'This is but a sample of my arts,' the woman in black said in great humility. 'There is no limit to what I might do when I am given sufficient time.'

Why, thought Scheherazade, did she imagine a sinister undertone to everything this woman said? Then she heard the delight in Dunyazad's laugh and decided there was no reason to be suspicious of something that would make her sister so happy.

'But come!' Omar called from behind them. 'The evening gong is about to sound! We must be on our way!'

And indeed, as soon as the servant had spoken, Scheherazade heard the deep sound of that gong that announced the end of the king's court and the beginning of his repose.

'Yes, sister, let us go now,' Dunyazad paused in midspeech as she unsuccessfully attempted to stifle a petite yawn, 'for we must present our well-prepared selves to the king.'

'And I hope he will be well pleased,' Scheherazade replied in an attempt to sound as light-hearted as her sister. But, she further thought, even if they had survived the afternoon without mishap, what could they expect this evening before a king who seemed to come ever more under the spell of the swords? Still, there was no helping it. Enchanted or no, the king awaited.

The two women turned to follow Omar to the king's apartments.

Dunyazad covered her mouth again as her second yawn became much more apparent than her first.

'You must excuse me, sister,' Dunyazad remarked. 'I do not know what has come over me.'

'It is no doubt your erratic sleeping schedule,' Omar said from where he walked before them. 'Though you are young, you must remember that you will not live forever!'

'That, and the pampering of the bath and other preparations,' Dunyazad agreed dreamily. 'They have made me so relaxed, I half feel like closing my eyes and taking a nap.'

Omar tittered at that. 'Surely, your sister is a great jester. The king awaits!'

'The king awaits,' Dunyazad agreed, her voice slower than before. Scheherazade glanced at her sister and noticed that she seemed to be having some trouble keeping her eyes opened.

'The – king – awaits,' Dunyazad repeated, and yawned again immediately thereafter. She pointed with some delight at a place upon the floor. 'But – those cushions await – as well. Dear sister, you will – excuse me for a moment.' And with that, she fell upon the cushions and began to snore loudly.

'What is the matter?' Omar shrieked. 'What is amiss?'

'My sister has fallen into a deep sleep,' Scheherazade remarked slowly, for even she was startled by the suddenness of this event.

'Is your sister then so lazy,' Omar demanded, 'that she will risk the wrath of the king?'

But Scheherazade knew Dunyazad well enough to discern the true reason for this event. 'This sleep does not come from laziness,' Scheherazade announced. 'It comes from enchantments!'

'Enchantments?' Omar cried in a voice even higher than before. 'There are no enchantments here!'

Most certainly, Scheherazade thought but did not say, and the king has further not separated a single head from a single body these past three hundred nights!

'But come,' Omar insisted, 'we are late for your appointment with the king!'

In this, at least, the large servant was correct.

Scheherazade glanced one more time at her sleeping sister before hurrying after him.

This night, she would have to face the king alone.

## Chapter the Twentieth,
## in which our storyteller
## develops a loss for words.

Lucky it was that Scheherazade never began to tell her stories without some preparation. So had she paused in her tale of the night before with a firm idea of what would next occur, and that idea remained with her despite the difficult circumstances of the previous few hours.

As they approached the king's apartments, she instructed Omar to let her sister rest and not to disturb Dunyazad in any way until Scheherazade had returned to the harem. While her sister slept, the storyteller did not believe that she was in any immediate and further danger. Rather, she was quite certain that Dunyazad had been put out of harm's way so that Scheherazade and the woman in black might confront each other without interference, as one woman to another. And Scheherazade further reasoned that, should she survive this evening with the king, that confrontation would follow quickly thereafter.

So it was that Omar again ushered Scheherazade to the great double doors that led to the king's apartments. And the queen was greatly relieved to see that the guard who had earlier befriended her still retained his post, although the man stationed upon the other side of the door was new to her.

Both guards bowed low as the queen approached. Scheherazade commended the two of them upon their fealty, and further asked after the man who had been wounded the day before.

'Alas, my queen,' the first guard replied with a great grimness of tone and manner. 'He seems to linger, half dead and half alive. The cuts upon his body do not wish to heal. It is as if the sword that struck him down had a spell upon it.'

'Let us pray to the Almighty that such a thing would not be,' Scheherazade replied.

'And may we also pray for your continued safe-keeping,' the guard replied politely. 'But, if I may be so bold as to ask a question

151

of my queen, where is your sister?'

'She is alas, indisposed,' Scheherazade replied.

'There does seem to be a lot of that going around the palace,' the guard added soberly. And, with that, he opened the doors to the king's chambers beyond.

The king greeted her somewhat distractedly.

'Ah. There you are at last. I had begun to get the slightest bit – I had a very bad day at court – people kept asking for judgements when all I wanted was to get my hand around – but why do I talk of such trivial matters? Where is your sister? I had come to expect her as a fixture of our evenings.'

But Scheherazade had thought long upon what sort of answer she might give to this very question from the king. 'Even the most pleasant of diversions might become routine. Perhaps, this night, I thought that we might ravish without any further distractions.'

'Most thoughtful,' the king replied, although he still seemed more distraught than pleased. 'I wish I were not so tired. Pardon? Did you say something about – lances?' He frowned up at the ceiling. 'I could swear that someone did.' His eyes returned to Scheherazade. 'Yes, ravishing. A most pleasant prospect. If only my hands did not long so for the feel of naked steel!'

Alas, thought Scheherazade. Her husband's conduct was becoming, as the wise woman put it, one bale short of a hay cart. Still, even if she could not use her body to calm him, she still had her most formidable weapon at her command.

'Perhaps, my king,' she therefore remarked, 'you should rest upon yonder couch and allow me once more to tell my tale.'

'Seal rings?' the king shouted. 'Someone mentioned—' He paused and blinked. '—oh, I suppose they didn't. Rest? Yes, that sounds most efficacious. And your story sounds most reassuring. How sweet that I might forget my cares so that I might hear of the cares of another. Pray continue.'

Scheherazade hurried to continue her tale before any other voices, real or imagined, might interrupt:

ONCE AGAIN RETURNING TO THE TALE OF THE
MERCHANT AND THE *DJINNI*,
WHICH CONTAINS THE TALES OF THE THREE
SHEIKHS, THE THIRD OF WHOM IS RELATING THE
TALE OF THE FISHERMAN AND WHAT HE CAUGHT

' " "So did the sultan agree to hear this strange youth's tale, which would tell why the youth was half of flesh and half of marble, and would further describe those events leading up to the lake full of fish of four colors, who refused to be cooked properly.

" " " "I am glad you have agreed," the youth replied, "for, when one's lower half is composed of marble, one does not get out to entertain oneself overmuch." And with that, the youth began his tale:

## THE TALE OF THE YOUNG MAN AND THE FISHES

' " " "Know you that once, upon this very spot, there stood a great kingdom which was ruled wisely by my father until he reached the age of seventy years. I was his son and his prince, and when my father passed on to Allah's mercy, it was left to me to rule this land.

' " " "So it was that I married my cousin, a woman who was my uncle's daughter, and we dwelt together in great happiness for a time, until that evening when my wife traveled to meet her sister.

' " " "That night I slept all alone, save for the company of two female slaves whom I had equipped with fans, one to fan my head, the other to tend to my feet. But I found that, with the absence of my wife, sleep did not come so easily as it usually did. So did I rest there with my eyes closed, and, after a time, the two slaves must have surmised that I was asleep, for they began to talk between themselves in low tones.

' " " " 'It is such a shame about the king,' said one.

' " " " 'But it is so blatant,' said the other. 'How could he not know?'

' " " " 'It is only that he is so pure and innocent, and without an ill thought for anyone that he does not suspect,' the first slave replied.

' " " " 'But his bride is so open in her lust!' the other insisted.

' " " " 'It is true that she is among the loosest of women,' the first agreed. 'But she only acts so when her husband is asleep.'

' " " " 'And her husband does sleep prodigiously.'

' " " " 'Even that is not entirely natural. For I understand that upon every evening, the king's wife gives him a draught of noxious herbs that makes our king fall into a profound and untroubled sleep. Then does she put on her best clothes to go out and make love to half the kingdom.'

' " " " 'And the king does not suspect?'

' " " " 'How can he when he slumbers until the harlot returns? And, upon her return, she waves another concoction beneath his nose so that he will awake, revived and refreshed.'

' " " " 'She is truly the worst among women.'

153

""""'It is a shame that no one dares tell the king of her true nature.'

""""And then the two women fell silent, except for their fanning, and I eventually fell into a shallow and troubled sleep. The conclusion I drew from this conversation was as inescapable as the dusk following the dawn. As is often the case in these tales, my wife was an adulteress!"'"'

## THE KING INTERRUPTS

'Adulteress?' the king cried aloud. He began to twitch in the most agitated of fashions.

Oh, dear, Scheherazade thought. Perhaps she should not have begun this story after all.

'Lances? Riding? Pillows? Seal Rings?' the king continued, his arms flailing about him upon the couch.

'No,' he screamed even louder, 'swords!' And with that word, the king became utterly still, every twitch and spasm vanished. And so were his apartments completely without sound or motion, until a moment later when Sharyar most casually remarked, 'Most certainly, swords.'

Scheherazade stared at her husband for a long moment, for this most recent display left even a storyteller such as herself totally speechless. She had known before that the king fought against great sorcery; sinister spells that caused him upon the one hand to rave about sexual innuendo, or wantonly to cut with swords upon the other. At first, she had thought that these two symptoms were the result of a single curse. Now, however, the king appeared almost to have cured himself of the rigors of one spell by the mere mention of the instruments of another magic. It seemed that there was not one sorcery at work here, but two.

The king muttered something upon his couch. The word was too soft for Scheherazade to hear, but whatever it was, it was accompanied by a noticeable twitch.

Scheherazade wondered what effect this revelation would have upon her fate. It made her lot no easier. She would have to be doubly quick and clever in her storytelling, or the king would slip beyond her powers of persuasion from a spell that promoted beheadings, or three swords that did the same.

But who wielded such power? The Sultana? The woman in black, who might or might not be called Sulima? Scheherazade

154

wished fervently that Dunyazad was here, so that she might have someone to talk to.

But there was no more time for talking. There was only time for storytelling. And, Scheherazade knew now, if she made a single false step within that story, the tale's ending would be death.

## Chapter the Twenty-first,
## in which certain things
## come to an untimely end.

So it was that Scheherazade rushed to continue her tale. And, as she spoke, she noticed the twitching on the part of the king at first decreased and then ceased entirely, due, she was certain, to the soothing sound of her voice.

This, then, was what she said:

### THE TALE OF THE YOUNG MAN AND THE FISHES, WHICH IS TOLD IN TURN BY ANY NUMBER OF PEOPLE WITH WHOM YOU ARE NO DOUBT BY NOW FAMILIAR

""""What was I then to do?" the youth further remarked as he related the tale of his wife's infidelities, which this storyteller does not in the least endorse, but rather has presented as the beginning of a moral lesson.

""""I decided that I must determine whether or not these stories that I had heard were true," the youth continued. "For, as the wife of the king, my bride had all those things which money and power could provide: a palace to live in, a hundred servants to tend to her needs, jewels in every color of the rainbow, talking birds from China and Africa, all those things you would come to expect. And, if you would pardon my lack of humility, I am not unpleasant to look upon, either. What, then, might she be seeking from another?

""""So it happened that my wife returned from her visit, and upon that very evening I formulated a plan which would lead me to the truth. We spent the evening in our usual way, partaking of both food and conversation in that intimate manner that I had once thought spoke of love. And, as was her habit, as we were about to retire for the night, my wife gave me a cup of mulled wine that she had specially prepared.

""""This night, however, instead of drinking this wine, as was

157

my custom, I waited for my wife to look the other way and quickly spilled the contents of the cup into one of the upper folds of my robe. Then I lay quickly back upon my couch, and feigned a deep sleep complete with snores.

'"""So you sleep again, Oh curse of my existence!' my wife said as soon as she thought me at rest. 'Now shall I take my leave of you and spend my night with a real man!'

'"""With that, my wife dressed and perfumed herself, and placed her finest jewels and bangles about her wrists and ankles, and lastly strapped my sword to her midsection. Only then did she take her leave.

'"""I waited until she was barely out of my chambers, and then rose to follow her, for I was now determined to learn the whole truth of this. Who indeed, could take my place in this woman's emotions? Had I made some error in my treatment of my bride? Perhaps it had been a mistake to marry within the family?

'"""Fully a thousand questions passed through my head as I pursued my bride from the palace to the well-to-do sections of town, and then to the not-so-well-to-do quarters, and from there to the hardly-doing-well-at-all part of the city, and then from there to those neighborhoods where people were living in such a way that doing-well was not a part of their vocabulary, and onward from there to a location that I had never witnessed before, even more downtrodden than all those locations before, and indeed so squalid that the area didn't even deserve the recognition of a name.

'"""And, when at last my wife had reached these most wretched of localities, she called out in a loud voice, 'I have escaped again from my misery, and come back to you, Oh my beloved!'

'"""She was greeted by a great fit of coughing that continued at such a length that I marveled at how the cougher might find a way to breathe.

'"""Oh my beloved!' my bride called with a laugh. 'You have such a way with words!' And with that she skipped gaily across the mounds of refuse and rotting vegetables that seemed to litter every inch of this quarter of the city, until she came to a mound that at first looked no different than any of the others, until I realized that this particular mound sported a door.

'"""At this, the rotting wood of the door was flung aside, and in the doorway stood a fellow dressed in the most disheveled and despicable rags imaginable. It would be difficult to describe him in any polite tones whatsoever, for he was a man of indeterminate color, since there was no way to ascertain the true shade of his complexion under all those mounds of dirt that were caked upon his skin.

'""" 'Bewarrr!' he said upon seeing my wife, or some such, for it was a noise that sounded mostly like some cross between the clearing of a throat and the hawking of a great quantity of phlegm. 'Garrr Snorkarrr!'

'""" 'It is so wonderful to be in your presence after having suffered so long with my cur of a husband,' my wife replied in great delight. 'He is so despicably clean!'

'""" 'With that, the filthy fellow paused to spit forth a large wad of mucus. But an instant later, he had stepped forward and placed his hands upon my bride. 'Snarr Gfaarrkle!' he growled as his gnarled hand left an oily trail of soot along the hem of her garments.

'""" 'My bride frowned at this. 'I know how upset you are when I cannot come more often. But it is so difficult to get away from my husband. He is so unsavorably rich.'

'""" 'Skrrakk barrr skrakk!' he replied gruffly. Bits of half-eaten food seemed to emerge from his mouth to rest upon his lips.

'""" 'With that my bride gently brushed her lips against his, and then paused thoughtfully to chew that which she had found. 'There is no one else but you. Who could possibly match your grime?'

'""" 'Harrf Gruffle!' he said as great quantities of drool proceeded from the corners of his lips towards his chin.

'""" 'Oh, how delightful!' my bride exclaimed. 'My husband has the most despicably dry chin. Please, may I lick your slobber?'

'""" 'Snarr Glubble!' the man replied as small bubbles of foam flecked his lips. My wife leaned quickly forward and artfully licked every bit of dribble from his chin.

'""" 'This only leaves me hungry for more,' my bride spoke in the tone of a lustful beast. 'Your nose is mine!'

'""" 'And before the filthy fellow could turn away, my bride had covered his nose with her mouth and proceeded to make a series of deep, sucking sounds.

'""" 'She smacked her lips with great satisfaction when she was done. 'No food in the palace satisfies me so fully! It is so rich and salty!'

'""" 'The filthy man spoke next in an entirely different voice, both far softer and more clear in inflection.

'""" 'Thank you. My anger always leaves me when you clear my nose. I do not know what I would do without you.'

'""" 'Then let us adjourn to the bed,' my bride said in a tone of voice that held more innuendo than every single remark she had made to me in the entire course of our marriage. Then did the two of them disappear inside the refuse-covered hovel. And, as quietly as possible, I followed them within and hid in the plentiful shadows, for the place was as devoid of light as it was filled with garbage.

' " ' " 'I watched as my wife led the decrepit man across the room. Bits of rag fell from him as he walked, along with other things, insects, perhaps, and bits of hair and skin. As they reached the far corner, I saw that what she referred to as a bed was nothing more than another pile of refuse and rags, even more disconcerting because some of those rags appeared to be moving.

' " ' " 'You arre so good to me, my darrrling,' the man remarked, his 'r's rolling together as if fluids were once again collecting in his nose and throat. 'Say therrrre is no one in yourrrrrr life but me.'

' " ' " 'I am only happy surrounded by your lice!' she cried as she pulled the man to her and thrust both of them down upon the bed of roiling rags. There followed a brief period of great animal passion, punctuated by frequent growls, cries and coughs on the part of both parties. At last, my wife went limp, and her lover indulged in a hacking fit of great lasciviousness. I then noticed that my wife had further passed out entirely from ecstasy, her hand only occasionally moving to scratch at a passing flea.

' " ' " 'It was too much for me to bear. I leapt forward, and grabbed the sword from where she had discarded her scabbard, and slashed at the filthy man in the throat.

' " ' " 'Grarrarrarrarr!' he screamed, as a great dusty exhalation of noxious fumes emerged from that place where I had cut. Surely, I determined, I had killed him in my fury, and further, if I remained to study my handiwork, there was every likelihood that I would be felled by the noxious fumes. So it was that I returned the sword to the scabbard and quit the neighborhood.

' " ' " 'I then returned to the palace and fell into an exhausted sleep, and was only awakened at first light by my wife holding a concoction of herbs beneath my nose. I leapt up, ready to hear my wife's confession, but instead she wept copiously before me.

' " ' " 'What is wrong, oh my beloved?' I asked, although I suspected that I already knew her answer.

' " ' " 'Someone very near to me has died!' she wailed.

' " ' " 'No doubt it must be a relative that has died, for you to be affected so,' I replied, for I must admit that there was a part of me which was enjoying my wife's misery.

"""""A relative?' she replied, as if temporarily surprised by the thought. 'Oh, most certainly, a relative. I will never survive my grief!'

"""""And then, what relative is that?' I pressed for a true answer.

"""""I have just heard that my mother is dead,' my wife said. 'And you must construct a tomb for her mortal remains.'

"""""That indeed is sad news,' I agreed in astonishment, 'but still we all know that our parents must die.'

"""""And that my father has been killed in the holy war,' my wife continued, 'and that my eldest brother has been stung to death by a scorpion, and my youngest brother was killed when a building fell upon him.'

"""""This is an entire catalog of grief!' I further agreed. 'No doubt you would wish more than a simple tomb, but rather an entire house of mourning to give you solitude in your grief.'

"""""My wife could but nod her head as she continued, 'And further did my sister lose her life beneath the hooves of a marauding camel, and my two nieces lost their lives in a freak desert mudslide, and my elderly grandmother has choked to death upon a date!'

"""""Perhaps, I thought, there might be a few too many coincidences in these deaths. Could she be using them as a ploy to divert me from the truth? So it was that once again I asked, 'And yet, before I give you this house of mourning, is there nothing else you might wish to tell me, say, as an example, what you do to while away your hours after I am asleep?'

"""""And additionally were my second cousins devoured by jackals,' my wife continued quickly, 'and my third cousins lost at sea during the worst of storms, and my fourth cousins—'

"""""Yes, most certainly I shall build you a house of mourning!' I said, for I never much cared for her cousins, either living or dead. And further did I reason, if she was not prepared to tell me the truth in this matter, at least she would be out of my way in her mourning, and I might proceed with my life without her.

"""""So it was that it took my workmen a month and a day to construct a suitable place for my wife to mourn within. For when it was done, it filled up an entire wing of the palace, and was equipped with complete facilities for my wife's daily needs, as well as a tomb with every modern appointment.

"""""Then did my wife disappear for a great length of time within her house of mourning, and I was further informed that certain remains were transported to the tomb, although the exact nature of those remains was not explained to me.

'""It was only later that I discovered that the remains that my wife had brought to the tomb were no relative at all, for none of her relatives had truly died, although now that my wife had indicated their various demises, she no longer encouraged those relatives to visit us, which was a blessing in itself. Rather were these remains not remains at all, but the still somehow living body of her filthy lover, whom, my wife discovered, beyond that ability to retain great amounts of dirt about his person, further had the ability to linger seemingly forever upon the brink of death, and neither die nor dramatically improve.

'""So it was that my wife would disappear with regularity at morning and evening, and I would hear great wailing and mourning coming from within her private walls. And this behavior continued for months, and then months after that, so that a whole year had come and gone and still was my wife lost in her wailing.

'""Well, let me tell you, the patience of even someone as royal as myself can be tried with time. And further came the day when I chanced upon her lingering about the door to her morose apartments, where she sadly sang the following song:

'""'When you passed by my tent door
I said goodbye to all the world.
Your hovel was my life to me
And I would be your garbage girl.

'""'If your sweet voice recalls the tones,
The dearest way you called my name
With coughs and wheezes so sincere,
The deepest love you will proclaim.

'""'If you come back the way you went,
I pray you take my body up,
And press me to your muddy breast
And with your drool I'll fill my cup.'

'""And this was followed by numerous other verses of equal depravity.

'""This poetry was at last too much for me to bear. 'These verses are not words of grief,' I declared, 'but of a naughty passion!'

'""'You have found me out!' my wife said with great defiance. 'For my lover lies within this enclosure.'

" " " " 'Then he lives still?' I said in amazement.

" " " " 'At that, my wife nodded her head. 'He is very good at lingering. Also, now that I think upon it, at drinking great quantities of wine and beer.'

" " " " 'It is astonishing,' I marveled, 'after the wound that he received.'

" " " " 'Yes, and he is twice the man that you are, even with the wound!' my wife declared. 'Although, now that you mention it, his stamina has not been all that great of late.'

" " " " 'But I had had enough of being cuckolded by my wife. I drew my sword as if I might strike her down where she stood.

" " " " 'Wait a moment!' my wife cried, as if she might be (however unlikely this might seem) realizing this connection for the first time. 'Look upon your sword! And look upon the wound in my lover's throat! Truly, they are a match!' She thereupon pointed all her fingers at me in a most threatening, and perhaps even clawlike, manner. 'By those dark powers within me,' she declared, 'you are now in trouble!'

" " " " 'And with that, her hands described certain fantastic symbols in the air, and she declared, 'May your lower half turn to stone!'

" " " " 'And no sooner had the words left her mouth, than it was so, and my lower half transformed into that marble that you can see there still.

" " " " 'No,' she murmured as she regarded her treacherous handiwork, 'this is not vengeful enough. I must do something even more severe!'

" " " " 'So was it that she took the four islands of my kingdom and turned them into mountains, and further took all the people of my kingdom and turned them into fishes in a lake between those mountains. Truly, you could see that she was peeved.

" " " " 'But this was not the end of her vengeance, for with marble legs I could not move from the palace, and she returned to visit me upon every day thereafter, and further did she give me a hundred lashes upon my back upon every day, and then she would place a shirt made of camel hair over the open cuts, and then – and then—" The prince hesitated, as if this last thing was almost too terrible to say aloud, "—she would practice her poetry!"

## THE SULTAN RESPONDS TO
## THIS MOST DIFFICULT OF SITUATIONS
* * *

163

'"'The sultan thought about this situation most seriously, before he mentioned, "I believe I may have met the woman. Does she like to rhyme things with scathe?"'

'"'A shiver went through the human half of the king. "Then you *have* met her. Praise be that you have not developed any marble appendages!"

'"'The sultan nodded at his good fortune. "But you say that your wife visits you every day to torture you with the lash, the hair shirt, and poetry?"'

'"'The king agreed, further saying, "Indeed. She is due at any time now."

'"'"Perhaps then we may save you from your fate," the sultan replied, "for I have a plan."

'"'And so did the sultan disappear through a nearby door. And, but a moment later, the king's wife arrived from the opposite direction.

'"'"Aha!" the woman cried as she came into the room. The sultan was astonished to witness from his hiding place nearby that this was the same woman who magically walked through walls to upset fishes. He was indeed finding answers to his riddles. Now, if he could only solve the king's dilemma as well.

'"'"It is time for your daily torture," the woman continued with an evil smile. "By now, you are well aware of the routine. First, I will reopen all your wounds with my lash. Then shall you have a shirt of coarse hair placed between your clothes and your wounds, to make certain you suffer even more. And then, and only then," she paused to laugh spitefully, "shall I grace your ears with my latest verse."

'"'It was only at that last remark that the king let out a groan of pain and misery.

'"'But his wife only laughed more at his outburst. "This, then, is how I repay you for almost taking my lover away from me. Thus I give you only what you deserve, although my opinions may be abetted by the fact that I have an essentially nasty personality!" She paused for an instant to consider her next move. "Let us see. Today, shall I lash you from top to bottom, or from bottom to top?"

'"'But she paused again as she heard a great coughing come from just without the door.

'"'The whip dropped from her hand, and her voice was filled with wonder as she asked, "Can it be?"

'"'As if in answer, a great wad of phlegm came sailing through the entry way.

164

‘"'"It can be no other!' the wife exclaimed.

‘"'"So it was that a man covered in equal parts by dirt and rags appeared in the doorway.

‘"'""It is my king of grime!" the woman cried in rapture. "My sultan of sewage! You are even more filthy than you are usually. I have to admit, I rather liked your appearance since the servants have been dusting you off. But I will not quibble about a little dirt! Come to my arms, my drooling devotion."

‘"'""So you say," the man said in a weak voice that had to struggle to overcome those fluids which filled his lungs, "but you have shown me little consideration."

‘"'""What do you mean, Oh my titan of trash?" the woman asked in great concern.

‘"'""You lash your husband every day," the man explained, "so that his cries for help keep me awake during the day, and his cries of pain and misery keep me from sleep at night. If not for this, I would have been cured long ago!"

‘"'""I had not considered those consequences, oh my caliph of crud," the woman wailed most piteously. "I shall lash him no more, and further shall free him from this place!" And with that, she used her hands to outline certain mystic symbols in the air, and the king was once again all of flesh.

‘"'""I am whole again!" the king called. "Praise be to—"

‘"'But his wife interrupted. "Enough of this uplifting prattle! Get from this place before I cause your death!"

‘"'And so did the king, who could spot a reasonable request when one came his way, gladly make use of his new legs to vanish.

‘"'His wife turned back to the filthy man, and her recently furious face was suddenly full of smiles. "Now," she said, "oh my ruler of rubbish, we will no longer be disturbed."

‘"'""What are you talking about?" the filthy man replied with the greatest of displeasures. "The moans of that king are among the least of my complaints!"

‘"'The woman's distress at this remark was so great that she fell to her knees. "What then disturbs you, oh my wazir of waste?"

‘"'""It is all these fish outside my door, constantly jumping in and out of the water," he replied in the most displeased of tones. "And further do they all rise up every night at midnight, and curse their fate, especially your use of poetry!"

‘"'""Then is everyone a critic?" the woman groaned. "I shall set this right as well, so that you may have your rest!"

‘"'"So saying, she quickly left the palace and walked to the shore of the lake. And she knelt upon that shore, and cupped both her hands and dipped them into the water. Then did she pull her hands from the lake and said certain words over the water that graced her palms. With that, the water in her hands vanished, as did the lake beyond, and all the men who had been fishes became men again, and the depths of the lake again became cities and markets, and the four mountains once more became the four islands of the kingdom.

' " 'Once this thing was done, she hurried back within the palace to her still-weakened lover.

' " " 'I have done all that you requested, Oh my master of manure! Now shall I have my reward!"

' " " 'Indeed you shall," said the other man as he lifted up his sword. And, when she saw his sword, this deceitful woman realized that she had been deceived as well, for this was not her lover after all, but the sultan who had visited the king, who had further torn his garments and rolled about in the lakeside mud in order to disguise himself. But she could realize no more, for at that point the sultan took his sword and clove her in two.

' " 'So did the sultan leave that palace, and he marveled that the outer walls of the palace were no longer made of deep black stone, but now of gold, and that there was a great city before him where once stood a lake. And as he walked down that avenue that led away from the palace, a young man came to greet him, and the sultan realized that this was the same young man who had been bewitched.

' " 'The king thanked him most heartily, and the sultan asked him, "Now that you have been delivered from bondage, oh King, do you wish to remain in your city, or would you care to journey to mine?"

' " 'At this, the king laughed, but he quickly added, "Forgive me, Oh greatest of sultans, but do you not know the great distance that lies between your kingdom and mine?"

' " 'The sultan replied that it had taken him but an hour to reach this lake, and a day more to find the palace.

' " " 'But that was when this place was bewitched by sorcery," the king explained, "for, were you to return to that place now, you would find nothing but a desert. Indeed, now that my lands have been restored to their rightful location, we would have to travel for a year and a day to gain your kingdom."

' " " 'A year and a day?" the sultan said in a tone of great distress. "Still must I return!"

' " " 'And I shall travel with you," the king announced, "for, after spending an eternity trapped in marble, it is time for a vacation."

'"'So it was that, after many other adventures too complicated to relate at this time, the sultan finally returned to his kingdom, to the great astonishment of everyone at his court, who thought he had surely met with evil companions and worse luck.

'"'The sultan complimented his retainers on how well they retained his kingdom during his absence, and then called for the fisherman who had begun his adventure. When the humble man came before the sultan, the king then did declare that, in honor of that great adventure, from this day forward the fisherman would be the keeper of the royal treasury, with all the many benefits such a position entailed.

'"'And so did the fisherman catch a great prize indeed.

## WE RETURN TO THE TALE OF THE THIRD SHEIKH

'"So it was that I told the story while I still wore the body of the dog who was so inept that he could not chew the butcher's wares," the third sheikh continued to tell the *djinni*, "and so was most fortunately brought home by that merchant and placed in the presence of his most excellent daughter, who not only recognized my true nature but promised to restore me to my true form, and further promised to deal with my wife in any manner that I desired, if I would only tell her a story of sufficient diversion.

'"And when I had concluded my tale, the butcher's daughter commended me for my tale, and further pitied my condition, and forthwith returned me to human form. Then did she ask me what retribution I might have upon my wife, and I replied, 'She is among the most stubborn of creatures. I would think it only fitting that I turn her into a mule.'

'"And so it was done, and so was this mule that you see before you once my stubborn and spiteful wife. And that is my tale."

## THE TALE OF THE MERCHANT AND THE *DJINNI* RETURNED TO AT LAST

'"So," the third sheikh added, "is this tale worth a third of the merchant's blood?"

'"Truly," the *djinni* replied, "it is a tale of unsurpassed marvel, and fully worthy of one third of the merchant's blood, and perhaps one third of my blood as well!"

'So did the *djinni* turn to the merchant and say, "Truly, it is ignoble to die for the improper placement of one's refuse! And that you have killed my son? When one thinks upon it, he could not be much of a *djinni* to be killed by the pit of a date. Now that he is gone, I will no longer have to suffer through that loud flute music, and he will no longer leave his carpets and magic lamps scattered about the ravine! No, for stories such as these, this is a fair exchange!"

'Thus was the merchant allowed to go free, while the *djinni* and the three sheikhs determined to form a social club.'

## SCHEHERAZADE PAUSES FOR BREATH

And with that, Scheherazade was still.

'That was a most excellent story,' the king declared. '*Swords*! Oh, pardon of pardons, where did that come from? You must certainly have another tale to follow that last one.'

'Yes,' Scheherazade agreed, 'most certainly.'

Unfortunately, at the moment, she could not think of another word.

## Chapter the Twenty-second, in which things go from bad to verse.

Scheherazade could not bear this loss of words. She had to say something, didn't she? If Shahryar were to get started again with his swords, there was no knowing where the carnage would end. But Scheherazade's mind was too filled with other thoughts for her mouth to work properly; thoughts of a sleeping Dunyazad, a worried father, a dead servant, a dying guard. How might she construct a story when all of her world was unraveling around her.

Maybe, she considered, if she might concentrate on other matters for a brief period, her stories would come back to her.

'Perhaps,' she began brightly to her king, 'I could continue my stories in a more relaxed fashion if we were to pause for a moment upon yonder—'

But before she could even utter the word 'couch' there was a great commotion at the door.

'No one keeps me from the apartments of my son!' a haughty and all-too-familiar voice announced.

The guard was in the room an instant later. 'I am sorry, Oh my master, but there was no way—'

The king raised his hand for silence, as if there was no explanation necessary.

'There you are, Oh great light of my existence!' the Sultana said as she hurried past the apologetic swordsman.

The guard bowed deeply and vanished. He might be a brave man and a skilled warrior, but he had no defenses against a mother's tongue.

But the Sultana no longer propelled herself towards her son. Rather, she had stopped mid-apartment to stare at Scheherazade. 'And what is she doing here?'

'Oh sweet mother,' the king replied most apologetically, 'she is my wife!'

'Is that reason enough?' the Sultana replied dismissively. 'Soon, you will tire of her. By the way, have you been practicing with your new swords?'

The king's hands twitched at the very mention of the new weapons, and Scheherazade could see a smile form deep within the wattles of the Sultana's face.

'Why don't you bring out that most excellent present,' the Sultana continued, 'so that we might both admire—' But before she could take another step closer to her son, the two were separated by a vast quantity of black smoke.

'Oh, no you don't!' said a most spiteful voice from within the cloud. 'I was responsible for killing all those three hundred who came before, and I shall be responsible for beheading this one as well. I will not have you breaking my curse!'

At that, the smoke cleared, and there was the woman in black, the same woman who had tended to Dunyazad, and no doubt caused sleep to overcome that fair child!

But the Sultana only laughed at the other woman's dramatic entrance. 'Who do you think you are? No woman can take my son away from me!'

The woman in black did nothing but laugh in return. 'I am nothing so weak as a mortal woman. I was captured upon my wedding night by a foul *djinni* and transformed into one of their kind.' She snapped her fingers, and tiny lightning bolts danced in the air.

At this revelation, King Shahryar's eyes opened wide, and he said but one word: 'Sulima.'

Sulima. Scheherazade remembered at last where she had heard that name previously. With an awful and inevitable feeling of dire consequence, the story that her father had told her about the *djinnia* and the king came back into her consciousness. And this was Sulima!

'It is so nice that you remember my name, Oh my lover,' Sulima said with a smile that made Scheherazade shiver. 'You are such a fine rider, I have resolved that we will do so again.'

This was too much for the king. His eyes lost their focus as he cried, 'Rider? Lances? Seal Rings?'

'This woman in black is displeasing me,' the Sultana remarked. 'But we know how to deal with women who displease us, don't we, my child?' the Sultana asked her son.

'Swords!' he replied. '*Cut! Slice! Tear! Maim!*' The king shivered and began to drool.

The *djinnia* shook her head sadly. 'You had to give him those swords, didn't you?'

The Sultana glared back at her. 'What are you implying, you shameless apparition?'

'Well,' Sulima replied in the haughtiest of tones, 'it certainly wasn't *my* enchantment that turned him into a raving lunatic!'

'My son, a lunatic?' the old woman shouted. 'He'll have your head for that!'

With that, the Sultana snapped her fingers and the doors to the armory flung themselves apart.

Scheherazade gasped, but Sulima did nothing but snicker. 'Did you learn such magic in the nursery? I have no need for such mundane spells. The king is *mine*.'

With that, she fixed her gaze upon the king, and did but a single dance step, accompanied by the most subtle turn of the head and twists of the wrist.

The king stared back at the enchantress. 'Yes, Sulima,' he said in a voice that held no tone, 'we must ride.'

'No!' the Sultana screamed. 'No woman is good enough to ride my son!' She made a certain motion with her hands, and all the drawers and restraints within the armory opened, exposing the weapons for all to see.

'What is amiss?' the king asked, startled from the spell by the extreme noise. 'Oh, yes, I remember now! *Swords!*'

'No, Shahryar, you must watch my dance,' Sulima instructed, as one foot glided behind the other and her hips undulated ever so slightly.

'Yes, Sulima,' the king replied in that same toneless voice, 'I have a fine, long lance.'

'Enough of this!' the Sultana announced with a clap of her hands. 'Weapons erupt!'

With that command swords, daggers, shields, armor, bows, arrows, slings, stones, and even lances clattered into a great pile at the armory door.

'*Swords!*' Shahryar managed, before Sulima increased the pace of her dance, skipping from one foot to the other and thrusting forward her well-endowed chest.

'Yes, Sulima,' Shahryar continued, as he again lost all emotion, 'would you like my Seal Ring?'

Sulima laughed as she continued her subtle and debilitating dance. 'So shall I put all men under my spell, whether they be men or *djinn*, for men have been the ruin of my innocence!' She glanced at the Sultana and Scheherazade. 'And, while I am at it, I shall kill all women as well!'

171

'Ride my lance, Sulima,' Shahryar said as he staggered across the room towards the dancer, 'and I shall pierce your Seal Ring.'

'This will not be!' the Sultana cried in agony. 'Swords! Fly to your master!'

The three swords flew straight for Shahryar, the one of the far right sailing straight to his right hand, and the one to the left soaring to his left hand. The king's eyes lit with a killing fire as his fingers closed around the two hilts.

'Swor—' he began.

Unfortunately for his killing fire, the third sword's hilt hit him directly in the belly. Shahryar doubled over with a mighty cry of surprise.

'Oh, dear,' the Sultana remarked. 'I should have known that three swords were too much. It was such a nice round number, though. So poetic.'

'Did someone mention poetry?' Omar inquired.

The three women jumped in surprise as they turned towards the eunuch.

Scheherazade took a step away. At the moment, no one seemed to notice.

'There is no time for poetry!' the Sultana demanded. 'There is only time to obey!'

'Of course,' Omar agreed with his usual obsequiousness, 'no one ever contradicts the Sultana.'

'Then pick up one of yonder swords,' the Sultana ordered, 'and drive it through this woman in black!'

The large man turned to regard the woman in black. 'Sulima,' he whispered as his pale complexion grew paler still, and then he added in a louder voice, 'Oh yes, I recall. You are the sorceress, are you not? My, I don't believe anyone ever contradicts a sorceress either, do they?'

'Then you shall kill this wretch of a mother for me,' Sulima instructed. 'Obtain any of those weapons littered about the room, but do it now!'

'Only after you have killed this vile sorceress!' the Sultana insisted.

'After you have plunged a blade between this crone's wattles!' Sulima required.

Omar paused and smiled at both of the combatants.

'I believe this occasion calls for a poem. And so did he continue:

\* \* \*

172

# CHAPTER THE TWENTY-SECOND

'The noble Sultana
Is a woman of power,
Yet the great Sulima.
Shall have her own hour.'

Unfortunately, Omar did not have the most appreciative of audiences.

'I don't think I called for a poem,' the Sultana remarked darkly. She picked up one of the swords herself as her son struggled to his feet.

Scheherazade took this opportunity to remove herself an additional pair of steps from the conflict.

'You will soon know the fate of all those who dare mock the Sultana!' she began as she raised the sword behind her shoulder, quite close to the rising king. 'My son shall—'

The king stood. The hilt hit him right between the eyes. Shahryar collapsed back down upon the ground.

Omar continued to smile beatifically, but he now appeared to be sweating.

He spoke again, his little fingers pointed upward towards Heaven:

'The palace harem
Is a place of peace,
Where unpleasant emotions
Should be released.'

To his surprise, both women nodded at the wisdom of this verse.

'I'll release you!' Sulima announced as she advanced upon the Sultana.

'Not before I release you first!' the Sultana retorted as she raised her fists.

So did the *djinnia* attack the other with her hands, and the mother of the king did respond in kind. Sulima was very swift with her blows, but the Sultana's weight made her very steady, so that the place where the two met reminded Scheherazade of nothing so much as a rock standing against the sea. For the moment, at least, they appeared evenly matched.

With a great groan, Shahryar staggered to his knees, so that his chin was at the precise level of their flailing fists.

Sulima hit him with her right fist, infused with the power of the *djinn*. And then the Sultana met him with a left fist, filled with the power of motherhood.

173

The king groaned again as he collapsed.
Even Omar stepped away as he hurried verse number three:

> 'Yes, these are great women,
> Worthy of anointment;
> Now if you'll excuse me,
> I have an appointment.'

With that, Omar was gone.

And, from the way his great bulk obscured the vision of all who watched him, only he realized that Scheherazade fled before him.

In the distance, both the escapees could hear the Sultana curse Sulima, and Sulima curse the Sultana.

But all that came from Shahryar was a groan.

## Chapter the Twenty-third,
## in which Scheherazade finds that the sun looks
## brighter upon the outside of the palace.

But when Scheherazade paused to take a breath in that great cavern where she had much more recently found herself, she was interrupted by the great booming voice of the *djinni*.

### OZZIE INTERRUPTS THE TALE

'SO, IS THAT THE END OF YOUR STORYTELLING?' Ozzie's voice boomed from overhead.

'Certainly not,' Scheherazade replied smoothly, for, after you have been faced by husbands with swords, and, even worse, that husband's mother, the intimidation of a loud *djinni* quickly pales. 'My storytelling will simply travel outside the palace with myself, and continue until this very moment, for am I not currently telling my own story?'

'And you are telling it very well,' the young and clever man known as Achmed remarked, 'and at great length, too, for, while you talk of whole evenings of storytelling, and all those events that have occurred in between, still have we heard your entire story in but a single sitting.'

'TIME IS AS NOTHING TO THE RACE OF *DJINN*,' Ozzie explained. 'I HAVE BUT TO MAKE CERTAIN MYSTIC ADJUSTMENTS, AND YOU MIGHT TELL YOUR STORIES ETERNALLY.'

'So it sometimes feels,' murmured the man called Sinbad, who was once a porter before he had to devote his life to eluding the Queen of the Apes.

'YOU WOULD DARE TO QUESTION OZZIE?' the *djinni* roared.

'Most certainly not,' the old man who called himself Harun al Raschid interrupted most pleasantly. 'All that one might suggest is that perhaps we should give this woman a moment to rest.'

'PERHAPS,' the *djinni* replied in uncertain tone.

'And I might fill the time most divertingly,' the old man continued, 'by telling the tale of the three mystic farts, and how they changed a kingdom.'

'PERHAPS NOT,' Ozzie quickly replied, all uncertainty fled.

'Then what do you wish of us?' said the fair Marjanah, servant to Ali Baba, and the equal in cleverness to the young Achmed.

'YOU ARE HERE BUT TO AMUSE ME WITH YOUR STORIES,' Ozzie replied in the manner of one used to being obeyed. 'IF THERE IS MORE, PERHAPS I WILL LET YOU ALL LIVE FOR A LITTLE WHILE.'

Ah, thought Scheherazade, this was another of those *djinni* bargains, as I have spoken of so often in my tales, where it appears that the humans are at the mercy of these beings both powerful and cruel. Only the cleverness of men and women might bring such as this to a successful end.

'And yet I was busily telling my tale when you interrupted me,' she most gently indicated to their captor. Many in the crowd of listeners, which also included the brave Aladdin as well as a hundred or more residents of the Palace of Beautiful Women, called out encouragement. 'If you feel as if you lack for entertainment, the fault can only be yours.'

At that, the *djinni* did not immediately reply but rumbled for a moment in thought, much like the sound of a distant earth tremor.

'I SUPPOSE I DO NOT FEEL COMFORTABLE UNLESS I OCCASIONALLY THREATEN PEOPLE,' Ozzie admitted at last. 'NO DOUBT IT IS AN OLD *DJINNI* HABIT. PRAY CONTINUE.'

Scheherazade nodded pleasantly, as if the powerful creature's threats were the sort of thing she heard every day, and resumed her story:

## SCHEHERAZADE RESUMES HER ESCAPE

So it was that Scheherazade and Omar exited from that increasingly chaotic scene, passing from the king's inner chambers to his outer chambers, and thence through the great set of double doors which led to the palace.

It was at this point that Scheherazade found her further progress impeded by a crossed set of lances.

'Where are you running to?' the chief among the guards asked Scheherazade.

Omar answered for her. 'Rather should you ask, "What are we running from?"'

Both guards turned towards the open door.

'I will murder you for this!' Sulima shouted from within the king's apartments.

'My son does all the murdering around here!' the Sultana replied firmly.

The third voice, which resembled nothing so much as the howling cry of some beast of the desert, was no doubt that of the king.

'I fear that it might mean my life if I were to remain in that room,' Scheherazade admitted.

'Shahryar!' Sulima's voice echoed from within. 'By that power that I hold over you, rip this woman into pieces!'

'Shahryar!' the Sultana's voice counter-commanded, 'for the love of your mother, take up those fine swords and dice this woman into tiny bits!'

At this point, the third voice from within had been reduced from a howl to a gibber.

The guard that Scheherazade knew well looked to his fellow. 'Do you wish to investigate the noises within?'

'If that is truly a question and not an order,' the second guard replied after a moment's thought, 'my answer would have to be no.'

'What if you were to fetch the rest of our fellows from the guardhouse,' the first guard suggested, 'and approach this as a group?'

Before the second guard could answer, there erupted a series of screams and growls from the interior of the king's chambers.

'Very well!' the second guard immediately added in a much more willing tone. 'I leave at once! Of course, it may take me quite some time to gather all the guards. Perhaps I shall send some of the others ahead while I attempt to locate any who have temporarily strayed—'

But by that point in his reply, he had already disappeared around a distant bend in the corridor.

The remaining guard turned back to regard Scheherazade. 'I could not speak frankly until he was gone. You say that you are afraid to remain within these chambers?' The guard nodded grimly. 'Though it might mean my head, I am afraid I must agree.'

'Then you will let us pass?' Omar cried, great tears of joy streaming down his face. 'I believe such generosity calls for a poem!'

Scheherazade decided to ignore the possibility of poetry, and instead asked, 'What is the name of our benefactor?'

'My given name is Hassan,' the guard said as he executed the slightest of bows.

Scheherazade had to admit that he did have the most magnificent of smiles. It was a shame, indeed, that she was already married, but she had already told far too many adultery stories to become personally involved in such an adventure.

'I think I must escape this palace,' she confessed instead.

'There are some times when we must change our entire lives so that we might survive,' the guard agreed in the most solemn of tones.

'I do have a poem on that subject as well,' Omar suggested.

'Still, I fear for my sister,' Scheherazade confessed. What was it about this guard that made her so want to confess? 'She appears to be placed under some sort of a sleeping spell—'

'I will make certain that your sister is delivered to your father,' the guard assured Scheherazade.

The storyteller shook her head, doing her best to remove the foolish smile from her face. It would not do to feel too safe and secure when in this guard's vicinity. If she was going to survive this dilemma, she had to depend upon her own wits.

'Is something amiss?' the guard asked in great concern.

'Oh no,' Scheherazade quickly replied, realizing that her recent actions might seem confusing in the extreme, 'most certainly, I shall be greatly relieved if you see to my sister.'

Recognizable voices came again from the king's chambers.

'Now what will you do for Sulima?' came the *djinnia*'s insinuating tone.

'Kill for Sulima!' returned the guttural reply of a voice just barely recognizable as that of the king.

'Nonsense!' an older but even more commanding tone interrupted. 'Tell what my boy will do for his mother.'

'Kill for the Sultana!' the king replied in the exact same tone that he had used before.

'Why should he do anything for you, crone,' Sulima remarked in a voice filled with venom, 'when he sees me do my dance?'

'Because the blood of kings runs through his veins,' the Sultana replied triumphantly, 'and royal blood is thicker than any magic!'

But the king, for his part, simply repeated one word over and over: 'Kill! Kill! Kill!'

'Perhaps there is no time for poetry after all,' even Omar admitted.

'I believe,' the guard agreed, 'that this palace may not be safe for any of us.'

# Chapter the Twenty-fourth,
## in which our heroine discovers that even death is relative.

'Still,' the handsome, bold and extremely competent guard assured Scheherazade, 'there should be no trouble removing yourselves from the palace. As the king has slipped away from his contact with the world around him, much of the palace has also fallen into disarray.' The guard paused, and looked from one side and then to the other before he continued. 'I must further tell you that your father has been greatly concerned about your welfare. Though it may cost him his head, no doubt he would be glad to help.'

'Then let us be off!' Scheherazade insisted.

'I wish you might choose another phrase.' Omar rubbed at his substantial neck.

But their forward movement was stilled by the sound of trumpets.

'Oh, dear,' Omar said for them all. 'Complications.'

All three hurried over to a nearby window that looked out upon the palace grounds.

'Announcing a royal visit!' announced one of the many palace criers from the courtyard below. 'The king's brother, Shahzaman, has arrived.'

'Shahzaman?' Scheherazade repeated, as the story her father had told her long ago came back to her, concerning the two brothers and their adulterous wives, and how all this head-chopping business began. And then she fully recalled the origins of Sulima, and how she had used both brothers, as all my audience no doubt recalls.

'Our necks are even less safe than they were before!' Omar insisted.

Scheherazade did not understand the eunuch's concern. 'Won't Shahzaman take care of his brother and set the kingdom right?'

'You forget who was the original executioner among these two

179

brothers,' Omar said in the most emotional of fashions. 'When Shahzaman sees the chaos that has erupted around this palace, the solution will become obvious to him, because it is the only solution he knows. Chop off a few heads, and things will right themselves.'

'And if there are still problems?' Scheherazade asked.

'Chop a few heads more!' was Omar's fevered reply. 'There is no way we may safely confront such logic, not to mention swords.'

'But Shahzaman and his retinue now occupy the courtyard,' Scheherazade pointed out most reasonably. 'There is no way for us to bypass such a company.'

'No way out in the open, perhaps,' Omar agreed.

The handsome, bold, extremely competent and no doubt intuitive guard, seeing the gist of what Omar implied, cried aloud, 'The secret passages!'

'The secret passages?' Scheherazade once again asked, for that seemed to be her function within this conversation.

Omar paused to look to his right and to his left. 'The palace is honeycombed with them. In parts of this ancient building, there are more secret ways than there are public corridors.'

'I know of a few,' the guard, who was not only handsome, bold and extremely competent and intuitive, but knowledgeable about his surroundings, agreed in a low voice.

'I know of dozens!' Omar added. 'Palace eunuchs tend to have a lot of extra time on their hands.'

'The noble King Shahzaman is entering the palace, and he is not well pleased that he has not received an official greeting!' the caller called from the courtyard below.

Scheherazade paused to consider. As queen, she was probably the highest ranking member of the royal family still in her right mind. 'Perhaps I should go down and greet him,' she suggested.

'It would surely be your head, before you uttered a word!' Omar answered. 'For a king to be greeted by a woman, even the queen? Do you have no grasp of palace politics?'

Unfortunately, Scheherazade thought, her grasp of palace politics was becoming far too great; for wherever she grasped it, her head was forfeit.

'Then there is no way we may prevent the mass slaughter of the palace denizens?' she called out in frustration. 'No way to speak of these things directly?'

'There are far too many things that cannot be spoken of directly,' Omar replied in the most reasonable of tones. 'Why do you think that I employ poetry?'

180

'I will go,' said the bold, intuitive, handsome, extremely competent guard. 'I am wearing a uniform, which gives me a certain authority. This should give me license to speak a whole sentence or two before I lose my head.'

'Must you?' Scheherazade asked, for such a course of events seemed wasteful in the extreme.

'It will give you a little extra time for your escape, my noble queen,' said the handsome, bold, extremely competent, knowledgeable about his surroundings and ultimately self-sacrificing guardsman.

'King Shahzaman is now about to climb the stairs to the king's private chambers,' the caller announced from below, 'and he is even less pleased that everyone is avoiding him!'

'I must be off!' And the guardsman who was all those things bowed most courteously to Scheherazade, then ran towards that royal retinue now ascending the stairs.

'But what of the secret passageways?' Scheherazade asked.

'There is one behind this very curtain,' Omar replied, nodding toward a heavy drapery to their right. He moved quickly to pull the cloth aside, then pressed a panel within the ornate tile design upon the wall. A doorway six feet high and four feet wide slid away in the wall.

'Follow me,' Omar instructed.

'The king has reached the second floor, and he is becoming downright displeased, not to mention out of sorts, that no one has yet—' the caller hesitated. 'Who are you?'

So the guard had finally met the king. Scheherazade paused, waiting for she knew not what.

'We must go now!' Omar insisted.

The large servant was correct. The guard's sacrifice would be meaningless if they were to die as well.

So it was that Scheherazade followed Omar into the darkness. Omar's bulk fit easily within the hidden passage, which was almost as wide as the more public hall that it ran next to. Scheherazade stepped within the hidden hallway, and the doorway slid shut silently behind her.

'These passageways were constructed when this palace was built in the distant past,' Omar explained in a low voice, 'and are constructed with the assistance of the most cunning and complicated devices, although the true purpose of some of these mechanisms have been lost in the mists of time.'

Scheherazade was impressed. Apparently, no matter what her

true feelings were about this large fellow, he was the ideal guide to show her through this second, secret palace. If only her thoughts were not so much with the bold, handsome – and no doubt recently deceased – guard.

And hopes that might have remained were shattered when she heard the caller's voice: 'King Shahzaman will show his displeasure by executing – no, wait a moment.' This was followed in short order by a scream.

'Oh, no!' Scheherazade cried.

'Please,' Omar cautioned, 'do not call out. If you wish to observe, there is a place just along here where you can look out.' He indicated a delicate latticework as covered many of the halls and rooms of the great palace. There was sufficient space between the ornately carved trees and birds to observe what transpired in the rooms beyond. Scheherazade suddenly wondered if every latticework within this palace held such a secret way?

Scheherazade's eyes focused on the hallway beyond exactly as King Shahzaman's retinue began to march on by. And, when she looked at the first man to pass her hiding place, she could tell from his regal bearing, his resemblance to his brother, and the crown upon his head, that he could be no one but King Shahzaman.

Scheherazade's heart almost stopped, for striding next to him was the bold and self-sacrificing guard!

'You see, I simply had to execute somebody,' the king explained. The guard quickly nodded in agreement.

'It is one of the trials of being a monarch,' the king continued. 'The day just doesn't go right unless you have blood on your hands, don't you know.' He clapped the guard upon the shoulder. 'But you are the only one whom I have found with any knowledge of the palace! How could I possibly execute you? As the wise man says, I will not slice off my nasal passages to persecute my facial features. Besides, that caller was beginning to get upon my nerves. His voice had a certain exceedingly unpleasant piercing quality, don't you think?'

The guard, knowing his place around royalty, could do nothing but nod further.

'Now where are my brother's chambers?' Shahzaman asked.

'Immediately ahead,' the guard replied in his strong voice. 'I feel, however, that I should tell you there has recently been an altercation within.'

'Altercation?' Shahzaman said with a great passion. 'I will execute any who harm the peace of this palace. Who is the cause of this?'

At this, the guard appeared less than pleased. 'Though it might mean my head, I regret to inform you that one of the prime participants was your mother.'

'Oh, my,' Shahzaman replied with some disappointment, 'I suppose I can't execute my mother, or my brother, at least without good reason. Was there no one else present?'

'Well, I could swear I heard the voice of another woman, though no human passed my guard.'

'Another woman?' Shahzaman said with rather more satisfaction. 'Let us hope she has none of these blood limitations.' He sighed. 'Sometimes, relatives can be so frustrating.'

Perhaps, Scheherazade thought, Shahzaman could actually remove one of her impediments to happiness. Perhaps she could even hope for some sort of successful resolution after all. Shahzaman stepped within Shahryar's quarters, followed by the guard and Shahzaman's retinue.

Omar snapped his fingers and whispered for Scheherazade to follow.

'The view will be much better from here,' he further explained. And indeed, Scheherazade now looked into the primary room of the king's apartment, that room where they had often made love, and the room in which Sulima and the Sultana had fought.

'Aha!' Shahzaman called out upon seeing the woman in black. 'You are definitely not a relative! Prepare to die!'

'Fool of a king,' Sulima retorted. 'Do you so soon forget someone with whom you were all too familiar?' And with that, she performed the slightest of dance steps.

'Sulima!' Shahzaman cried out in horror. 'Pillows! Lances! Riding! Seal Rings!' And these later exclamations were accompanied by that same sort of twitching so prevalent in his brother.

So much for her hope of early resolution, Scheherazade realized.

Sulima sneered at the twitching monarch. 'I do not like to share my couch before old crones. I shall come for you later!' She thereupon disappeared in a cloud of smoke as dark as her garments.

'Kill! Kill! Kill!' called King Shahryar from that place where he was huddled upon the floor.

'Yes, Shahryar,' Shahzaman agreed, 'there will be some killing done here this day.' He turned to the Sultana. 'What has happened to this place, mother?'

'This has happened most recently,' the Sultana replied. 'For since that time that your brother returned to his home, he had immediately discovered a method whereby he could ease his mind upon every night, which was to kill a maiden upon every evening.'

'Most reasonable,' Shahzaman agreed.

'And so this method worked well for him for three hundred nights,' the Sultana further explained. 'But on the next night, the vizier who supplied the king found himself at a loss for new maidens.'

'Ah,' Shahzaman remarked most sympathetically. 'Lack of victims? I've often had supply problems when performing multiple executions. I remember one period when I was particularly peeved and was slaying three a day – you know, one before every meal? Does wonders for the appetite, may I tell you. Anyway—'

'Not now, boy,' the Sultana insisted. 'Listen to your mother.' She further explained, 'So it was that this vizier turned to his own family and married off his daughter to Shahryar.'

'A pragmatic man,' Shahzaman agreed.

'Yes, but the vizier's daughter,' the Sultana continued urgently. 'She's a—' And she had great difficulty speaking that final word. '—a storyteller!'

Shahzaman was almost overcome by shock. 'So she has my brother under her spell? Shahryar always was too good an audience. He would watch for hours as I pulled the legs off frogs.'

'Those were simple, happy days,' the Sultana agreed. 'But what if she works her wiles upon you as well?'

'Have no fear, Mother,' Shahzaman reassured her. 'I never listen to anyone.'

'Well,' his mother replied with a satisfied smile, 'I am glad I raised at least one son fit to be king. Then what will you do?'

'There is but one inescapable conclusion,' Shahzaman said firmly. 'Scheherazade must die.'

## Chapter the Twenty-fifth,
*in which Scheherazade learns the secrets of a very large palace, and a very large heart.*

So they were back to death again. Scheherazade supposed she should be accustomed to this by now. But unlike his brother Shahryar, who in his actions was often befuddled but at the very least malleable, Shahzaman seemed single minded and even relentless in his pursuit of executions. As of that moment, Scheherazade's destiny did not seem to be of long duration.

Shahzaman and the Sultana marched from the king's quarters, followed closely by Shahzaman's retinue. Scheherazade waited for the bold, handsome, sympathetic and still-somehow-among-the-living guard to close the doors before she spoke.

'What shall I do?' she said, her voice barely a whisper.

'Perhaps it is time for a quiet poem,' Omar replied most conscientiously, quickly beginning the following rhyme:

> 'Thus does this fair flower face
> A world of a thousand harms,
> And yet might she find solace
> Within these chubby arms.'

Scheherazade felt another flash of anger at the large fellow's suggestion, but, when she looked upon him in the dim light of the passageway, with that imploring gaze, that quivering lip, and that single tear falling from an eye, he presented the most pitiful four hundred pounds that she had ever seen.

Omar continued:

> 'Excuse me if I stare
> And tug at my tunic
> For my heart must ask
> Could I be your eunuch?'

Scheherazade still could not bring herself to be harsh. She hardly knew this large man, and he knew equally little about her life, and

185

yet Omar seemed to be showing feelings that he hid from the rest of the world, and she could not rail against his honesty. Besides which, if she was going to stand any chance of escape, she would have to enlist the large man's help.

'Thank you, but no,' was her reply. 'Could you forget that I am a married woman? Oh, most certainly, my husband may be slightly out of his mind at present, but I believe that to be a temporary condition. No, Omar, I believe it would be better if we remained only friends.'

'Friends, friends, always friends!' Omar said in a voice edged close to despair. 'What do women want from a eunuch?'

'This woman needs to find a way out of here,' was Scheherazade's straightforward reply, 'before someone elects to take my head.'

'Oh, most certainly,' Omar quickly agreed. 'What could I have been thinking of?' He paused, and looked to the left, and then to the right. 'We will take the stairs,' he announced.

'The stairs?' Scheherazade replied. 'Will we not risk discovery?'

'Not the stairs without,' Omar corrected her gently. 'There are hidden stairways within these hidden passageways, not to mention hidden windows, hidden doors, hidden trapdoors, hidden ventilation grates, hidden levers, hidden pulleys, and other hidden simple machines. And there are whole hidden rooms beyond, sleeping chambers, storerooms for food and valuables, as well as great rooms for meeting and gardens open to the sun.'

'This is all very informative,' Scheherazade replied, 'but would it not be better if we were now hiding in these places at this moment?'

'Oh,' Omar answered. 'Perhaps it would. Forgive me, my queen. I hear and I obey!'

He moved so quickly down the passageway that Scheherazade was hard pressed to follow. Even though their surroundings were shrouded in gloom, Omar further never seemed to make a false step, calling back to his charge, 'Turn here!' and then, 'There is a single step up,' and later, 'Watch out for that loose board.' Scheherazade reflected that the eunuch must have spent many, many hours hiding and watching to have this sort of a knowledge. Perhaps, because of this, he knew far more about Scheherazade than she had previously thought.

Omar held up his hand. 'Be still, my queen. I must open the way to the stairs.' He took one step forward and two steps back, then jumped up and down in place.

A piece of the floor whirled silently out of the way, revealing a stairway that led below.

'It is how it is done,' Omar answered Scheherazade's silent question. 'The exact reasons are, alas, lost to antiquity.'

She descended the stairs after the sure-footed Omar. On this lower level, they did indeed pass through a series of rooms, some quite small, but some as large as Scheherazade's own rooms in the harem. But the existence of the rooms did not startle Scheherazade so much as the fact that there were people living in them. And as they passed through the rooms, the people waved and called out greetings to Omar and a welcome to the queen. And Scheherazade was further surprised to learn, after she had seen fifteen to twenty of these inhabitants, that they were mostly women and children.

'Who are these people?' she asked Omar as they continued their flight.

'Escapees from the palace for the most part. Women who would have become wives or consorts of the king, and thus victims of the king's sword. There are few places to hide in the wide open city beyond the palace gates. The best location to conceal oneself is where those who search for you will not look. No place, therefore, could be better than the palace.'

'But they seem well fed, even happy,' Scheherazade said as she heard a child's laugh trail down a connecting corridor.

'It does take a great deal of food for me to maintain this magnificent bulk,' Omar said with a trace of pride. 'However, I sometimes take even more than I need to survive, and transport it here. Others pass them meals from the palace kitchens. The population of the palace is so greatly reduced of late that there is much extra food about. And, of course, they do have gardens and livestock pens in those hidden places among the roofs.'

'And they do not have to face the rigors of my husband's court?' Scheherazade asked with a smile. 'Or the wrath of the Sultana? I tell you, Omar, this place sounds a little like Paradise. Shall I stay here as well?'

Omar frowned at that suggestion. 'For a short time, perhaps, although I might like to have you near forever – forgive my boldness. Your freedom is more important than any petty whim of mine. For have not the poets often said:

> 'My wish grew warm upon this day.
> It sizzled like kebab,

But you must go, my kebab falls,
To be smothered by my flab.'

Omar's rhyme was succeeded by a muffled sob.

'Only a short while?' Scheherazade asked, although she had to admit that her regret was not so great when she considered that, in leaving this palace, she also managed to leave Omar's poetry.

'I am afraid so. Many people pass from the public palace to these private ways, and we could not guarantee that all of them would remain silent, especially if there is a price upon your head. Your capture and death are so important to some that these secret ways might well be violated.'

Omar's summary of the situation made far too much upsetting sense to Scheherazade. 'Then what should I do?' she demanded. 'Where should I go?'

'Of that I am uncertain,' Omar replied. 'But I know the very person to ask.'

*Chapter the Twenty-sixth,*
*in which Scheherazade discovers some words to the*
*wise, and some directions out of the palace.*

'We must go this way, now,' Omar informed Scheherazade, even though the large man had seemed to walk them into a corner.

He turned three times, skipped once upon the left foot, whistled sharply and waved his right hand. A trap door opened in the ceiling, and a rope ladder fell before them.

'It is how these things work,' Omar explained even though Scheherazade had not asked the question. 'The exact reasons are lost in antiquity. Oh,' he added as an afterthought, 'we go to see the wise woman.'

'The wise woman?' Scheherazade asked, for she had never heard of such a person.

'There is always a wise woman,' Omar explained. 'They are part of the standard furnishings of any palace.' He climbed the ladder with a grace that Scheherazade would have found surprising if she had not already known Omar's moves. She followed quickly behind.

Now did they fit through narrower ways, where Omar's bulk rubbed the walls at either side. 'These ways are not much used by those of my noble girth,' came his muffled voice from the other side of his large form. 'But we must make an exception, for the sake of your life.' And these corridors went on for some time, as had the ways below, except that these new places were ill lit, with the occasional low ceiling and continuous refuse upon the floor. Twice, when Omar paused to rest before her, Scheherazade thought she could hear other things moving through the refuse; smaller things, no doubt, but things most certainly equipped with sharp teeth and unclean claws.

'We are here!' Omar cried at last, as he thrust himself out of the narrow corridor into a wider place with an audible pop. As he moved forward, Scheherazade could see sunlight. She walked forward as well, and found herself at the entranceway to one of the

189

hidden gardens that Omar had previously described. Though it was bordered by high walls on all four sides, this place was full of vegetation of all shapes and colors. Coming from the darkness of the corridor to see this splendid array, Scheherazade almost felt that she had simply learned to see all over again.

'Halt!' a woman's voice cried. 'No man may pass this way and live!'

'What?' Omar replied in a voice that was greatly offended. 'You mistake me for a man?'

A woman with a drawn sword approached them along a path through the vegetation. 'My apologies, Omar. I should have recognized your wattles.'

Omar sniffed in agreement. 'We are here to see the wise woman.'

'She had mentioned looking forward to speaking with – Scheherazade, is it?' the armed woman replied. 'She did not mention anything about eunuchs.'

'We do our work so quietly, many people forget us,' Omar said most humbly. 'I will follow most unobtrusively, so that you might ignore me completely.'

A great cry of anguish arose from the forest before them.

'It is the wise woman,' the swordswoman announced. 'She requests the presence of Scheherazade now!' She set off on the path at a run, and the storyteller thought it best to follow her.

'She is subject to fits,' their guide called over her shoulder as she ran. 'They are especially acute when she is having her visions.'

'From all I understand,' Omar called back sympathetically from where he took up the rear, 'having visions is not among the easiest of occupations!'

The swordswoman did not deign to answer that remark, but instead redoubled her speed as an animal-like howl erupted from the bushes ahead.

'She is here, wise woman!' the armed guard called as they came to a clearing well hidden by the surrounding trees and underbrush.

In the middle of this clearing there sat cross-legged an emaciated woman with skin stretched over purple veins. She raised one quivering hand as the three others approached.

'Wait!' the cracked voice announced. 'Don't tell me! Your name is – unnnhh!' Her forehead creased as if she were in pain. 'Scheherazade!'

'Yes, that is most certainly true,' Scheherazade replied, impressed that the woman would so easily discern her name. 'And we have come—'

The wise woman waved away her words. 'There is no need for you to speak further! You have come because – errk – ennggggg— ' Her mouth spasmed into a most unpleasant expression. '—you need to escape from the palace.' She frowned. 'But you are the queen. Why do you need to escape?'

'I am pursued by most deadly—' Scheherazade began.

'Say no more!' the wise woman instructed. 'Gakkkk!' Her tongue lolled out of her mouth for an instant before it was snatched back within those toothless gums. 'Sceerrgh! You are pursued by not one but – snibble – two separate parties that hold only one thing in common between them, and that is – arkark – their desire for your death!'

'That is most correct,' Scheherazade agreed.

'Please don't interrupt,' the wise woman snapped. 'You are – ragnorak! Rrrmagedged! – being pursued at this very moment by the elite guard of Shahzaman!'

'This is the very reason we have sought refuge—' Omar began to explain.

'Sought but not found!' the wise woman snapped. 'Orrubb-bbulll! Nasteeeee! For they have breached your defenses, and even now search the palace's secret corridors.'

'So soon?' Omar said in horror. 'How close are they to discovering us?'

'They are not close. Orrrooooooo!' The wise woman suddenly bent over double. 'They are here.'

As if they had been only waiting for the wise woman to speak those words, a dozen members in the purple and gold uniforms of Shahzaman's elite guard burst from the bushes at either side. Four of them surrounded the swordswoman, while the other eight turned their attention to Scheherazade.

'There she is!' said one of the elite guard with great perception.

'Prepare to die,' another added with great purpose, 'you who have cursed King Shahryar!'

'Excuse me for a moment,' Omar said to Scheherazade. The storyteller wondered if the eunuch would now grovel in a pitiful attempt to save his life.

But, instead of groveling, Omar tapped his right foot twice, his left foot three times, waved both hands in the air, belched most loudly, and said the word 'Avocado!' three times in rapid succession.

Great spikes of slightly rusted metal rose from the ground to instantly impale the eight elite guardsmen who threatened Scheherazade. In the ensuing confusion, the swordswoman made short work of the four guards who remained.

'No one is quite sure how that works,' Omar explained, even though Scheherazade was now far too confused to ask a question, 'for the reasons have been lost to antiquity.'

Scheherazade felt something rasp against her hand. She looked down to see the dry and ancient fingers of the wise woman feebly touching her own. 'But there is more that I must tell you, my child. There are others who pursue—'

This time, she was interrupted by a chicken.

'Could it be?' Scheherazade said, turning to Omar.

'Sulima would have no trouble finding us within a place that is her second home,' Omar most grimly agreed.

'Arrcnarkk! That cry will be followed by the call of a goat, and the call of the cow.'

Again, as if they were prompted, Scheherazade heard a distant bleat followed by a phantom moo.

'Beware! Swarrxxx! They are bewitched!' The aged woman began to flap her arms up and down, as if they were wings. 'Come back!' she called. 'Break the spell! Loopegaroux!' Her head began to move in quick forward jerks, as if she was butting against something with invisible horns. 'All is forgiven!' Her closed mouth began to move back and forth, as if she chewed grass with her gums.

A light flashed at the other end of the clearing, followed quickly by two more.

'Where am I?' A servant woman stood where once there had been only the shadow of a chicken.

'What time is it?' a second servant said from where was once the ghostly image of a goat.

'We must attend the queen!' the third announced, now no longer a spectral bovine shade.

'You have been bewitched!' Scheherazade announced. 'But now all is well.'

'Urrgahh!' the wise woman called. 'Eeyyouugah! It is Sulima. You have foiled her for the moment. But she will attack you in another way. For her power is so great – Oogumboogum – that she can transform any woman and bewitch any man.'

'Any man?' Omar bristled. 'I'll have you know that I was unaffected, unless of course, you mention that time when I introduced her as the new servant without realizing her true nature. Not of course that I fit into this man category anyway.'

'You can see how – crabbledabble – difficult it can be to battle such a power,' the wise woman commented most simply. 'There is only one hope.'

'And what might that hope be?' Scheherazade asked when there was no further information forthcoming.

'I'm getting to that!' The wise woman's eyes rolled back into her head so nothing was showing but the whites laced with veins. 'Buffpuff! Listen carefully. Oggnoggg! You have but one chance. You must consult the wise woman!'

Omar frowned at that. 'Aren't we already consulting the wise woman?'

'No,' the aged voice croaked, 'the other wise woman. Snarrk! Hendrak! The one who dwells in the marketplace.'

'Oh,' Omar remarked, '*that* wise woman.' He further added, 'Every marketplace has a wise woman as part of its standard provisions.'

'She is much wiser than I! Goggoogppoooppo!' The wise woman made shooing motions with her palms. 'Now you must depart. Quickly! But I will leave you with three – oolong! lapsang! – pieces of advice.' So great was her concentration, that the old woman bent almost double. 'Boomboom! Lead with your right! Zambam! Never eat at a place called "Mom's". Zappow! And know your strengths and when to use them.'

'Come,' Omar said close by Scheherazade's ear. 'We must go, and quickly!'

Scheherazade frowned back at the clearing as she followed Omar back the way they had come. 'How could she possibly know so much?'

'If we could truly fathom wise women,' Omar counseled sagely, 'we would no longer need them.' He stopped before a certain bush and pressed the greenery aside. There was a stairway leading down.

'To save yourself, you must leave the palace, and at once,' Omar explained as he led the way below. 'And I cannot go with you, for a woman traveling with a eunuch would be far too conspicuous.'

'But where shall I find this wise woman?' Scheherazade asked.

'It is simplicity itself,' Omar replied, 'for the marketplace is immediately adjacent to the palace's outer wall, and the woman keeps her counsel in a hidden space to the rear of the stall of a certain Hassan, who is a seller of carpets. Ask to see his finest carpet, but refuse to pay more than fifty dinars. That is the signal that you are to see the wise woman.'

Scheherazade said that she understood. Omar paused at the foot of the stairs to push aside a loose stone within the wall and pull free a dark cloak.

'Here, I have saved a disguise for just this sort of occasion.' Omar paused to study Scheherazade's appraising gaze. 'Well, perhaps it wasn't saved for you, but you must forgive a eunuch his indiscretions.'

Scheherazade accepted the cloak, and thanked Omar for his assistance.

'Now we must use the secret door,' Omar explained as he looked to the right and then to the left.

'Don't tell me, but it is time for a new series of arcane movements,' Scheherazade quickly replied, sure she at last understood how things worked around here. 'It's how these things work, for reasons lost in antiquity.'

'No, actually the door opens outward from this very knob. See?'

Oh, Scheherazade thought. There was a knob there, wasn't there?

Omar pushed open the door in the wall. There, beyond, Scheherazade saw the crowds of the city at the edge of the marketplace.

'I will continue to watch you from afar,' Omar said wistfully.

Not, Scheherazade thought, if she could watch Omar first. But he had helped her greatly, so she said nothing. Instead, she stepped quietly through the doorway.

'I think,' Omar added, 'that we have time for a parting poem.'

Somewhere in the distance, Scheherazade could hear a series of shouts.

Omar began anyway:

'Would that this moment
We could hold so dear—
But I hear the guards
And I'm out of here!'

* * *

The door slammed behind her.

And so, as the morning sun rose towards its zenith, Scheherazade stepped out of the palace and hurried quickly towards the market-place.

## Chapter the Twenty-seventh
## in which Scheherazade gets the rug
## pulled out from under her.

So it was that Scheherazade found herself in the midst of market day, surrounded by a hundred times a hundred as many people as she had seen in all her time within the palace and harem.

'Make way! Make way!' someone called behind her.

She quickly stepped to the side of a stall and turned to see the deep red robes of a dozen members of Shahryar's personal guard hurrying down the street. She averted her face and pulled up her veil so that it covered much of her nose as well.

She noticed a woman of middle years minding a display of vegetables, a woman who also looked most disapprovingly at the passing guards. Perhaps, Scheherazade considered, she might be able to gain some information if she were to feign ignorance.

She therefore approached that frowning woman and asked the following question: 'Who are these people who hurry through the market?'

'It is one of the king's special patrols,' the other woman said with distaste. 'They are truly a ruthless group. In times past, I would say they were searching for a new bride for the king, as we all know of our monarch's predilections.' She looked to her left, and then to her right, and then leaned forward to talk in a lower tone. 'Now, however, have you heard? He has married the daughter of the vizier, one Scheherazade, and she has kept him occupied for a week and more. Now there is a worthy woman! Perhaps we will have peace within our kingdom at last.' She stood straight again and shook her head. 'Still, do I pity the poor soul who is the new subject of the dread guard's search.'

Scheherazade attempted to nod pleasantly at all this, as if she was hearing gossip that did not both praise her and inform her that she was the subject of a merciless search.

'Might you tell me where I might find Hassan the rug seller?' she asked.

197

'That bandit?' the other woman replied with a laugh. 'He is on this very lane, some twenty stalls down, upon the left. You will be able to see his wares from a distance. But I warn you, look at both sides of anything he might sell you. And keep a regular acquaintance with the location of your purse!'

Scheherazade thanked the woman and hurried on her way, past stalls selling ripe fruits and aromatic nuts, and others offering colorful scarves or exotic animals or leather goods of fine design, or any of those other varied items shipped from all the corners of civilization. And so was she also constantly assaulted by voices raised to either side, urging the passers-by to stop and see all the bargains of a lifetime.

So it was that she walked by ten stalls to her left and ten to her right, and then another ten in either direction, and she saw immediately before her a great display of carpets, all of them rich with red and yellow designs.

She paused at the very front of the carpet seller's stall, and saw a portly man with an expression that resided somewhere between the friendly and the crafty.

'Are you then Hassan?' she asked of the man.

'I can be no other, for are not these the finest rugs in all of the marketplace?' Hassan replied. 'And who might be my honored customer?'

Scheherazade pulled her dark cloak closer to her shoulders. 'I am but a poor tradeswoman.'

'Is that so?' Hassan's smile grew wider still. 'Then I am certainly the most honest of all the merchants within this market.'

Scheherazade realized that he did not sound totally convinced. Perhaps she should have thought to change from that rich clothing that peaked out from beneath the cloak before she left the palace. Still, her credibility was not of the greatest importance. She was here to speak with the wise woman, and in order to do that, she would have to follow the directions that Omar had given her.

'Very well,' she replied to the merchant. 'I want to see your very best carpet.'

'That is much more like it!' Hassan rejoined enthusiastically. 'It does no good for a woman of quality such as yourself to pretend poverty.'

He reached into a great pile of rugs behind him and brought forth a deep ruby brocade with a design upon it of the most delicate pink.

'This is the finest of the fine,' he said as he laid the carpet out before her. 'Now may I ask you how much gold that you wish to spend?'

'Gold?' Scheherazade could not keep the astonishment from her voice. It was not until this moment that she recalled she had escaped from the palace without a single dinar in her possession.

'Merchants must be flexible,' Hassan replied as he sensed her distress. 'I do not necessarily need hard currency. After all, we might barter for some of that gold about your arms and ankles, not to mention all those precious stones worked into your hair.'

Oh yes. No doubt one of the problems with courtly life was that she had begun to take this sort of costume for granted. She smiled graciously at the merchant, as if this sort of barter was what she had intended all along.

'Very well,' Hassan agreed with a smile of his own. 'You have struck me with your openness and charm. Since I can tell that you are a woman who knows the value of a dinar, I am willing to give you this rug for barely more than I paid for it, say two hundred and fifty dinars?'

Scheherazade then remembered her next instruction from Omar. 'I am sorry,' she replied, 'but I cannot spend more than fifty dinars for the finest of carpets.'

'Fifty?' the merchant cried in disbelief. 'What, do you wish not only myself to starve, but also my wife and five small children? Surely, I have not made the worth of this rug abundantly clear. But I tell you, since it is such a quiet day in the market, perhaps I can sacrifice a bit this once to put food on the table. Two hundred dinars and it is yours!'

'I am sorry,' Scheherazade said demurely, 'but fifty dinars is my limit.' Shouldn't he be showing her the way to the wise woman? She had no idea how long she might stand here without encountering another group of soldiers.

The merchant knocked at the side of his head. 'Surely, I have something trapped in my ears! I could have sworn you still said fifty dinars. What, are you from some foreign land, and do not know how to haggle? You should have at least, out of respect for my merchandise, raised your offer to seventy-five. But I tell you. I will give you one more opportunity, although it will mean that three of my five children will have to go without a midday meal. One hundred and fifty dinars!'

Scheherazade looked to her left, then to her right. Had not she just heard a cry of 'Make way! Make way!' somewhere else in the marketplace? She turned back to the merchant, and said firmly, 'I am sorry, but fifty dinars is the only amount I can offer.'

'Fifty dinars!' Hassan shouted as he clutched at his chest. 'Why don't you simply stab me where I stand? It would be an equal crime to such an offer!'

Yes. Scheherazade was quite sure she heard the shouts of the guards mixed in with the noise of the market. She leaned toward the merchant. 'Could there possibly be another Hassan hereabouts who is in the carpet trade?'

But Hassan was beyond answering simple questions. 'Fifty dinars!' the merchant said in great agitation. 'Fifty dinars, fifty pitiful – Wait a moment. Do you want to see the wise woman?'

'Yes, precisely,' Scheherazade answered.

The merchant placed his hands in front of his face. 'Why don't you say so? I absolutely loathe this password business. Go, quickly! She is in the back, behind those piles of merchandise. Although that is a fine rug you are passing up.'

Scheherazade thanked him most graciously and walked swiftly in the direction the merchant had indicated. She knew she was close to her goal when she heard the howl.

'It is – capandgown – Scheherazade, is it not?'

Apparently, this wise woman also had similar reactions to this vision business. She pulled aside a carpet that was acting as a doorway to the rear of the stall.

'Yes,' Scheherazade agreed. 'I—'

'Of course!' the wise woman said 'You were – lincolnlogs – sent by the wise woman!'

It took a moment for Scheherazade's gaze to adjust itself to the dim illumination within this alcove, but when she could see, she found this particular wise woman looking oddly familiar. It was more than simply the pained expression and the quivering limbs; even more than the emaciated condition of her body, not to mention the pale skin laced with blue veins.

'Are—' Scheherazade began.

'No – Worcestershire – I understand your question even before you speak it,' the wise woman replied. 'She is my sister!'

'Your—' Scheherazade ventured.

'Exactly,' the wise woman agreed. 'But I do get a lot of referrals. It is good to keep business in the family.'

'The—' Scheherazade began.

'No,' the wise woman interrupted. 'I understand your – armadillo – question before you can even think of it!'

Scheherazade frowned. Had she been going to ask a question?

'Perhaps I am moving too fast,' the wise woman remarked. 'It is an occupational – blastfurnace – hazard. But come, I know your problem, and I know its solution. Of course, you have virtually nothing to fear at the moment from any member of your family. Sulima, however, is another matter. I imagine she should be arriving here right about – now.'

Now? Scheherazade looked about to see the rug behind her savagely ripped out of the way!

'At last!' the woman in black snarled. 'I shall have my vengeance!'

Her hands reached out for Scheherazade, and the tent was filled with her vile laughter.

## Chapter the Twenty-eighth,
### *in which a member of the race of* djinn *once again stomps upon the storyline.*

Truly, this was the end for Scheherazade.

### OZZIE AGAIN INTERRUPTS THE TALE

'THEN DOES ONE OF MY KIND WIN AT LAST?' Ozzie roared. 'HAVE YOU NOTICED? IT HAPPENS SO SELDOM IN THESE TALES. THIS IS A MOST EXCELLENT CHANGE OF PACE. TELL ME, WHAT WAS THE MANNER OF YOUR DEATH, AND HOW HORRIBLE WAS THE *DJINNIA*'S RETRIBUTION? THIS TALE WAS ALMOST FINE ENOUGH FOR ME TO LET YOU LIVE!'

Scheherazade looked up to the glowing green head that gloated above them. 'I am not quite finished with my tale,' she remarked. 'Besides, if I am already dead, how could you possibly "let me live" as you have so graciously suggested? Or, for that matter, how could I be telling this tale?'

'See here,' the many pieces of Kassim interjected. 'I am a living exception to that rule. Well, perhaps not exactly living, for I am six times six pieces, but I am still speaking. Aren't I?'

'Speaking, most certainly,' Achmed agreed. 'Making sense, we are not so certain.'

But Scheherazade thought, the rules were indeed different down here in this enchanted cavern that housed the Palace of Beautiful Women. So could Kassim, the brother of Ali Baba, be cut into smaller and smaller segments and still somehow survive. Even the dreaded cave itself, one Mordrag by name, had been a thing of enchantment, keeping all of its hundreds of women captives fed and entertained until it in turn was defeated by Ozzie the *djinni*. And there were further wonders here as well, such as the *djinni* of the lamp and the *djinni* of the ring who had so aided Aladdin during his adventures, and who Ozzie had tricked into

203

filling that bottle in which the gloating *djinni* himself had once been trapped.

Magic was everywhere. She remembered something that the third wise woman had told her. But that was a part of Scheherazade's story, the same story that she should resume. It was sufficient for the moment that she remember she was in a magic place, and that perhaps it was a magic she could use.

'It seems to me,' said the clever young Marjanah, 'that this *djinni* is doing everything he can to see that the storyteller does not succeed.'

'WHAT DO YOU MEAN BY THAT INSINUATION?' Ozzie demanded. 'I WILL HAVE YOU KNOW THAT OZZIE IS FAIREST AMONG THE FAIR.'

But Marjanah's statement seemed to meet with general agreement by many members of the largely female audience.

'Let her speak!' said one.

'And without interruption,' another agreed.

'It is only fair that you allow her to tell her story in the same way that Sinbad and Ali Baba were allowed to tell theirs!' said a third.

'Ook ook ook!' added a fourth.

Ozzie looked up to the stalactites in frustration. 'I AM GOOD ENOUGH TO LET THEM LISTEN IN THE AUDIENCE. WHAT DO THESE WOMEN WANT?'

From the cries of outrage that now rose from the hundreds of listeners, apparently the women wanted something besides Ozzie's condescension.

'AND WHERE ARE YOU GOING, SINBAD?' the *djinni* further asked.

The thin and somewhat nervous former porter stopped in his attempt to climb within the darkened and most inaccessible recesses of the cave. 'I could have sworn I heard an ook ook ook,' was his explanation.

'SO?' Ozzie demanded. 'COULD THIS BE WORSE THAN MY TERRIBLE VENGEANCE?'

'You must understand,' Sinbad said as he looked first to the left, then to the right, surveying all of the female audience. 'Getting killed by a vengeful *djinni* is one matter. The Queen of the Apes is something else altogether.'

Ozzie took a moment to regard all that now transpired before him. 'OBVIOUSLY, THERE ARE THINGS HERE THAT EVEN A VIRTUALLY ALL-KNOWING, ALL-SEEING *DJINNI* HAS DIFFICULTY ATTEMPTING TO

COMPREHEND. IT COULD BE A HUMBLING EXPERI-ENCE, IF I WERE TO HAVE A HUMBLE BONE WITHIN MY BODY, WHICH OF COURSE I DO NOT. SO, WHAT SHALL IT BE? DEATH NOW TO ALL CONCERNED, OR MORE STORY?'

On this, all agreed most readily and instantly. There should be more story.

'SEE?' Ozzie hooted in triumph. 'AREN'T THINGS MUCH MORE PLEASANT WHEN WE ALL AGREE? ESPECIALLY WHEN EVERYONE AGREES WITH ME, FOR I MAKE THE RULES AROUND HERE. MOST EXCELLENT.'

Scheherazade decided it was time for her to raise her voice again.

'Not that I wish to disagree with you,' she began most sweetly, 'for I wish to continue my tale, for, indeed, there are certain subtleties of meaning and intent that will not become apparent until the tale's very conclusion. And I further understand that I might tell this story in its entirety, for somehow you have used your *djinni* magic to suspend time so that none of us need to eat or drink or in other ways attend to the functions of the body. Still, magic or no, any story, no matter how fascinating, may not go on forever. I feel that you sense this as well, and this is the true meaning of your interruptions.'

'THEN YOU AGREE THAT I MAY INTERRUPT?'

'It is not for me to agree or disagree,' Scheherazade replied most reasonably, 'for are you not a *djinni* of almost infinite power?'

'YOU ARE MOST WISE,' Ozzie agreed. He allowed one green hand to materialize so that he might blow contentedly upon his fingernails.

'Then let me show you that wisdom in another way,' the story-teller quickly added. 'I am sure that someone as all-knowing as yourself can see that our audience grows restless despite your magic. Give us a few moments to rest and refresh ourselves. The differences will be remarkable, and worth any minor inconveni-ence that you might suffer. Those around me will be able to listen with new ears. And the words that pour from my tongue will be ever more clear and filled with wonder than those I have spoken before.'

'VERY WELL, IT IS A BARGAIN.'

Achmed spoke for a second with Marjanah, then looked up at the *djinni*. 'Tell us, Harun al Raschid! Perhaps, while we rest, it is time for one of your tales.'

'Really?' the elderly storyteller replied, immediately rising to his feet. 'Let me see. I know a good one. How about "The Tale of the Parrot, the Toad, and the Fart that was Heard all the Way to China?"'

'THEN AGAIN—' Ozzie began.

'I am sure that must be a most excellent tale,' Achmed answered quickly, 'but I was thinking that perhaps we might honor our host's earlier request. Surely, a storyteller as venerable as yourself must know stories in which clever *djinn* better themselves through the use of their powers.'

'I most certainly do!' Harun al Raschid replied most cheerfully.

'WELL,' Ozzie added somewhat grudgingly, 'I SUPPOSE THAT WOULD BE ALL RIGHT.'

'Very well,' the elder replied most merrily, for he was obviously warming to his task, 'I shall begin with "The Tale of the Great *Djinni* Oggog, and the Magic Lamp He Filled with Farts".'

So did Scheherazade move away from her place of honor as another storyteller took over. And she discreetly motioned to Marjanah, as well as Aladdin and Ali Baba, to follow her as she walked to the spring that bubbled up within that cavern so that she, and perhaps the rest of them, might refresh themselves with a drink of water. Even now, she would have only a few minutes available to her, and Scheherazade had to tell as many as possible about what would soon happen, and how they might use it to their advantage.

*Chapter the Twenty-ninth,*
*in which Scheherazade is lost and saved,*
*on any number of occasions.*

So it was that they at last managed to quieten Harun al Raschid after he had told but six different tales of different *djinn* and their magical farts, the first four of which, at least, Ozzie enjoyed quite vociferously. And, when the elder had sat himself down again, Scheherazade at last resumed her tale.

THE TALE OF SCHEHERAZADE IN THE MARKETPLACE
WHEN SHE HAD MET THE WISE WOMAN
AND THEY WERE FURTHER CONFRONTED
BY THAT VENGEFUL *DJINNIA* SULIMA,
AND WHAT HENCEFORTH TRANSPIRED

'Oh, dear,' the wise woman said upon the *djinnia*'s arrival. 'Must we play our part so broadly?'

Sulima stopped mid-cackle to stare at the old woman. 'How dare you question the behavior of a *djinnia*?'

'I question it,' the wise woman said calmly, 'for I know that, upon that exact moment you set foot within this little space that I call home, you shall be instantaneously transported back to that place you would call home yourself. I would – etchasketch – imagine that would be the palace.'

At that, Sulima laughed again. 'What puny powers do you use to turn away a *djinnia*?' She took a step forward. 'Oops.'

And she was gone.

'That was very well done,' Scheherazade said most admiringly.

'That's why they call me the wise woman,' the other agreed. 'But, now that we have given you a minute away from danger, we must lead you upon the next step of your journey.'

'I am upon a journey?' Scheherazade asked, for, until this instant, she had not been precisely sure of her plans.

'You are if you wish to remain alive,' the wise woman replied,

207

"which – Zoomazooma – I see that you do. And to do that, you must now visit the wise woman.'

'But—' Scheherazade began.

'No, I do not mean my sister who dwells within the palace, for she has sent you to me, who has five times as much knowledge as my younger sibling. Nor do I mean myself, sometimes referred to as the other wise woman, for you are still in such danger that even my own extensive knowledge could not guarantee your safety. Now I must send you to another who holds five times as much learning in all things that matter, she who is known as the other other wise woman, the wisest of the wise.'

'Wiser than—' Scheherazade ventured.

'Any other woman? Most certainly.' The wise woman laughed shortly. 'And any other man? We need not even bother speaking that sort of nonsense!'

'Where then—' Scheherazade attempted.

'Will you have to travel next? Only a few feet, but farther than you have ever gone before. We – hullygully – wise women do love paradoxes. Listen closely to what you must do. Go back out to Hassan and ask him for the carpet that goes far away. Do you under – of course you do. Once he has given you this item, sit upon its very center and say the following words: "Fly, carpet! Fly, fly, fly!" Then will the carpet take you where you must go.'

'And once—'

'You reach the third wise woman? Have no fear. She will know every answer before you even have arrived.

'You are most welcome,' the wise woman added before Scheherazade could thank her. 'Now go, and quickly.'

So it was that Scheherazade pushed aside the hanging carpet and reemerged in the sunlight of the marketplace. There before her was Hassan, deep in conversation with a pair of the king's guards. Scheherazade froze upon the spot, like a woman who has seen her own death. Why had the wise woman not told her of this danger?

'What would you look for?' Hassan called out in astonishment. 'I have nothing but carpets here.'

'Still we have orders to search all the stalls,' one of the guards insisted.

Scheherazade attempted to overcome the panic that was within her. Perhaps, if she was quiet, she could hide again behind the carpet.

It was then that the second guard looked straight at her. But he raised no alarm, and she realized why.

It was that same guard who had watched the door of the king's chambers. He smiled ever so slightly for an instant, then turned to his fellow.

'There is no further need to search here,' he announced with great authority. 'On to the next stall.'

The other guard nodded most briefly and both proceeded to their right. Scheherazade paused until the two were lost within the crowds of the market, then walked quickly to Hassan.

'The wise woman has asked me for the carpet from far away,' she said.

'I would expect no less,' was Hassan's reply. He turned and pulled a rug from the very bottom of one of the piles. 'It is here to do with as you wish, although I trust that someday you, and the carpet, shall return.'

Scheherazade thanked the merchant as she looked upon the faded red rug spread before her. It was a carpet which appeared unexceptional in every way, except perhaps that it had been well used over the course of years.

'Are you sure you do not wish to buy that other carpet?' Hassan added with a certain hope. 'It can get very chilly in the upper air.'

But Scheherazade was determined to follow the wise woman's directions most precisely, and so sat on the very middle of the carpet, and said those words that she had been told to repeat.

'Fly, carpet!' she said. 'Fly, fly, fly!'

And the carpet rose, straight into the air.

'May you have a most pleasant journey, my queen!' a voice called from below.

Scheherazade was uncertain if it was the voice of Hassan, or instead that of a certain bold, handsome and self-sacrificing guard.

## Chapter the Thirtieth,
### in which Scheherazade discovers there is more than one kind of palace, and that there are many kinds of danger.

Thus was Scheherazade lifted above her troubles, and indeed above the palace and the entire city which she had always called her home. The carpet lifted her gently but swiftly, first above the merchant's stall, then above the marketplace. For the first moment, Scheherazade could hear calls of surprise and wonder from those in the crowd who looked her way, but the voices were soon lost beneath the rush of the warm summer wind, as she rose so high that the palace and all of the city were spread before her.

The carpet then shifted slightly beneath Scheherazade, and she realized that they were leaving the city behind and flying towards the distant mountains, a journey that she understood would take three days by caravan, but now seemed to take only a matter of minutes. And so comfortable and secure did she feel upon this journey that she ventured to look over the side of her magical conveyance. There, below her, were all the works of man, but so small were they in the bright sunlight that they reminded her of nothing so much as jewels sparkling in a field of brown, so that the fertile and tilled fields looked like nothing so much as deep green emeralds, and the lakes and ocean appeared to be great hunks of turquoise, and the ever-closer mountains seemed to be capped by snow-white pearls.

All the world seemed to be spread before her for her to observe. Scheherazade laughed in delight, and realized that now was the first moment she had had without care since that day she had decided to marry the king. And, as much as she treasured that moment, she realized that, once this carpet had taken her to her destination, she would have to contend again with those who pursued her, as well as her own concerns for her sister and her father, and what might happen to them because of her actions.

The carpet shifted slightly again, and she saw that she was

already far closer to the mountains than she would have imagined. In point of fact, the carpet was already descending with that same swiftness that it had reached its original height, at the same time angling its flight so it now appeared that it would fly straight into a mountain peak.

For the first time since she had begun this strange adventure, Scheherazade felt the slightest amount of trepidation. Still did she reflect upon the words of the wise woman, and, while those words were not always entirely comprehensible, when she could indeed understand them, they always turned out to be true.

Still did they fly straight for the mountain. As they approached, Scheherazade realized they were not flying directly towards the forbidden stand of rock at the very peak, but slightly lower, where a band of trees grew below the snow line. She imagined it might hurt slightly less to smash into a copse of trees rather than a wall of granite, but this somehow seemed to be of little consolation.

She wondered if there was some way to stop or divert this flying carpet, but she feared she might doom herself even more quickly if, for example, she would stop the carpet dead, and it then plummeted from the air to the still-distant ground below. She also considered closing her eyes against her impending doom, but decided that, if these were indeed her last moments upon this earth, she might as well witness them in their entirety.

Still did the carpet fly on without changing course, and still did the trees loom ever closer. She hoped for an instant that the rug might be able to fly between the branches, but the evergreens ahead of her grew so densely together that she could see nothing but a mass of green. Perhaps she would close her eyes after all.

Something groaned ahead. Scheherazade blinked as she saw all those trees upon either side bend to one side or the other, leaving an open space for the carpet to fly. And there, behind the trees, rather than the granite face of the mountain, was a cave large enough for them to enter with ease.

So Scheherazade found herself plunged into darkness as the carpet plummeted within the cave without losing speed in the slightest. She might have screamed at that moment, but the great rush of wind around her prevented her from hearing anything whatsoever.

And then, as swiftly as she had been plunged into darkness, she was brought again into light, as the carpet brought her into what must have been a great internal chamber, lit somehow by glowing stalactites above her. And beneath her was a great palace, so

212

extensive that it might have fit the great home of King Shahryar three times within its walls. And further did the palace shine in the strange light of the cavern, the walls glittering as if they were lined with jewels, and the minarets sparkling as if they were roofed with gold.

The carpet spiraled down towards the floor of the cavern, slowing as it traveled. Scheherazade realized that they were now headed for a clear and flat patch directly before the palace gates. And there, in the area immediately beyond the gate, waited a great quantity of people. No, upon closer inspection, she could be far more specific. They were in actuality a great quantity of women.

'Greetings, Scheherazade!' they all cried in unison as the carpet gently settled back upon the ground.

So, she was expected.

One of the women walked quickly forward. She was quite young, but strode with an authority that spoke of a great confidence.

'We have been waiting most anxiously for your arrival,' the young woman said.

'And I have been waiting most anxiously to arrive,' Scheherazade admitted. 'What is this place that the carpet has brought me to?'

'Ah,' the young woman replied quickly. 'I forget my manners. We welcome you to the Palace of Beautiful Women. I am a fairly recent arrival here myself. My name is Marjanah.'

'The Palace of Beautiful Women?' Scheherazade asked in wonder. 'Is there a story behind that name?'

'There are indeed as many stories behind this palace as there are women living within its walls,' was Marjanah's reply. 'But we do not have time for them at the moment, for I have been sent by the wise woman. I am to bring you before her immediately.'

'Ah,' Scheherazade agreed, 'I shall see the wise woman at once. Am I then to learn of my fate?'

'It is more complicated than that, most noble Scheherazade,' Marjanah replied most soberly. 'Now that you have arrived, every one of us within the palace shall learn of our fates.'

*Chapter the Thirty-first,*
*in which a wise woman gets ahead of herself,*
*not to mention everyone else.*

'This is a most magnificent place,' Scheherazade said as Marjanah led her through the gate and up the marble path to the palace. 'It is, however, most unusual.'

'Yes,' Marjanah replied as she looked up at the jewel-encrusted front of the great structure before them, which was at least a hundred cubits in height and twice as wide. 'The Palace of Beautiful Women is no doubt unique, not only for its size, appearance and location, but also for the fact that it was created by the very cave we now see around us.'

'Then this cave we are now within is a thinking being?' Scheherazade asked in astonishment.

'You could call it that,' Marjanah said with a great dryness of tone. 'It certainly is a talking being. It calls itself Mordrag.'

'*Pleased to make your acquaintance,*' came a great, deep, booming voice from high above them. '*There is always room for another beauty.*'

'Mayhaps I should say *he* calls himself Mordrag,' Marjanah added, 'for does not that sound exactly like a male?'

'Mordrag?' Scheherazade asked with a frown. She looked towards the ceiling, but could see no particular point from which the voice might have originated. 'What does he want from us?'

'Apparently,' Marjanah answered, 'simply to keep us here. We are well fed in this place, and offered many pleasant diversions, but we are prisoners and cannot leave. He does ask us for occasional entertainments, dancing, perhaps, or storytelling. But far less than has been asked of us by any other male.'

'And that is all?' Scheherazade asked in astonishment. 'It seems beyond comprehension.'

Marjanah paused to turn to the storyteller. 'Indeed, Scheherazade, but think upon this. Who among us can truly comprehend the mind of any man?'

Well, Scheherazade agreed silently, that was most certainly true. Aloud, she further asked, 'Then am I too a prisoner here?'

'No,' Marjanah answered before she turned back to the path, 'I believe you are our salvation.' She mounted the marble stairs, which were lined with borders of rubies all of the deepest reds. 'The wise woman will be able to explain it much better than I.'

They walked in silence then through the great hall that led into the palace, and indeed words would have been lost to Scheherazade when she gazed upon the decorations and trappings within this palace, for they were to the designs within Shahryar's palace as that palace might have been to a hut made of sticks and mud. So were there animals portrayed in great murals along each wall, and each animal was etched in precious metals and jewels, so that a tiger was formed from gold and onyx, a sweet dove in flight from diamonds, and a peacock's tail seemed to contain every form of gem that Scheherazade had ever seen. There was similar wealth apparent in the tapestries in the wall, which had gold and gems woven into every picture, and in the statues that graced the corners and even the great candelabrums that lit the hall.

'Mordrag spares no expense,' Marjanah commented at last. 'Actually, I believe he has a tendency to overdo.'

It was true. Surrounded by nothing but gold and a glitter, Scheherazade felt her head begin to hurt. After a while, she imagined, one might grow used to the glare, if one was trapped here for a great enough time. She thought again about her guide informing her that all the women here were being held captive. Must a woman be a prisoner, no matter where she traveled?

As they proceeded down the hall, they passed a number of doorways, and each door led to a room full of ornate furniture, and various other opulent appointments. And in each of these rooms crowds of women would look out as they passed, and all would hail Scheherazade with greetings.

'So all here know of my arrival?' Scheherazade asked.

'When all are trapped within a palace that is itself within a cave,' was Marjanah's reply, 'a new arrival is great news indeed.'

They passed yet another room filled with well-wishers. Scheherazade turned back to her guide. 'How many women are there here?'

'Hundreds at the very least. The palace is so great that it would be nearly impossible to make an exact count. And, of course, there are new arrivals whenever Mordrag's agents can supply them.'

'Then not everyone arrives by carpet?'

216

'No, most arrive as I did, kidnapped by thieves and brought here in return for – what?' Marjanah paused to frown. 'That I do not know. But whatever drives these thieves, it must be great indeed, for you see their successful achievement all around us.'

They reached a broad marble stair. 'We must climb here,' Marjanah explained, 'for the wise woman dwells in the innermost recesses of the palace.'

So they climbed past floor after floor, each one furnished in the most extravagant of styles, although one floor's furnishings would be primarily of silver, and the next of gold, and the third all of pearl. When they reached this floor, Marjanah announced, 'Now we must travel deeper still within the palace.'

They traveled down a smaller hallway than the one below, but the designs upon the wall were no less opulent, for they were composed of the largest pearls that Scheherazade had ever seen. Now, at the end of this hallway was a further doorway, and that doorway led to an enclosed garden, whose top was open to the air above.

'It is here where the wise woman dwells,' Marjanah explained as she again led the way.

They stepped through the doorway, and Scheherazade realized that what she thought would be a garden was not a garden at all. Rather, it was little more than a mound of dirt, from which grew a few small bits of moss and lichen, not to mention a mushroom or two. The walls of this enclosure were painted black as well, to make this interior seem even darker than it might otherwise.

'Nothing much grows underground, besides those odd trees and bushes before the palace, but those are Mordrag's doing,' Marjanah explained with a note of apology in her voice. 'The wise woman prefers to have as little to do with Mordrag as possible. Come, she is at the top—'

But the remainder of Marjanah's sentence was lost beneath the prodigious wailing that descended from above, telling Scheherazade the wise woman's precise location. The storyteller and Marjanah climbed the hill side-by-side.

At the very top of this mound of dirt there seemed to be a flat plateau. It was from that plateau that Scheherazade next heard the voice of the wise woman.

'Greetings – winstonchurch – Scheherazade! Yes, I am the – mauricecheva – the wise woman, and you did notice that I greatly resemble those other two, lesser wise women! Well, of course – howdydoo – they are both my sisters! And no – buzzal –

I don't think that should be a problem, but I appreciate your concern.'

So this wise woman had answered Scheherazade's first half dozen questions before the storyteller had even set eyes upon her! Scheherazade only wished she knew what some of those questions had concerned.

Actually, the upper reaches of the dirt pile were quite well illuminated by the glowing stalactites overhead. So it was that the two women who climbed the hill finally came upon a third woman who was even more amazingly frail and thin than those other wise women Scheherazade had previously consulted. And the quivering of her arms and head appeared even worse that that of the others as well, and the blue veins beneath her skin were so prominent that they appeared almost to glow in the spectral cavern light, and her grimaces as she spouted nonsense words were as filled with spasmodic pain as anything Scheherazade had ever seen. Truly, from appearances alone, this woman should be the wisest among the wise.

'Forgive me – bugsbun – but I sometimes see so far into the future that I lose all around me. Sometimes I even lose myself – colonelsan – what was I saying?'

Perhaps, Scheherazade thought, if she were actually to speak her desire, it might help to focus the concerns of all of them.

'I am—' she began.

'Of course,' the wise woman interjected. 'Foolish of – normanschwarz – me to forget. You will be the savior of all those trapped within the Palace of Beautiful Woman, and you will do it with your own talents.'

'Sav—' Scheherazade began, but stopped to sputter, 'My own tal—'

'Certainly – charlesde – and I do not think that next is a foolish question either. Those forces rallied against you will find this cave in the not too distant future. It is difficult for me to look so briefly ahead, but their very numbers will lead to some interesting conclusions.'

'Then you—'

'Have known that you would be coming for quite some time? But did nothing to remove you from your situation with King Shahryar? You must understand. For things to work properly, we must wait for that time when you yourself are ready to join us. I may be able to read the future, but a wise woman certainly knows enough not to toy with Destiny.'

'But—' Scheherazade attempted.

'In answer to your next six questions, yes, yes, no, yes, no, and only with parsley. Now that I have got those out of the way, please listen, for I have certain important lessons to impart.'

'What quest—' Scheherazade once again started, but the wise woman raised one quivering hand for silence.

'Many have said, and it is true that no man controls his Destiny,' the elder began, 'for, after all, do not women control it for him? On the most simple level, what would a man not do for his mother, his daughter, or his beloved? Not that men need to know this, for, by and large, they make much less of a fuss when we pretend to let them run things. Occasionally, this illusion of power will grow out of hand, and must be redressed, but most subtly, so that the men do not suspect the true nature of things.'

Until this moment, Scheherazade herself had not suspected the true nature of things. But, upon a certain reflection, it made a great deal of sense.

'There are, of course,' the wise woman continued, 'far more potent weapons – marilynmon – that we females may use than say, mother love or a daughter's devotion. And the time that is coming may be an occasion where we must use every weapon in our female arsenal. But there is one thing that you, of all of us, must re-member. The greatest power comes from that you already know, and do so well.'

With that, the wise woman's gaze left Scheherazade and rose to the great ceiling of the cavern. 'That is all that I have to tell you. You may go now. I look forward to what I have already seen.'

Scheherazade wondered if half the reason such elders as this had such a reputation as wise women was that they also were so cryptic? Still, as there was no more to be gained by staying here, she allowed Marjanah to lead her from this austere pile of dirt back within the over-opulent palace, and thence to find an unoccupied room where she might rest from her travels. Marjanah suggested they look upon the opal floor, where she believed there might still be an unoccupied wing.

Before they could reach their goal, however, the air around them was filled with the sound of bells.

'It is the alarm!' Marjanah informed Scheherazade.

'Does that mean danger?' the storyteller asked in turn.

'Perhaps,' Marjanah agreed after a fashion. 'What it means more exactly is that we've been invaded by a group of men!'

*Chapter the Thirty-second,*
*in which past and present come into ever closer*
*proximity, and the future cannot be far behind.*

## OZZIE BEGINS TO FRET

'WHAT IS THIS ABOUT THE POWER OF WOMEN?' Ozzie bellowed to interrupt the flow of the narrative.

'Pardon?' Scheherazade asked, for she was always startled by interruptions, and none could be more startling than an angry, floating green head.

'WHAT THE WISE WOMAN SAID,' Ozzie continued, his anger now simmering down to petulance. 'ABOUT THE FE-MALE ONLY ALLOWING THE MALE AN ILLUSION OF POWER. DOES THAT APPLY FOR EVERY SPECIES?'

'Oh, you mean in my tale?' Scheherazade replied in the calmest of tones. 'That illusion is nothing more than a storyteller's device. But you must wait to the end of my tale before you may see how artfully I have woven this theme into the whole.'

'OH,' Ozzie replied, as if he even now did not quite understand. 'PARDON ME. OF COURSE, WHAT ELSE WOULD IT BE? YOU MAY CONTINUE.'

'Very well,' she agreed as she passed a small note to Marjanah. The two women had been passing these notes back and forth now for some little time, since somewhere in the midst of the tale of the three fishes, and Ozzie did not seem to mind. Indeed, as long as Scheherazade continued to tell her tale, Ozzie did not even seem to notice. 'So do I return to my tale,' she added.

## SCHEHERAZADE CONTINUES HER TALE OF THE PALACE OF BEAUTIFUL WOMEN, A STRUCTURE QUITE CLOSE TO THAT PLACE WHERE ALL OUR HEROES NOW RESIDE

## EXCEPT OZZIE INTERRUPTS ONE MORE TIME

* * *

'WAIT A MOMENT BEFORE YOU BEGIN,' Ozzie again objected.

'Is there some other point that you wish to discuss?' asked Scheherazade with remarkable patience.

'IN THE INTRODUCTION TO YOUR STORY, PRE-CISELY WHO DO YOU MEAN BY "HEROES"?'

'Why,' the storyteller remarked most sweetly, 'it is simply another way of referring to the principals within my tale.'

'PRINCIPALS?' Ozzie asked with somewhat more satisfaction. 'THEN THAT MIGHT INCLUDE *DJINN* AS WELL?'

'Most certainly,' Scheherazade agreed with the most gracious of smiles. 'Any deserving *djinni* may be a hero.'

'VERY WELL,' the *djinni* said, his voice swelling with a certain arrogance. 'I JUST WISHED TO DEMONSTRATE WHO WAS IN CONTROL HERE.'

'And you have done so most admirably,' Scheherazade answered, if possible, even more pleasantly than she had before. She received a note in return from Marjanah, and glanced at it most briefly before she added, 'May I continue?'

'PLEASE DO.'

'I believe I shall do so most directly.'

## THE TALE IS RESUMED WITHOUT ANY FURTHER INTRODUCTION

So it was that Marjanah and Scheherazade descended the stairs to get a better look at the commotion.

'Are men often upon these premises?'

'This is the first time since I have arrived,' Marjanah confessed. 'I do not believe they are allowed hereabouts with any great frequency.'

From the tremendous commotion that rose from the great hall below them, Scheherazade would imagine that men were a rarity indeed.

'I suppose that Mordrag does truly not provide for everything,' she remarked.

'Yes,' said another, a well-dressed woman who was climbing those same stairs the others were descending, 'but there is such a thing as decorum.'

'Ah, Scheherazade,' Marjanah remarked, 'may I introduce Princess Badabadur. She was captured at much the same time as myself.'

'After being fooled by a lamp salesman who fancied himself a magician!' she remarked disdainfully. 'But that is another story.'

'I am sure there are a great many here who have interesting stories,' Scheherazade agreed, thinking that, if nothing else, she might be able to use this place to rekindle her failing imagination.

'But what transpires below?' Marjanah asked with a smile.

'Certain of our sisters, desperate for male companionship, have allowed their desires to overcome their better judgement,' the princess explained. 'Some dozens of them are below unclothing our visitors.'

'It is most disgraceful,' Marjanah agreed. 'Could it be anyone we know?'

'Well,' the princess replied, 'I could not be certain, but I believe I saw Fatima down there among the front ranks.'

## THE TALE IS INTERRUPTED BY ANOTHER

'Fatima?' Sinbad called from that place where he had again sat in the audience. 'Then she is here after all?'

'Oh, most certainly somewhere hereabouts,' Scheherazade agreed. 'It simply depends whether she is among those tens of hundreds of women yonder in the audience or the palace beyond.'

'I must locate her at once!' Sinbad stood, looking wildly about him. 'It has been my one life's goal to find her. So I swear!'

'Now, master.' The young man known as Achmed slapped the other upon the back. 'It has not been your only life's goal.'

'Well,' Sinbad admitted, 'I've also been escaping from the Queen of the Apes, of course. But that is not so much of a goal as it is born of desperation.'

'But you have already found the Queen of the Apes here once,' Achmed pointed out, 'by hardly looking at all.'

Sinbad shivered violently. 'That is quite true. There will be a more auspicious time to look for Fatima. I will resume my seat.'

'And I will resume my tale.'

## SCHEHERAZADE ONCE AGAIN MANAGES TO RESURRECT HER TALE OF THAT TIME WHEN THE PALACE OF BEAUTIFUL WOMEN FIRST FOUND MEN

'Unfortunately,' Princess Badabadur remarked, 'while these may be the first living men in known memory to enter the Palace of Beautiful Women, from the manner in which the welcoming committee is ripping their clothes from their bodies, these men will not be among the living for long.'

Another approached them up the stairs, a slim woman with especially fine hands and dainty feet. 'This welcoming is beyond me,' she said to those gathered above her. 'Never have I seen such savagery.'

'This is the fair Fatima,' Marjanah introduced the newcomer in turn, 'who, alas, has lost in love.'

'And I suppose,' Fatima replied, 'that the rest of you are above this sort of thing?'

'I am pledged to brave Aladdin,' the princess acknowledged, 'who through the clever use of a pair of *djinn* has won my love, although I am quite certain that I shall never see him again.'

'And I am promised to clever Achmed,' Marjanah added, 'whose bright tongue is second only to his sweet lips.'

Scheherazade, however, was sadly silent. She wished she could share the same endearments for her own husband. But, while she had begun to feel a certain fondness for King Shahryar's well-meaning gestures in his brief periods of sanity, the combination of his mother's enchanted swords and Sulima's dread spells seemed to have guaranteed that the king would never visit sanity again.

'I should never have expected you to share my feelings,' Fatima admitted. 'It is hopeless, sisters. You were not kept in a palanquin for months at a time, a promised gift to a distant monarch, a woman who further, due to shipwreck and misadventure, never reached her goal. I feel that my longings will never be requited!'

'Wait a moment!' Princess Badabadur exclaimed. 'I thought I heard another sound above those women's shrieks.'

Marjanah moved to a nearby window and stared off into the distance before she replied most excitedly. 'It is even more men. And this time, I believe I recognize some of them as our fine companions. Do you know what this means?'

'Most certainly,' Fatima agreed, the hope returned to her voice. 'Soon there will be more than enough men to go around.'

## Chapter the Thirty-third
### in which the story becomes more complicated for everyone concerned.

What more could there be?

Scheherazade thought it best to connect her tales to the others.

'What happened next you will all more or less agree upon. The men had arrived and recruited those three eunuchs, whose life work it was to guard Princess Badabadur, into their cause, even though they had to battle the minions of the dread bandit One-Thumb in order to do so. However, Mordrag the cavern would not let those women within the palace go without a battle of his own, so he in turn reanimated a number of corpses that the men who would rescue us had already killed, which Kassim, or at least his disembodied head, attempted to control with no luck whatsoever.

'It was at this juncture the hidden trap door to the adjacent cavern full of treasure was discovered, and Aladdin reclaimed the ring and the lamp, both of which held separate *djinn*. So were the two *djinn* released to fight Mordrag, except that, since lamp *djinn* have very little respect for ring *djinn* and vice versa, their fight was ineffectual at best.

'So it was that Mordrag decided that all of the humans had become too much trouble. He would crush us all and start with a brand new Palace of Beautiful Women. And so he would have, if Ali Baba had not discovered that bottle which contained Ozzie.

'When the woodcutter released this *djinni*, Ozzie made short work of the enchanted cavern, causing Mordrag to fall into a deep sleep for a hundred years. And Ozzie, clever spirit that he was, also further trapped his two fellow *djinn* in the jar from which he had originated, thus insuring no further competition within the cavern. Also, since the jar was now filled, there would be no way for anyone to lure him back inside.

'However, this is not the end of the tale, for in his imprisonment,

227

Ozzie had heard of the cavern's love for storytelling, and this sounded like a fine diversion to the *djinni* as well.

'So it was that Ozzie declared that he would not kill all of us, at least not quite yet, until three of us, Sinbad, who was once a porter, Ali Baba, the woodcutter who met the forty thieves, and myself, humble Scheherazade, were to tell stories. And if those stories were of significant drama and wonder, the noble Ozzie would then free us all.'

'VERY NICE,' Ozzie thundered. 'FOR THAT SUMMARY ALONE, I SHALL LET ALL OF YOU LIVE FOR ANOTHER QUARTER HOUR. IN FACT, YOUR STORY WAS SO FILLED WITH MARVELS, THAT I AM ALMOST TEMPTED TO LET ALL YOU HUMANS LIVE AND GO FREE. ALMOST, I SAID, BUT NOT QUITE.' The upper reaches of the cavern rumbled with the *djinni*'s laughter.

'But noble *djinni*,' Scheherazade protested, 'that is not truly the end of the tale.'

'WHAT, THEN,' Ozzie roared in great displeasure, 'WILL THIS TALE LAST FOREVER?'

'No,' Scheherazade replied. 'It is nearly done. But in preparation for the final story, I shall tell you a tale of your future.'

'YOU WILL CONTINUE ONLY IF I GIVE YOU PERMISSION!' Ozzie insisted in the most ominous of tones.

'If you say so, oh most powerful sir,' Scheherazade said most meekly, as befitted her sex and station, 'but I did so want to tell the following tale:'

### THE TALE OF THE GREAT *DJINNI* OZZIE, AND HOW HE BECAME KING OF EVERYTHING

She paused to look up at the great green head.

'OH. WELL, I SUPPOSE AN EDUCATIONAL STORY OF THAT SORT WOULD BE MORE THAN ADEQUATE.' The *djinni* coughed delicately. 'SIMPLY BE SURE TO EMBELLISH IT PROPERLY.'

'Ah,' Scheherazade replied. 'Do you mean in this fashion?'

### THAT FINAL TALE OF THE MIGHTIEST OF THE MIGHTY; THE MAGNIFICENT *DJINNI* OZZIE

WHOSE NAME MEN MIGHT FEAR FOREVER,
AND HOW, THROUGH HIS OWN CLEVERNESS,
HE BECAME MASTER OF ALL THINGS,
ARBITER OF THE FATES OF ALL LESSER BEINGS,
AND SUPREME RULER BESIDES

'YES,' Ozzie replied, 'I THINK YOU ARE BEGINNING TO GET THE SPIRIT OF IT.'

'Very well,' Scheherazade replied. 'If I might continue?'

THE ACTUAL TALE,
WHICH IS SO FILLED WITH SUPERLATIVES THAT
TO SPEAK THE TITLE TOO OFTEN
WOULD OVERLY DAZZLE THE LISTENER,
BEGINS HERE

'Aha!' another, female voice cried from overhead to interrupt the story before it had ever begun. 'I have found you at last!'

'WHAT?' Ozzie cried out in frustration. 'WE CAN'T HAVE ANY INTERRUPTIONS! NOT NOW, WHEN WE'RE BARELY GETTING TO THE GOOD PARTS!'

But directly across from the great green head there formed an equally great black cloud. 'You have not yet dealt with Sulima. I will not be denied!'

'IS THAT SO?' Ozzie replied with a great haughtiness of tone. 'I'LL HAVE YOU KNOW I'M EXACTLY THE TYPE TO DENY YOU.'

The cloud wasted no time in resolving itself into the black-clad yet very shapely form of Sulima the sorceress.

'THEN AGAIN,' Ozzie further remarked, 'CANNOT WE GO SOMEWHERE AND TALK?'

Sulima smiled at this, and it was an expression that froze Scheherazade's blood.

'Why do we need to go anywhere,' Sulima said most seductively, 'when I can dance for you at this very moment?'

Scheherazade used this opportunity to give yet another instruction to Marjanah before quickly calling up to the *djinni*, 'If you pause at every interruption, I shall never be able to finish my tale!'

'YES,' Ozzie agreed as he pulled his gaze from the *djinnia* and once again regarded the hundreds of humans beneath him, 'YOU ARE QUITE CORRECT. ALL THINGS SHALL HAVE THEIR TIME AND PLACE. I MUST HEAR THIS FINAL, MOST INTERESTING STORY BEFORE I KILL ALL THOSE INDIVIDUALS BENEATH ME IN A MOST LINGERING, HORRIBLE AND PAINFUL MANNER. AFTER THIS MINOR MATTER IS ATTENDED TO, I SHALL HAVE TIME APLENTY TO LISTEN TO THIS *DJINNIA*'S CONCERNS AND EVEN TO WATCH HER DANCE.'

'Men!' Sulima managed to spit out the word, even though it did not contain a single 's' sound. 'I am not here to satisfy your pitiful needs, for my needs are supreme. Rather, I am here to prove the natural superiority of a *djinnia* to a pathetic, swelled green head!'

Ozzie became greatly incensed at this remark, partly from the effrontery of it, and partly from the ragged cheering that the effrontery brought from some quarters of the Palace of Beautiful Women.

'YOU DARE TO SUGGEST THAT YOU MIGHT MURDER THESE INSIGNIFICANT HUMANS,' Ozzie thundered most imperiously, 'WHO I HAVE SO LOOKED FORWARD TO DESTROYING IN A MOST VENGEFUL AND HIDEOUS MANNER?'

'No,' Sulima remarked with an equal haughtiness, 'I will kill only Scheherazade, for she has foiled my plans for far too long. The rest I will simply make eternal slaves to my will. And, within that group, you shall be my easiest conquest!'

The crowd below was once again becoming restive, for, under this most recent plan, even though the majority of them would not be killed, still there was that matter of becoming eternal slaves.

'If you two are eternally to argue up there, perhaps I should forget about my story completely,' Scheherazade remarked, 'which of course could be retitled:

'THE MOST MAGNIFICENT TALE
OF THE GREAT *DJINNI* OZZIE,
AND HOW HE SUBJUGATED
THE LOVELY BUT WEAK SULIMA
TO HIS WILL SO THAT SHE MIGHT BE AT HIS SIDE
AFTER HE CONQUERED THE WORLD.'

\* \* \*

'MOST EXCELLENT!' Ozzie agreed most heartily. 'HERE, TRULY, IS A STORYTELLER WITH FORESIGHT! I MUST HEAR THIS STORY AT ONCE!'

But Sulima was not amused. 'It is a pity that you will have to hear the tale with dead ears, for I fear that I will have to kill two here today.'

But Ozzie only laughed. 'IT IS NOT AS SIMPLE AS THAT!'

'I should say not!' said another new voice. Scheherazade turned to see a number of guards climbing out of a hole in the ground in front of the palace to surround the Sultana and her two sons, Shahzaman and Shahryar.

'It was good of you, Sulima, to find this vile woman Scheherazade for us,' the Sultana chortled triumphantly. 'Now our superior forces will crush you both!'

It was at this juncture that the women in the audience began actively to complain.

'Who are all these people?' said one.

'This was once a quiet little palace,' added another.

'This sort of thing never would have happened when Mordrag was in charge,' a third agreed.

'Where did they come from?' Scheherazade asked.

'Oh,' Marjanah said matter-of-factly. 'I imagine there is a trap door there.'

'Oh.' Scheherazade was beginning to understand. 'Much like the passage that I entered through?'

'Quite so,' Marjanah agreed. 'They seem to be littered all over the cavern. It is very easy to get into this place.'

'But,' Princess Badabadur added, 'at least when Mordrag was in charge, it was absolutely impossible to leave.'

And still did the troops of Shahryar and Shahzaman pour onto the palace grounds. Scheherazade imagined that the Sultana had brought every man they could find. If this were the case, it meant that a certain bold, handsome, and in many other ways highly desirable guard would no doubt be among them. Ah, well, Scheherazade sighed. If luck was with her, she would get to see him one final time before she died.

But she must not think this way. The wise woman had given her certain advice which had in its turn led Scheherazade to develop certain ideas. She knew well that it was within a storyteller's power to manipulate fact and opinion in certain ways in order to shade the outcome of a story. Scheherazade hoped she could use some of this hard-won skill in negotiating what was ahead of her.

So far as she could see, she was being visited by not one or two but three different ways to die, two of which wished her death most actively. She was further surrounded by some hundreds of lonely women, many of whom had for years been kept in forced seclusion, along with numerous soldiers and the last ragtag remains of a couple of bands of thieves and cutthroats. And everyone about her seemed about to leap into battle with everyone else.

This meant, essentially, that everything was going according to plan, thanks to certain written exchanges she had made with her fellow adventurers. And yet they were missing one final element.

Achmed, Aladdin and Ali Baba all gathered around Scheherazade. Sinbad joined them a moment later, muttering an apology concerning his search for Fatima. All of them were trained swordsmen, thanks to their earlier adventures, and quite able to repel at least the first attack of the guards. Not that Scheherazade thought it would actually come to that. If Sulima and the Sultana were to attack her, it would no doubt be with the same sort of sorcery they had thrown at her before.

'I have no more time to waste with foolish, overgrown *djinn*,' Sulima declared. 'I will now cast a spell to turn Scheherazade into a garden slug to be crushed beneath my feet!'

'You will never be able to complete your spell, vile witch,' the Sultana retorted, 'for I have equipped both my sons with enchanted swords, and one will slay you as the other murders Scheherazade.'

And Scheherazade saw that both Shahzaman and Shahryar had been given one of those swords that had appeared to have a will of their own. Shahzaman stared at the weapon before him, and his hair appeared to be matted with sweat.

Shahryar, upon the other hand, was swinging his weapon about with abandon, and had already managed to cut substantial portions out of two guardsmen who had had the misfortune of standing too close. The king smiled and drooled quite contentedly.

'NONE OF YOU WILL MOVE ANYWHERE!' Ozzie announced as he furrowed his great brow. And Sulima froze in mid-gesture, although Scheherazade could see anger flashing in her eyes at the sorcerous imprisonment. And the Sultana was similarly frozen, as were the two swords of the kings, so that, no matter how Shahzaman and Shahryar might tug and push and twist them, they would not move.

'WE SHALL HAVE SOME PEACE HERE, AT LEAST FOR THE MOMENT,' Ozzie announced. 'SCHEHERAZADE. YOU MUST TELL YOUR STORY, NOW.'

Ah, this was it, then; the final element of the plan.

And Scheherazade began to tell the most important story of her young life.

*Chapter the Thirty-fourth,*
*in which the storyteller begins*
*an adventure beyond description.*

THE TALE OF THE GREAT *DJINNI*, OZZIE,
MOST HONORED OF ALL HIS KIND,
AND HOW HE CONTROLLED ALL THOSE AROUND
HIM,
EVEN THE MOST POWERFUL SULIMA,
A *DJINNIA* OF AWESOME ABILITY,
AND THE VENGEFUL SULTANA,
WHO HAS BROUGHT BOTH HER SONS,
SHAHZAMAN AND SHAHRYAR,
KINGS IN THEIR OWN RIGHT,
TO HELP CONDUCT HER FEARSOME RETRIBUTION,
SO THAT SCHEHERAZADE MIGHT FINALLY FIND
THE PEACE AND CONCENTRATION TO CONCLUDE
HER PROPHETIC TALE OF HOW THAT SAME OZZIE
MIGHT EXPERIENCE A MOST GLORIOUS
AND UNEXPECTED FUTURE
WHERE HE MIGHT ETERNALLY RULE ALL
THAT HE SURVEYS

'YES,' Ozzie remarked, his smile turned to a grimace of concentration. 'THAT WILL DO QUITE NICELY. NOW, IF WE MIGHT GET ON WITH THE TALE?'
'Oh, most certainly,' Scheherazade replied demurely.

SO DOES THE STORYTELLER
RETURN TO THE MOST AWESOME
OF ALL HER TALES
SO FULL OF WONDER THAT
IT WOULD MAKE ANY LISTENER
FORGET ANY OF THOSE OTHER STORIES
SHE HAS TOLD PREVIOUSLY,

235

### AND SO DOES SHE CONTINUE
### MOST PRUDENTLY
### AND WITHOUT FURTHER DELAY

'Once was there a great *djinni*, who had lived a thousand years and more, and so had gained great wisdom. For, not since a series of unfortunate incidents with King Solomon, had there been a *djinni* of such great power and resource.'

'YOU HAVE SPOKEN QUITE ENOUGH ABOUT KING SOLOMON,' Ozzie interrupted.

'Yet this is the first time I have mentioned Solomon and the *djinn*,' Scheherazade replied in all innocence, 'save for that earlier story that I related.'

'AND A GROSS EXAGGERATION IT WAS, TOO,' Ozzie insisted. 'I'LL HAVE YOU KNOW THAT I WAS NOT A PRISONER FOR MORE THAN TWO OR THREE HUNDRED YEARS.'

'Very well,' Scheherazade replied. 'There will be no more mention of the great King Solomon and how he subjugated and humiliated all of the race of *djinn*, for that was in the past, and we are now concerned with your future.'

'MUCH – BETTER,' Ozzie replied. His voice was even beginning to show a certain fatigue.

'So, shall I return to my story?'

### THE TALE OF THE MOST MAGNIFICENT OZZIE,
### WHO DOES NOT WISH FURTHER TO REMEMBER
### CERTAIN EMBARRASSING INCIDENTS IN THE PAST
### CONCERNING KING SOLOMON
### AND HIS TRIUMPH OVER ALL THE *DJINN*,
### SO THAT WE WILL CONCENTRATE
### INSTEAD UPON OZZIE'S GLORIOUS FUTURE,
### FEATURING HIS SUBJUGATION OF
### THE BEAUTIFUL SULIMA
### AS WELL AS THE AGED, INFIRM,
### PERHAPS EVEN DODDERING
### YET TYRANNICAL SULTANA
### AND HER TWO SONS,
### ONE OF WHOM IS SURELY DEMENTED

At that, certain of the guardsmen around the frozen Sultana and the ineffectual kings started to mutter darkly among themselves, and looked capable of acting independently from their rulers.

'One move towards Queen Scheherazade,' called Kassim from where he was piled within the bags at Ali Baba's feet, 'and I will have my brother throw my many parts upon you, and I shall bleed all over you!'

The guards appeared not to know what to make of this, but the very unsettled nature of the threat was enough to make them lose their nerve.

'Men!' an authoritative voice broke through their ranks. 'There is obviously great sorcery at work here. While the two kings that we follow, as well as their beloved mother, seem inconvenienced by these spells, none appear to be in immediate danger. I believe we should exercise caution in our actions, so that we might not jeopardize them further!'

Scheherazade recognized that voice, and soon saw a certain bold and handsome head and shoulders to go with it. So she had seen him one more time. But she vowed now it would not be her last.

'CAN – WE – GET – ON – WITH – THIS?' Ozzie insisted. 'OR I SHALL BE FORCED TO TAKE – DRASTIC MEASURES!'

'Well, if you must,' Scheherazade agreed, 'although I was about to tell you of the clever way that you subjugated Sulima and bent her to your will so that she was devoted to you for life, if perhaps a touch more addled than she is at present.'

'DO – TELL,' was all Ozzie could manage.

And so Scheherazade resumed:

THE TALE OF OZZIE CONTINUES
PAST ALL THAT UNNECESSARY INTRODUCTORY
MATERIAL
AND PROCEEDS DIRECTLY TO ITS MEATIEST
PORTION,
IN WHICH OZZIE OVERCOMES
THE TOO PROUD *DJINNIA*,
AND RESTORES HIS FAITH IN MALE SUPERIORITY
WHILE TEACHING HER A LESSON
SHE WILL NEVER FORGET

Scheherazade thought she heard the most muffled of screams of rage from the direction of Sulima, but it was soon lost beneath the *djinni*'s laughter. But Ozzie's chuckle was interrupted in turn by a new commotion as three eunuchs carried forth a stretcher which bore a woman old enough to cause the Sultana to appear middle aged.

'WHO IS THIS?' Ozzie demanded.

'Well,' Scheherazade replied. 'It is no wonder I can never finish my tale if you continue to interrupt me.'

'OH,' Ozzie replied. 'SORRY.'

'You know,' someone in the restive crowd remarked, 'this entertainment isn't up to the sort of thing we used to get with Mordrag.'

'How true,' another agreed, 'but some of those guardsmen over there are kind of cute.'

'Very well, Scheherazade continued. 'I will resume my story in earnest. And this time I do not wish to be interrupted by anyone.'

## THE TRUE HEART OF THE TALE OF OZZIE, AND HOW HE IN A GREAT MOMENT OF INSPIRATION MANAGED TO HUMILIATE THE *DJINNIA* SULIMA SO THAT SHE LOST WHAT LITTLE HONOR SHE HAD, AND FURTHER DID HE TAKE ALL POWER AWAY FROM THE SELF-IMPORTANT SULTANA AS WELL AS THE TWO SWINE MASQUERADING AS HER SONS

'No spell is enough to restrain me from that abuse!' Sulima screamed as she shook herself free of Ozzie's powers.

'WAIT A MOMENT!' Ozzie bellowed.

But his moment was lost, for the Sultana shook herself free in turn as her two sons each managed to regain control of their frozen swords.

'No one can say such things about us!' the Sultana screamed. 'I cannot bear such humiliation. Kill them all!'

Shahzaman shouted in rage as Shahryar gibbered. The two kings advanced upon their twin targets, followed by their loyal guards.

'I WILL HAVE THIS UNDER CONTROL IN AN INSTANT!' Ozzie asserted.

'Kassim!' Scheherazade shouted. 'Ali Baba! Now is the time!'

The bag at Ali Baba's feet popped open. The woodcutter pulled forth a certain jar.

'I will kill the *djinni* first,' Sulima announced, 'so that I may take that time with Scheherazade to repay her for her lies!'

'BUT I MUST SUBJUGATE YOU—' Ozzie began.

'My sons will deal with the women, cutting out their lives with those cursed swords,' the Sultana asserted. 'In the meantime, I know of certain very unpleasant spells to use on *djinn*.'

'IT IS IN THE TALE!' Ozzie insisted.

Shahzaman ran purposefully towards Sulima while Shahryar skipped merrily towards Scheherazade, slashing the air jauntily with his sword. This time, the shout came from the wise woman at Scheherazade's side. 'Open it – richardnix – now!'

And Ali Baba pulled the cork from a certain jar.

# Chapter the Thirty-fifth,
## in which many things break loose,
## including the plot.

The center of that great room was filled with swirling smoke.

'Who dares?' Sulima asked.

'CURSES!' Ozzie realized.

'I can't see a thing!' the Sultana complained.

In an instant, however, the smoke had solidified into two great *djinn*, one as pale as alabaster, the second as dark as onyx.

'OH, BOTHER!' Ozzie further remarked. 'CANNOT ANYTHING BE SIMPLE IN THIS PLACE? NOW I HAVE TO TRAP YOU IN THE BOTTLE ALL OVER AGAIN.'

'I think not,' said the onyx *djinni* in the most polite tones. 'What say you, brother?'

'My thoughts are as yours, my dearest friend,' the pale spirit replied with equal affability.

'No, rather we shall work together to defeat you,' the dark *djinni* added as he nodded most cheerfully at Ozzie.

'And entrap you within that bottle for the rest of time,' his companion continued with equal merriment.

'YOU ARE WORKING TOGETHER?' Ozzie cried out in astonishment. 'BUT YOU HATED EACH OTHER!'

The two *djinn* paused to glance at each other most fondly. 'It is amazing what time together in the confines of a jar may do to bring you close,' they said, seemingly in the same voice.

'I WILL NOT BE DENIED!' Ozzie shouted with his usual bluster. The two *djinn* ignored his words completely, and began to work together on constructing the best possible entrapment spell. Perhaps Ozzie still could have defeated them if he was able to devote his full attention to turning back their efforts. But he, and everyone else, was somewhat distracted.

'Yes, rid us of Ozzie!' Sulima chortled. 'And he will no longer thwart my vengeance upon Scheherazade!'

'She is the beginning and ending of all our trouble!' agreed the

Sultana. 'For us to regain our respect as one great happy family, we must destroy Scheherazade.'

'Gibber gibber pillowing! Slobber slobber seal ring! Kill kill kill Scheherazade!' Shahryar managed.

'After I make short work of this vile temptress Sulima,' Shahzaman added, 'I shall help my somewhat inconvenienced brother to rid this world of Scheherazade!'

'Perhaps before we reinter certain *djinn*, we have another task before us,' said the pale *djinni*.

'Most assuredly, dearest companion,' his darker fellow rejoined, 'we should protect Scheherazade!'

'Guards!' the Sultana screamed. 'Forget killing anyone else until she has been hacked into small, disgusting pieces!'

'I beg your pardon,' interjected Kassim.

But the Sultana would not be deterred. 'Guards! You are ordered to kill Scheherazade!'

'We now know what we must do, unto our very deaths!' stated the brave if a bit bloodthirsty Aladdin. 'Protect Scheherazade!'

'WHAT IS THIS?' The great green head of Ozzie swiveled to regard the storyteller. 'PERHAPS THIS WAS ALL CAUSED BY SCHEHERAZADE!'

'Women!' the wise woman called from her spot where the eunuchs supported her still. 'Now is the time to elevate Scheherazade.'

'There is our goal!' came the ragged call from the guards.

'What a perfect target!' Sulima chortled.

'We defend her until our last breath!' Aladdin went on.

'Or until every piece is used!' Kassim added from his personal point of view.

'In a moment,' said both onyx and alabaster in the most reassuring of tones, 'nothing will defeat our protection spell.'

'I WILL KILL SCHEHERAZADE FIRST,' Ozzie announced decisively. 'THE REST OF YOU WILL BE NEXT!'

'I suppose this drama is a little better,' a member of the audience mentioned, 'although it still doesn't match up to Mordrag.'

'Gibber lance!' Shahryar managed.

'Death to all who offend our mother!' Shahzaman clarified.

'Yes,' added the Sultana, glowing with pride and power, 'and death to all those who do not defend my honor!'

'We are with you, Scheherazade,' called Marjanah, 'in whatever we must do!'

'Do you suppose,' another audience member conjectured,

'we might get one of those cute guards to charge over this way?'

And then everyone struck, at one and the same time.

The wise woman stood upon her platform to clap her hands. And all that was magic in the room became quite visible.

So could Scheherazade see something not unlike a shaft of sunlight emerge from Ozzie's eye, except that this shaft was of the brightest green. And she saw a pair of lightning bolts, save that these bolts were of the darkest black, originate from the palms of Sulima. Bright swirls of the deepest red emerged from the mouth of the Sultana, and orange halos had formed around each of the enchanted swords. It was even more impressive when she realized that most all of this magic was directed towards her, save that the twin *djinn* had wrapped her with a cloak made up of a hundred times a hundred brilliant lights, so that Scheherazade felt as though she wore the stars.

It was in that next instant that the lights all met in Scheherazade's cloak, green and black and red and orange, each glow adding to the next so that Scheherazade half imagined she stood at the center of the sun.

Inside this brightness, she heard the voice of the wise woman: 'Tell your story, Scheherazade!'

So the storyteller opened her mouth. But before she could utter a single syllable, a swirl of color emerged from between her lips, absorbing the great light around her. And where the color and light met, the two formed images which were very familiar to Scheherazade.

Here was a merchant who had the misfortune to toss the pit of the date into the wrong location. And here was the *djinni* who had responded, claiming revenge. And here were people turned into animals, and an entire city turned into fishes of four different colors, a king and a doctor whom the king should have trusted, a clever fisherman and the ifrit whom he had released, then captured and released again, and a young man half of flesh and half of marble. All these and more filled the cavern before Scheherazade, all the many men and women and beasts and spirits that she had given life through her stories. And all of them turned to look at Scheherazade, waiting patiently yet most expectantly.

'You have given them a gift,' the wise woman's voice filled the sudden silence within the cavern. 'Now, through the proper channeling of magic, they are prepared to give you a gift in turn.'

Scheherazade looked up at the amassed figures before her, and they nodded most knowingly in return so that she might know what to do, for she realized that all of those images were at her command.

'Very well,' she said quite simply. 'Make things right again.'

And since all these great beings before her were as close as her thoughts, they knew exactly what to do.

'I MUST NOT BE DEFEATED,' Ozzie called as the *djinn* and women of power approached him. 'I MUST BE SUPREME!'

'So you say,' Sulima said in the most derogatory of tones, 'as if any man is supreme. That you would think you could get the better of me!'

But neither of them had the slightest possibility of success, for they were faced by all the powers of the imagination. And all those powers worked as one.

'THIS WILL Not happen!' Ozzie squawked as his great head shrank down to a more reasonable size.

'Surely, you can defeat such a blowhard,' Sulima scoffed, 'but you will not be able to touch such as – get your hands off me. What are you doing?'

In an instant, *djinni* and *djinnia* were reduced to smoke. A second instant, and both of them had been returned to the bottle that had once been Ozzie's solitary home.

Ali Baba replaced the cork. 'This is the most satisfying occupation,' he further remarked.

'Now that we are rid of those pesky *djinn*,' the Sultana commanded of her sons and guards, 'destroy Scheherazade for your – oink!'

'My sword is – oink!' Shahzaman replied.

'Gibber drool slobber – oink!' Shahryar wholeheartedly agreed. For indeed, the entire royal family had been turned into swine, as had Scheherazade earlier suggested.

'Wait a moment!' Ozzie called from within his bottle. 'What of my promised superiority?'

'You will be in control of all your world,' Scheherazade reassured the once fearsome entity. 'It is just that your world now exists within a jar.'

'And I am not alone!' Ozzie said, his voice filled with grim realization.

'I will show you who will subjugate whom!' Sulima rejoined from much the same location.

'Well,' Scheherazade replied with no regret whatsoever. 'I am afraid you will have to fight this out between yourselves. What more can you expect? After all, I am only the one who tells the stories.'

'My, my,' came a comment from the audience. 'I must admit that the first act could still use some work. But when they got to that conclusion, Mordrag couldn't even hope to compare!'

'I whole-heartedly agree,' another added. She nodded towards a large group of very confused guards. 'Now what are we going to do about all these men?'

*Chapter the Last,*
*in which things are set as right as possible,*
*and life goes on not at all as before.*

So it was the certain final matters had to be dealt with, so that all could return to their lives the same or better than before.

'Wait a moment!' one of the more perceptive guards called. 'What have they done with King Shahryar?'

'Are you blind?' replied a regal voice. 'Do you not see your monarch before you?'

All the guards bowed before the king. Except, Scheherazade could see, he was not the king at all, but instead that same bold, handsome and self-sacrificing guard that she had so admired.

'What transpires before me?' she whispered.

'A wise woman must work – joedimag – with the materials at hand,' the wise woman replied. 'I am afraid that the poor king was one wall short of a hut, as the wise woman says. For am I not a wise woman?'

'Yes,' Scheherezade replied softly but urgently. 'But the guard?'

'I hope you do not overly object. We very much need a king to extract us from this situation, and this particular man was the best available.'

Scheherazade was still not convinced. 'But will not the others suspect?'

'No, all but you will see him as the king. And for the time being, even he will believe he is the king when he holds his court every day, although it will be far different at night. The actual king and his relatives, of course, have already been turned into swine, and are beyond objecting. Beyond them, who would dare to question a monarch?' The wise woman frowned, and added quickly, 'You will, of course, have to keep up the charade of storytelling and the threat of beheading for some little time, even though, of course, you will be involved in perfect marital bliss. I would imagine that about another – maggiethatch – nine hundred and ninety-odd nights would do.'

247

To the storyteller, it seemed a small price to pay. Scheherazade was at last beginning to see the wise woman's point. This had worked out rather better than she had expected.

'Now that we have found our queen,' the king who was once a guard announced, 'we must escort her home with all honors. And would somebody find a nice clean pen for these swine?'

'Then all is as it should be?' Scheherazade mused.

'It is drawing closer,' the wise woman agreed.

'We have both Ozzie and Sulima within this one jar,' Ali Baba said as he held his prize aloft. Even from a few feet distance, Scheherazade could hear a series of muffled shrieks and grunts emanating from within.

The two *djinn* who had once occupied ring and lamp before occupying this jar looked on with benign smiles.

'They will find peace together within that jar, good friend,' one said to the other.

'Either that, best companion, or they shall kill each other,' the second replied to the first.

'And what of the others? Bold Marjanah, whose wit first inspired me to tell that final story before Ozzie and the others?'

'It will be wit to wit,' Marjanah replied, 'for I am reunited with my Achmed.

'And I with my brave Aladdin,' chimed Princess Badabadur.

'And look!' came a voice from the crowd. 'Hundreds of beautiful women have found their future husbands!' And there were indeed a great many women holding down a great many guardsmen, for the women had snuck up upon these fellows in the aftermath of battle, and pounced upon them as they were listening to the resolution of the tale, so that each of the lovely women had a handsome man of her very own. A few of the men still struggled from where they were sat or stood upon, but even they were not struggling too greatly.

'So all then is truly—' Scheherazade began her final summary.

'But wait!' Sinbad interrupted. 'Where is my Fatima?'

'Ah, there is this one last item,' the wise woman agreed. 'But to find your Fatima, Sinbad, you first must approach another.'

'Another?' Sinbad replied.

'Ook ook chee!' came from the rear of the crowd.

'The Queen of the Apes?' the former porter cried out in horror. 'No, I will never – ook chee ook ook!'

And so did the wise woman through her arts transform Sinbad into the most handsome of bull gorillas. And when the Queen of the Apes saw her king, she ran immediately forward, and soon they were involved in the most romantic of embraces, at least by the standards of gorillas.

'So have they both forevermore been turned into gorillas?' asked Achmed, who was a close friend of Sinbad's, having shared many adventures.

'Certainly not,' the wise woman replied. 'This is simply a little something that Fatima needs to confront within herself. But only once they have truly joined as apes will they be returned to human form, for only then will they have discerned both parts of their natures.'

'Oh,' Achmed replied, as if he had understood what the wise woman had most recently said. 'But, if Fatima and the Queen of the Apes were always one and the same, how could we have seen them both in the same place upon our earlier ocean voyage? Not that we actually saw Fatima; that is beyond a hand or the sound of a laugh, but still I—'

'It is best,' the wise woman said, 'that any story should hold a few secrets. Now it is time to go. Everything will work out for the best. Who should know better? After all, I am the wise woman.'

So it was that all concerned left by the many trap doors concealed within the cavern and returned to their native lands, unless they were suddenly married and found that they had to make other arrangements. Ali Baba returned to his wife, and Kassim was made whole again, or at least as whole as could be managed, since a couple of the smaller pieces had been lost in the shuffle, by the twin *djinn*, who in turn elected to stay with Aladdin and the Princess Badabadur. Harun al Raschid returned to his very distant land where the populace did indeed enjoy a neverending series of fart jokes, and Sinbad and Fatima were returned to human form after a most enjoyable apehood, and then were accompanied back to Baghdad by Achmed and his new bride Marjanah, and all were showered with gifts from that elder Sinbad, who was rich again, at least for the time being, and was much relieved to see them.

And as to Scheherazade and her new king, they returned to their city as well, bringing with them what few members of the guard remained, along with their new wives. And, after Dunyazad was reawakened by the palace wise woman, and the sisters were reunited with their rejoicing father, the vizier, so did the king and queen immediately decree that their entire palace be recarpeted by a certain merchant named Hassan. And Scheherazade, who through her adventures had gained a neverending series of new ideas for her tales, told her stories for nine hundred and ninety-some nights more, and lived in peace and contentment with her king until this present day.

And what happened to the clever queen Scheherazade after she had told her tales? Well, the youngest of the three wise woman, who held her residence within the queen's palace, suggested that, rather than depend upon the more common rendition of how passed the thousand nights and the one night, the storyteller might write down the manner in which all these things actually occurred.

And that is precisely what she did.

*THUS ENDS THE STORY OF
THE FURTHER ARABIAN NIGHTS.
AND MAY ALL YOUR DESTINIES
BE AS SWEET!*